Beyond the S-Bend

or

the personal recollections of a deluded politician

Martin Pilcher

Copyright © 2006 Martin Pilcher

The right of Martin Pilcher to be identified as the author of this work has been asserted in accordance with the Standard Copyright License (US)

All rights reserved. No part of this publication may be reproduced, stored in a retrieval system, or transmitted, in any form or by any means, electronic, mechanical, photocopying, recording or otherwise, without the prior permission of the copyright owner.

This book is a work of fiction. Names, characters, places and incidents either are a product of the author's imagination or are used fictitiously, and any resemblance to actual persons living or dead, events or locales is purely coincidental.

ISBN 978-0-9556819-2-9

AADVARK-ZAP PUBLISHING (UK)

For defenders of democracy everywhere

Key players in Ambrose's First Cabinet

Chancellor of the Exchequer	Jocelyn Hubbard
Home Secretary	George Blossom
Foreign Secretary	Aubrey Fynch-Chilling
Overseas Development	Rashidi Eaglescliffe Mboya
Education Secretary	Hattie Chapelthwaite
Social Services Secretary	Lucy Bowens
Arts Secretary	Susan Palmero
Lord Chancellor	Clive Smeelie
Defence Secretary	Claude Napper
Employment Secretary	Mervyn Mallatratt
Health Secretary	Quentin Nesbitt
Scottish Secretary	Hamish McToot
Treasury Secretary	Leonard Welling
Industry Secretary	Harold Plumrose
Transport Secretary	Christopher Meelybean

ooo00ooo

Key changes after the re-shuffle

Aubrey Fynch-Chilling	Chancellor of the Exchequer
Claude Napper	Foreign Secretary
Rashidi Eaglescliffe Mboya	Deputy Prime Minister
Hattie Chapplethwaite	Defence Secretary
Lucy Bowens	Health & Social Services
Dr Mangal Bali Chakkar	Education Secretary
Scott Rignold	Overseas Development

ooo0Oooo

Other players

Amelia Covey-Crump	Ambrose's wife
Helga Vine	Ambrose's lover
Benjamin Finkel	Director of Communications No.10
Rodney Snodder	Head of MI6
Gloria Fitzbagley	Head of MI5
Sir Mallard Kane	Head of Civil Service
Hugo Snatch	Cabinet Secretary
Scott Rignold	Ambrose's parliamentary secretary
Trevor Skidmarsh	1st Police Commissioner
Kevin Doppler	2nd Police Commissioner
Sgt. Paul Pickering	PM's security officer
Ivor Pleeth	Head of Anti-Terrorist Squad
Damien Chick	Head of Drugs Unit
Jim Brigginshaw	MP Leicester Central
Dr. Mangal Bali Chakkar	Jim's replacement
Pandit	Mangal's dog
Lord Justice Sackbut-Slid	Lord Chief Justice
Lord Justice Selwyn-Smythe	Appeal Court Judge
Lord Justice Bantock	High Court Judge
Sir Roland Quince	High Court Judge
Samuel Packer	Crown Court Judge
Selina Sheen	a fashion model
Justin de Rose	BECTU Trade Union Leader
Norman Balls	Architect
Quinlan Frick	Arts Centre Manager
Karl Dung	Maestro of Sutchworth Sinfonietta
Sylvester Maloney	a ballet dancer
Angela Basoutar	Parliamentary Private Secretary
Francis Lilac	UK Ambassador to Spain
Florrie Finch	Housekeeper at No.10

ooo00ooo

If at first an idea does not seem absurd, there is no hope for it.
Albert Einstein

1

Although I say so myself, I am not a nutter. I know that lots of people think I am simply because I practise meditation and believe in spiritual healing. I accept that you would not normally associate such pursuits with a politician. But I am different. My critics do not bother me. I am happy as I am. And who am I? I am The Right Honourable, Sir Ambrose Covey-Crump, MP, Prime Minister of Great Britain and Northern Ireland. What a grandiose title. However, I shall mention it no further. My ego is not what this is all about.

As I look out of the window, my spirits are lifted by the simple pleasure of observing a fine, spring day. A perfect setting, not to gloat about my success, but to contemplate the progress of my administration. As the whole world knows, when I became Conservative Prime Minister, I did so as a result of the biggest electoral landslide in British political history. I shall not burden you with the statistics, the press and media have thrust those upon you enough as it is. Besides, it is very important that you understand right from the very beginning that numbers alone are not my abiding consideration.

Unfortunately, successive governments, both Labour and Tory alike, have failed to grasp the fundamental fact that, even when the economy is good, it does not automatically follow that everyone is happy. Usually, they are not.
Of course, there are many who are delighted at the fat profits such circumstances produce, but I am concerned with the majority who, in spite of everything, still toil with fear and uncertainty in their hearts. A vibrant global market place is not to be sneezed at but not at the expense of society as a whole. It was all very well for Margaret Thatcher to say 'there is no such thing as society', just look at what we have now.
A septic tank screaming out to be purged. I am resolved to bring about balance and harmony to this great nation of ours. In so doing, I reject absolutely the alarmist cries from the liberal left that the size of my majority is tantamount to a dictatorship. The chattering classes were as disillusioned as any of us by our appalling quality of life and that's why so many of them voted for me. Our manifesto was totally transparent. It promised the nation exactly what they wanted. Clear, strong, direction that put the dignity of human beings above all else.

Naturally, bearing this in mind, I instructed George Blossom, my Home Secretary to double the police force, the immigration service, customs and excise and the national coast guard. But more about that in a moment.

Most political leaders deserve what they get, talking of which, I must say a few words about Messrs. Blair, Brown and Howard. I shall be brief. It is important to set the record straight, particularly as my ascent into office continues to be pilloried by that scurrilous publication, The Guardian. It was they, let us not forget, who likened our manifesto to, and I quote, *a rather odious set of faeces that all common-sense voters will surely flush down the lavatory to the sewers of oblivion.* Well, they did not. And so to the facts.

Whatever one may think of Tony Blair, (and privately I think he's rather a nice sort of chappie, very quick on the uptake and superb at telling jokes) it was abundantly clear that the rigours of high office, particularly the whole debacle of Iraq and the weapons of mass destruction, had taken a serious toll on his health. As a doctor of medicine, albeit in the alternative sector of homeopathy and spiritual healing (and may I remind you that I was knighted for my services to the community, culminating in the creation of the Kaya Centre for Mindfulness) I was not surprised that he was literally carried out of number ten on a stretcher. I often wonder what that splendidly maverick actor Richard Harris must have thought when poor Tony blatantly pinched his dying line 'it was the food that did it' to the attendant press, as he was shunted, somewhat unceremoniously, into the waiting ambulance.

A duodenal ulcer was bad enough in itself, but coupled with a perforated appendix and a profoundly bifurcated colonic tract, the time had come to throw in the towel as gracefully as possible. Not surprisingly, the cycloptic Gordon Brown was ready and waiting in his corner, with his team of minders, to take over the reins of power in strict accordance with Labour Party constitutional procedure. This he did, with all the panache of a crumpled canapé sprinkled with dandruff. And then the silly man was hoisted by his own petard. All those stealth taxes against the middle classes came home to roost, and, as a consequence, they galloped en masse toward us like the Gaderene swine on speed. Serves him right. Hell hath no fury like the middle classes holed in their pockets.

Alas, Michael Howard, no mean strategist, if I may say so, would by now have some lucrative city directorship were it not for the unfortunate complications following his operation. He claimed that he resigned because he had failed to win the election. I beg to differ. Even before the general election, he was ill and worried about his health. Michael is a human being like everyone else (although there are some twisted souls at Westminster who try to imply otherwise) and shortly after his defeat, he began to take on a most unhealthy pallor.

I hesitate to compare it with something of the night and take exception to those who claimed he had less colour than a vampire; I have no time for such malicious remarks. It wasn't simply because we were close friends, (we are the same age and entered parliament within weeks of each other) that he mentioned his concerns to me. We soon agreed that it would be a good idea if I were to carry out a full body Reikki healing session in the strictest of confidence; after all, I am a spiritual healer and alternative medicine practitioner of some emminence. When my hands hovered above his lower abdomen, the source of discomfort was unmistakable.

I could have cured him in time, but time was not a commodity he could indulge in. Without further delay he was admitted to hospital for a routine operation to remove a gall stone. To the relief of many, everything went off without a hitch. Unfortunately, a week later, he was confined to a wheelchair, having succumbed to that dreaded hospital superbug, MRSA. Conventional medicine and indeed my own alternative methods could not prevent the bug from gaining the upper hand and, as his condition worsened, he was confined to St.Ethelred's, a private nursing home. Shortly afterwards, when I visited him, I could tell at once that, politically speaking, he was yesterday's news. I was proved right. With commendable courage, and before the media vultures could peck at his bones, there in the restful, flower-bedecked surroundings of St Ethelred's, Michael urged us to accelerate the proces of choosing a new leader. It was a pity that the rules could not be changed without so much bitching and back-biting but we got there in the end. By the time the contest took place poor Michael was attached to a kidney dialysis machine. Suffice to say, the records will show that I received an outright majority at the first ballot. All other contenders were firmly consigned to history. Enough said. And so to matters in hand.

There was much circumspection concerning my cabinet appointments. In the end I confounded everyone by appointing total unknowns. Certain sections of the press and the opposition (what little there was of them) took great pleasure in deriding my selection. Back bench no-hopers with a paucity of experience, was the general cry. Even the sober Telegraph could barely disguise its dismay - *a cabinet of questionable merit* - it intoned. Only the Independent struck a positive note, albeit a facetious one.

It must be remembered that the endearingly benign Sir Ambrose Covey-Crump, fashionably flawed in his machine-knitted, pea-green cardigan, floppy bow tie and sagging fedora, has confounded his critics many times before. We await to see whether this quaintly eccentric gentleman can yet again pull another rabbit out of the hat.

Privately, I rankle at the suggestion that I am no more than some kind of third rate variety act. An end of the pier magician. A fast fading anachronism. Isn't winning the election with the biggest landslide ever recorded, proof enough of my political skills?

I seek no revenge. Posterity will record my achievement. The democratic voice of Great Britain has spoken and I have arrived to serve it. Right now, I am at the centre of everything. Everything. My time has come and I intend to make the most of it. For the good of the nation. This battered and bewildered nation, yearning to regain its pride and self-respect. Its joy in living. Its place in history. I alone have the key to this savage parade and am about to turn it. To wrestle free the rusty lock of doubt and insecurity and fling wide the door to unbridled joy and happiness. Few can imagine it. Even fewer believe it. But just you wait and see.

I have a master plan.

2

It's Saturday night and Amelia is soaking herself in the bath whilst I brush my teeth (I still have my own, in spite of malicious rumours). I don't know whether it's because she's on her fourth gin and tonic or because she's just smoked her last Silk Cut, but tonight I find her more than a little testy. She enjoys the attention and all the trappings of power but resents the inevitable intrusion and scrutiny that comes with it. Publicly she never lets the side down but privately I'm always the first to experience the backlash. In an hour's time we shall be whisked away in the ministerial limousine to open a new Hindu temple somewhere in Leicester. The excursion itself seems to irritate her, as she will be required to cover her head and this, she assures me, will play havoc with her coiffeur, about which she is always incredibly sensitive. But this alone is not the cause of her sulkiness. It is the fact that we shall be accompanied by Jocelyn Hubbard, the Chancellor of the Exchequer, of whom she holds a less than charitable opinion.

"It's bad enough having to stand next to a man the size of a barrage balloon, but having to suffer his equally voluminous flatulence, especially in the confined space of a car, is more than any reasonable human being can be expected to tolerate."

"He is aware of his problem, my sweet, and has assured me that he will take the carbo veg tablets that I recommended. The strongest smell of the evening will probably be the incense."

"And what about curry, will we be obliged to eat that? I shall be livid if I get stains on my new dress."

"As far as I'm aware, there will only be a finger buffet, nothing more dangerous than a few chipolatas dunked in something by Pathak I guess."

The splash of a sponge is the only response, and I know, from experience, it is better to leave it at that.

I must admit that, personal habits notwithstanding, Jocelyn Hubbard is not the most attractive of men. In fact, his appearance is downright unprepossessing, one could almost say, bordering on the freakish. He has the bulk of a grisly bear and, when standing, must surely reach at least six foot eight. What is most extraordinary is his overall shape, which exactly resembles a pear. His shoulders slope at an alarming degree and quite how his braces remain in position is a constant source of fascination. His lower bulk is dominated by an enormous bottom and huge paunch which join seamlessly together to bear down on one like an ocean liner coming into dock. To make matters even more preposterous, is the size of his head. Compared to the rest of him it is tiny, and sits on top of a long neck with no discernible chin, like the knob of an old-fashioned clothes peg. His complexion is absurdly pale and he has small twinkly blue eyes with heavy red lids that look perpetually raw. It's as if someone had tried to caramelise them with a kitchen blow-torch. And he is completely bald apart from unruly tuffs of ginger hair that sprout outwards above his ears like clumps of mountain grass. Amelia says he reminds her of the Swedish chef in The Muppets. I'm inclined to agree.

But what a magnificent brain. Oh yes, no denying that. An Oxbridge double first in maths and economics, a professorship at the London School of Economics, and author of nearly thirty published books on strategic fiscal policy. His most recent, entitled, The Daemonic Dollar, was praised by Alan Greenspan as the most accurate assessment of American financial influence in the last twenty years. And this was the quiet genius who, had it not been for me, would still be sitting quietly unnoticed and unremarked upon in the back benches. Granted, he has the charisma of a cold suet pudding but what more do you want from such an intellectual colossus ?

The telephone rings. It is Jocelyn. There is no mistaking his voice. A deep gurgle in a subterranean drain pipe.

"Ah, Ambrose. I appear to have mislaid your prescription note for those tablets, when should I take them?"

That's what I like about Jocelyn, he always comes straight to the point, there is no room for idle chatter.

"Take two tablets in about half an hour."

"And subsequently?"

"Another two, every hour until you feel entirely comfortable."

"Good. I can't seem to loosen the cap, is it a left handed thread?"

"No, it's a snap fit, just align the tamper-proof arrows and prize it off."

"Right, splendid, thank you. I'll see you and Amelia later."

He rings off. That's the strange thing about geniuses, they can't boil an egg, or, in this case, open a bottle of pills. They need taking in hand.

Right from the word go, which is to say, when I appointed my cabinet, that is precisely what I did with each and everyone of them. Naturally, I did this on an individual basis and in a very personal manner. I was anxious to ensure that they understood how much I valued them as human beings first, and politicians second. Perhaps this is an appropriate moment for me to elaborate on the underlying philosophy by which I lead this government.

Policy is one thing, but achieving it is another matter. A distinguished film director, I cannot recall his name just now, whose talents sadly appear to be ignored these days and has subsequently taken to writing food reviews (and at one point became conspicuously rotund) once defined team work as (and here I must paraphrase as I cannot remember his exact words) *teamwork is everybody doing everything exactly the way I want them to but only when I say so."*

This to me, strikes at the very heart of effective teamwork. Of course, as we all know, the books on teamwork are legion, however, when it comes to politics, they are best left ignored. It is all very well talking about inclusivity and contribution and the shifting sands of team dynamics, but in politics, all bucks eventually stop with the Prime Minister. Given that undeniable fact, I maintain the right to lead my cabinet team, not from the front, or the rear, or indeed the centre, but from inside their heads.

I have no wish to get bogged down in deep philosophical issues, but suffice to say, (as equal legions of experts on motivational psychology will concur) winning the hearts and minds of people will never be achieved if those involved do not share a common set of values and beliefs. Put simply, if dissent and discord is to be avoided, then everyone must sing from the same hymn sheet. I therefore interviewed everyone of my cabinet members personally before formally appointing them, and invited them to share with me, not so much a hymn sheet, as a complete set of musical notes, with every change of key, every sharp and flat, every nuance of phrasing and articulation, clearly indicated. Metaphorically speaking, I instilled in them a burning desire to sing in glorious unison, like a blessed choir of angels. How did I achieve this in reality? As I said earlier, I hesitate to delve deeper, but, on reflection, perhaps I should grasp the nettle and take you into my confidence in an open and honest manner. I know you are eager to learn the secret of my success, a success which, I cannot in all humility deny, has stirred not only this great nation of ours, but many others throughout the world. It goes like this.

For most of my adult life I have been sustained by my practice of daily meditation and, as I pursued my calling in alternative medicine, the principles of spiritual healing. These are the tools I use. There's nothing particularly special in that. The key is to what extent. Tee hee. Whoops, please excuse that momentary lapse into frivolity, but we really must lighten up here. I mean, when we talk about meditation, it's no great deal, it's been around for more than two thousand years. Nowadays it has more adherents in the West than ever before. But ask yourself, when did you last meet a Buddha, or even a frightfully wise person? Exactly. Without wishing to diminish the achievements of such wonderful people as the Dalai Lama, when it comes to enlightenment, that glorious entry ticket into Nirvana, who do you know who's actually been there and come back? A rhetorical question, since, if the teachings of the middle way are to be believed, arrival, ipso facto, guarantees the long goodbye. In short, those who reach the far side never come back. Certainly, I've read quite a few accounts, (as possibly you have too), of what it was like, by those individuals whose assiduous practice have allowed them a passing glimpse. Total clarity, utter stillness, the incredible beauty of simple every day things are most often cited. But the experience, having arisen, always subsides. Not so with me! Well, I did say I would be open and honest, didn't I?

You see, what I'm driving at is that it's not a secret. Granted, the impact on one's life can be so profound that many are reluctant, if not incapable, of putting into everyday terms, exactly what their experience has been all about. Usually that's the point where all the issues get hopelessly bogged down in the intellectuality of it all. If you will pardon my saying so, that's also when everything becomes a load of old bollocks. I mean, some things can drive you absolutely potty. For example, such and such is not A nor is it B. But neither is it <u>not</u> A or <u>not</u> B. Well it must be something, mustn't it? Apparently not. But I disagree. You see, at the risk of being accused of gross self-aggrandisement, it takes guts to declare that when you experience enlightenment, you have a choice. You can either bring the message back and get on with it, or you can hold it tight in your heart, sharing it with nobody and simply ponder its ramifications for the rest of your life. I chose the former. Which brings me back to effective teamwork.

The past six months have seen unprecedented accord in cabinet. Why? Because everyone of my ministers received the same message, unwavering and uncluttered in its clarity and commitment. How? Well, that venomous, but fiendishly talented cartoonist Gerald Scarfe, drew a picture of Maggie Thatcher, in the guise of some ethereal eminence grise, offering her hand bag to me as I chaired the inaugural meeting of my cabinet. The caption read: *give them an inch and they'll take a mile.* Less inspired persons, such as the leader writers of The Guardian, accused me openly of brain washing. It's all water off a duck's back, as far as I'm concerned.

The Secretary to the Cabinet knows full well that on the day I made my appointments, I meditated for forty minutes in my private office. I came out of meditation and established the appropriate aura. Then, as previously agreed, on a personal basis with each minister to be, and without any coercion of any kind whatsoever, I submitted them to thirty minutes of cranial therapy.

As any practitioner of spiritual healing will confirm, the healer, in this case me, is merely the channel through which the cosmic energy flows. I placed my hands over their temples, not touching, but close enough to allow the message from the far side to resonate freely with our declared policies and in so doing, to fuse with my vision on how we would achieve it. This gave the receiver, i.e. the minister to be, a profound understanding of what they had to do to remain in office. Even as Prime Minister, I was merely the vessel through which this great message passed. The message from the far side that I had chosen to promulgate through the highest state of office that it was my privilege to hold.

Not surprisingly, some were more open to the process than others. It is a personal issue really. Fears, doubts, and insecurities can arise as much as gratitude and joy, it all depends on the inner self and one's individual karma. Throughout the sessions, I remained calm and centred, as my years of training and experience had taught me to be. I gave them my personal assurance that when the going got tough, as it most certainly would, I would support them, not only as a resolute Prime Minister, but in an holistic sense, as a Master would his disciple. That did the trick.

The one hundred day honeymoon that pundits twitter remorselessly on about has long been superseded. Indeed, our courage was not tested until nine months later when the first signs of public disorder broke out. I believe it was the carefully orchestrated work of anarchists. It occurred within days of the announcement in the commons by George Blossom, my Home Secretary, of our intention to introduce free mortgages for the police force. Clearly, this was not the time to be faint-hearted. George understood this. So did Trevor Skidmarsh, the Police Commissioner. Within days, one hundred and forty two people had been arrested, the majority of whom are now contemplating their futures for the next twelve months at Her Majesty's pleasure.

At the time of his appointment, George agreed wholeheartedly with me that community service was no longer a burden that society should be expected to tolerate. An amendment to the Public Disorder Bill was just one of many pieces of legislation to leap from the House of Commons to the House of Lords and on to the statute book as quickly as a greyhound from its trap.

I was delighted that the judiciary backed our proposals so convincingly and at such an early stage. The fact that so many of them had suffered crimes and misdemeanours against their persons and their property, doubtless tipped the scales of wisdom in our favour. Trevor Skidmarsh whinged and whined in the corridors about overcrowded prisons and low morale in the prison service itself but George took him to one side and showed him the first draft of a speech that he was to make to the House the following week. He soon caught the gist of our message.

The Treasury would be releasing twelve billion pounds for the construction of six new mega-sized prisons, (good old Jocelyn was right up there behind the eight ball) together with a comprehensive rehabilitation programme that would include both capital building projects and personnel recruitment. Naturally, I had already resigned as Chairman of the Kaya Centre for Mindfulness in order that no charges of impropriety could be levelled at me when the Centre would be invited to join the list of tenderers to supply and manage the specialist human resources.

What with our mortgage offer, dear Trevor went away like a dog with two bones. Wisely, George omitted to tell him that we intended to strengthen the law in order to make extensive use of compulsory purchase orders to ensure that the prisons were built within a reasonable time frame. It would not be a popular measure and some form of civil unrest was unfortunately to be expected. However, George and I agreed that, by then, as a result of our package of improvements for the police force, which incidentally included a generous clothing allowance, relocation expenses and assisted medical insurance, morale in the force would be so high and their recruitment programme so galvanised, that any act of public disorder would be dealt with effectively and efficiently, as never before.

In a way, it was no surprise that when George made his announcement the commons was in uproar. So indeed were members of the press and media. But I took everything in my stride. Later that evening, I meditated for two hours. I found that quiet centre where fear and anxiety no longer exist, where time stands still and life itself is revealed as a huge cosmos of nothingness.

For a moment, my spirit leaves its body. I see myself at the dispatch box. I am surrounded by hordes of devils. But the message from the far side is unmistakable. Forward noble Ambrose and defeat the forces of evil.

As I come out of meditation, I feel another tranche of controversial legislation is upon me.

3

Amelia is still sulking when the ministerial car arrives. We climb in and wait for Jocelyn, regrettably punctuality is not one of his strengths.

"I still think it's a mistake not to be accompanied by the Home Secretary," she says, settling herself into the soft leather.

"Please Amelia, I don't want to go through all that again."
And indeed, I do not. I know that deep down Amelia fully understands why Jocelyn, rather than George is present tonight. The Asian community, be they Sikh, Hindu, Muslim or Christian, are becoming anxious about the publication of our white paper on amendments to the immigration bill. Needless to say, their apprehension is based on rumours that bear no resemblance to the facts. Unfortunately, having a massive parliamentary majority does not prevent political commentators from postulating all sorts of erroneous opinion. Tonight, I shall publicly not only re-affirm my belief in a multi-faith society, but one free of all bigotry and racism. I shall gently remind them that, as a practising Buddhist, my purpose in life is to investigate the nature of reality, and there is no

greater reality than the conspicuous benefits to our society arising from the presence of peoples from other cultures and countries of origin, the Asian community being no less regarded in this respect. Jocelyn will then top and tail my speech by reminding them of the sums of money that the Treasury has ear-marked for the support and development of ethnic minorities in general. Obviously, we shall not mention our intention to stop immigration dead in its tracks for six months whilst we sort out the hopeless mess inherited from the previous labour government; that will be the subject of a commons speech later this year. No, the purpose of tonight, quite apart from opening their Hindu temple, will be the calm assurance that the Asian community is safe in our hands. Slowly, carefully, humanely, we shall move towards the sunny uplands of tolerance where the sweet smell of incense is not regarded as a health threat to asthmatics, as the National Front would have us believe.

"Sorry to keep you."

The car heaves to one side as Jocelyn appears and somehow manages to manoeuvre his bulk from the pavement to inside the car. He heaves to a standstill on the bench seat opposite us, the transport chappies having long since realised that a conventional limousine is too small to accommodate Jocelyn and two other persons together on a single bench seat. I think this a Daimler of some sort, it has one of those lovely radiators with gently flowing creases like a lion's mane with a perm. Whatever, it cost a small fortune to upgrade with the appropriate security measures which, so I am assured, includes bullet proof windows. These days you can never tell when some Al Qaeda inspired terrorist will choose to immolate themselves in the name of Allah, transforming you into toast in the process.

Two plain clothes policeman who have been loitering diplomatically outside, also join us.

"Are you ready to go, sir?"

"As ready as we'll ever be," retorts Amelia, "given the circumstances."

I smile solicitously. The word is given and we pull away, accompanied by two police cars and three motorcycle outriders front and rear. You can never be too careful and let's face it, these days there are sleeping terrorists cells even in Tonbridge Wells, let alone Leicester. I shall of course be addressing such matters in the fullness of time, national identity cards by next spring being one of them. For the time being, what with police recruitment and the prison building programme, George has enough on his plate. He's popping in tomorrow anyway to discuss progress on the motor torpedo boats for the coast guards and the laser portcullis system at Dover which, I must confess, I have not had the time to mug up on. I'll read it later in bed. I don't want to let George down, he might think I'm not one hundred percent committed to his proposals, whereas in fact I'm utterly delighted with the speed at which he has translated my vision into working projects. I do remain rather concerned about his high blood pressure though.

Nobody speaks until we pick up signs for the M1 and M25.

"Is the climate control working?" asks Amelia, rather curtly.

Sergeant Pickering checks the controls.

"Yes, everything seems to be in order."

Jocelyn eases himself.

"It's rather muggy for the time of year," he chortles, "you may want to alter the humidity settings."

Amelia's expression falls half way between murder and martyrdom. Luckily, Sergeant Pickering picks up the signals and within moments a cool wave of fresh air touches all our cheeks. Mild tension, having arisen, now subsides. I am relieved. I do not like atmospheres any more than the next person.

"Paul, have you got any Silk Cut with you?"

Sergeant Pickering flicks me a quick glance almost before Amelia has finished speaking. I nod in assent. He passes Amelia a full packet.

"I've got a light," she says, and makes a dog's dinner out of the whole process, finally blowing an arc of smoke triumphantly towards Jocelyn. He gives a smug, far away, half smile as Sergeant Pickering increases the ventilation flow.

Outside, I notice that the urban landscape has given way to motorways. There is something about the surreal lighting of such places that makes me feel uneasy.

It is irrational, I know, but neither is it helped by the flotilla of blue flashing police lights that I can't help thinking would be more at home on some Mephistophelean posse galloping towards the abyss. Something doesn't feel quite right but I cannot put my finger on it. We sit in silence.

Amelia puffs contentedly on her cigarette. She is aware of the hazard to her health and although she has promised not to smoke in public, a promise which, to her credit, she has kept, I would dearly love to see her give it up altogether. I believe she has the will power, she can be very determined when she puts her mind to it, but the desire is not yet there. It has to come from within. I do not believe in any of these external remedies and their exaggerated claims. The mind is the key to everything. Outwardly, Amelia appears a relatively happy person, she has a vivacious personality and great charm. She engages with people easily and they warm to her high spirits and general bonhomie. But there is a darker side to her which takes hold now and again. She can be prone to depression and self-loathing. I do not think she will give up smoking until she learns to love herself a bit more. I can do nothing to help her beyond offering my own love as unconditionally as possible. Being a human being that is not always easy.

The motorway speeds endlessly by. I observe Jocelyn sitting opposite, his huge bulk as impressive as a boulder dam. He is scribbling in a little hard-backed, black, notebook with an elegant gold propelling pencil. There are quite a few politicians in the Palace of Westminster who indulge in fountain pens, but Jocelyn is the only one I know who favours such an idiosyncratic graphological tool. For a man of such massive dimension, (his fingers are as fat and ugly as bunch of raw pork sausages) his handwriting is surprisingly neat and delicate. When I first encountered it, it reminded me of the narrow, forward leaning, carefully modulated strokes and curves that one sees in the letters of first world war officers and gentlemen. I wonder what he is writing now? His expression gives nothing away, but his funny little blue eyes dart across the page like tadpoles in season.

My gaze lowers to his feet. They are enormous, I suppose they have to be to balance a frame of such height. He is wearing a pair of rather incongruous leather brogue shoes. The heavy leather soles are like slabs of paving stone and the laces weave through six huge horizontal eyes like steel cables on a suspension bridge. There is double bow of gothic proportions, the loops drooping heavily like the ears of a bloodhound. Above them, a leather tongue with a coarse cut fringe, spills over the top with all the exuberance of a tropical palm tree.

"Jocelyn, I'm sorry to interrupt your thoughts, but are you aware that we shall be obliged to take off our shoes before entering the temple itself?"

"Oh yes indeed," he says, "and I have taken appropriate measures to facilitate that operation." He brings one foot to rest across an adjacent knee and, with a quick jerk of the hand, he grasps the leather tongue and pulls the entire edifice, laces, holes and bow, forward with a rasping snap. The bright orange underside of a large Velcro strip flops open and he whisks off the shoe as easily as one would an old carpet slipper. We all sit in semi-stupification as he gurgles with delight.

"Jolly good, aren't they? I spotted them in Footsies in the Strand."

"It's a pity they don't make police boots like that, sir," says Sergeant Paul Pickering, barely unable to contain his mirth.

"I should have a word with the Home Secretary, next time you see him," says Jocelyn, eyes twinkling, "after all, we are a radical government in every sense of the word."

Even Amelia laughs at that one.

Just as things appear to be lightening up, Sergeant Pickering's mobile rings. I hate the damn things and on occasions such as this, it makes me nervous. We all listen in. It sounds like trouble. He rings off.

"Well?" I say.

"A lorry has jack-knifed at junction twenty, near Lutterworth, all lanes are blocked, we're taking an alternative route via Market Harborough, it may delay us by about twenty three minutes."

"So be it."

Sergeant Pickering talks to the driver via the intercom, apparently the glass partition is bullet proof too. Their conversation is full of coded gobbledegook. It makes no sense to me and presumably none to any undesirables that may be electronically eavesdropping, if such a thing were possible, and it had better not be.

Five minutes later the car slows down and we leave the motorway and then turn right. I catch a glimpse of a road sign - A14 Huntingdon and Cambridge. John Major's constituency is somewhere about here I recall. I think Amelia and Jocelyn have both spotted the road signs too but nobody makes any comment; we've all read Edwina Currie's diaries.

The journey continues with a slight air of apprehension. Our police escort, blue lights blazing fore and aft, remains in formation. I guess there's nothing to worry about. I look at Sergeant Pickering's colleague who has not uttered a word since we left Downing Street. I find that rather unnerving, so I make a point of addressing my next comment to him.

"If we are likely to be more than twenty-three minutes late, I would like a courtesy call to be made to the temple, assuming that's not a security risk?"

Sergeant Pickering answers whilst his colleague remains as mute as a statue.

"Central control are monitoring the route ahead, sir, they'll give us an accurate revised ETA in due course."

"Thank you."

I don't know what it is about security but I never get a definitive answer. I shelve my irritation. Jocelyn continues to write in his little black note book and Amelia requests another cigarette. I close my eyes to meditate. With so many issues clammering for attention I am surprised at the one that arises now. It is an image of a tall, statuesque blonde with an incredibly long pony-tail. I recognise her as the assistant principal private secretary who usually hands me the ministerial briefs with a charming smile. I think her name is Helga. I don't know why she occupies my mind in this way. Nevertheless, it is a very pleasing diversion, so I go with the flow.

Time passes. I become aware of a change in speed and direction. I open my eyes just as Sergeant Pickering answers his mobile.

"We're just clearing Market Harborough, sir, the road ahead is clear, we should arrive at approximately eight forty."

"Good, only ten minutes late after all, I'm sure His Holiness the Swarmhi what's-his-name, won't take offence at that."

I search my pockets for his name, I've written it down somewhere. I just cannot get the hang of these Hindu titles, the trouble is they never comprise of anything less than six syllables. I peer out of the window and notice that the road is clear for the simple reason that police cars with flashing blue lights are positioned at every junction, including the ones with traffic lights. These become more frequent as we head towards the city centre. I am pleased to note that the huge sums of money we are injecting into the police force are being translated into visible operational resources; Trevor Skidmarsh clearly knows which side his bread is buttered on.

As our motorcade enters a broad, slow-bending, dual carriage way, the temple becomes visible. It is very impressive and beautifully lit up.

"Only three minutes late, by my timepiece," says Jocelyn, whose ancient silver pocket watch is as big as a beer mat.

"Prime Ministers are allowed to be late," quips Amelia, "it enhances their position."

"But not where Her Majesty, is concerned," I retort.

That raises a chuckle all round, even Sergeant Pickering's colleague manages a quick smirk.

And then there is a God Almighty explosion!

A huge wall of orange flame erupts into the night sky, completely obliterating the entire frontage of the temple. The force of the blast hits our car like a massive Atlantic roller, and we are thrust sideways into the metal crash barriers. We skid to a halt. My ear drums are pounding. Outside there is pandemonium.

"Get down on the floor!" yells Sergeant Pickering.

We obey instantly but it's easier said than done. Amelia hits the floor first, quickly followed by me. Then Jocelyn rolls on top of us like the original Graf Zeppelin. Sergeant Pickering snaps some code word into his mobile. The car surges forward with a tremendous burst of acceleration and for a while we are pressed together like sardines in a can. Suddenly everything is bathed in brilliant white light as bright as a floodlit football stadium. Above us, I hear the aggressive hack-hack of a helicopter rotor, and it seems to be coming closer. I hope and pray it's one of ours. Another horrendous bang and sounds of screeching tyres and wrenching metal.

"What's happening?" screams Amelia.

"Some bloody terrorist has blown the temple up," I shout, "and we were supposed to be in it, that's bloody what."

I seldom lose my temper with Amelia but stupid questions like that really take the biscuit.

"This a major security incident, sir," says Pickering from somewhere above us, "please follow my instructions."

"Yes, yes, just get on with it." I snap. Surely I can be forgiven for being a bit edgy?

"Please remain on the floor."

None of us are fool enough to disobey. I half expect to hear the whirr and clunk of machinery as a James Bond fold-away machine gun swings out of the boot. Such imaginings are the product of fear. I would squeeze Amelia's hand if I could find it but it is somewhere on the far side of Jocelyn's bulk. His black note book has fallen open by my head and I can read three lines of what looks like a short shopping list, beautifully inscribed.

1. *Frank Cooper's Original Oxford Marmalade (coarse cut 453 grams)*
2. *Go-cat breakfast biscuits (herring & tuna)*
3. *Felix Cod & Plaice (economy pack)*
4. *Erotic Review (Dec. back issue)*

Jocelyn is a bachelor and clearly has everything to live for.

Suddenly, another huge explosion erupts behind us, turning the sky orange and pelting the car with debris.

"Missed!" yells Sergeant Pickering, with more jubilation than I would have thought appropriate. He follows up with a stream of incomprehensible security jargon into his mobile.

The car surges forward again at what might be described as a reckless turn of speed, were it not for the gravity of the situation. We continue like this for what seems an age and then we brake heavily and lurch to one side as it begins to turn. Eventually we come to rest.

"You may resume normal seating positions now," says Pickering, like an airline pilot in a disaster movie.

The three of us disentangle ourselves and climb gingerly back up into our seats. We appear to be parked on the circumference of a huge roundabout and in every direction there are blue flashing lights.

"What now?" I enquire, trying to hide the tremble in my voice.

"Any chance of a bloody gin and tonic?" says Amelia.

"In view of the prevailing circumstances," says Jocelyn, apparently unshaken, "I would imagine that the security advice would be to abort our mission and return to base?"

"Yes, sir, that's exactly the direction I have just received, and in a few moments we shall be transferring to an army helicopter."

"Pity we didn't have one in the first place," mutters Amelia, sarcasm always being her fall-back position in times of stress.

As I take in the scene, I'm relieved to see that, as yet, the press have not arrived. It won't be long before that changes. God alone only knows what tomorrow's headlines will say. One thing is for certain, however.

Bloody Trevor Skidmarsh can start reading the small print of his pension, that's what.

4

There comes a time when a Prime Minister has to take control and this was certainly it. Early reports are that His Holiness the Swami what's-his-name and his retinue of twelve priests have all been killed outright in the initial explosion. They were all awaiting my arrival inside the main reception area, which took the brunt of the explosion. So far, nearly ninety bystanders have also been injured and the number is likely to rise. The worst news of all is that Jim Brigginshaw, our local MP, who was with the Swami, has cheated death but has been severely injured by falling masonry and is now critically ill and struggling for his life in intensive care. It is a security catastrophe, an intelligence disaster, and a political time bomb. If that wasn't bad enough, we now have to launch a public relations damage limitation exercise that will be scrutinised by the whole world. My personal reputation and the integrity of this government is on the line after a mere eighteen months in power.

As anticipated, the press were awaiting our arrival back at Downing Street, an event which, I am relieved to say, did not require me to shin down a rope from our helicopter into the gardens of number ten. Uppermost in my mind was the incompetence of Trevor Skidmarsh. Clearly, the man has been stupendously inept and were it not for the chance jack-knifing of that lorry, I may very well have become a mere footnote in history, to say nothing of my beloved Amelia and dear Jocelyn.

On arriving back at number ten, and after a few stiff drinks, I swung into action. I knew that George, my loyal Home Secretary would be beside himself with misplaced remorse.

I summoned him to my office with the sole intention of easing his conscience. At the same time I called for Benjamin Finkel, my Communications Director. This attack was not only a gross breach of security but its very audaciousness reflects badly on the integrity of our intelligence agencies. Damage limitation as well as the failings of the Police Commissioner were both occupying my thoughts when the two men entered my office. Regardless of the situation, you could not hope to see two more contrasting figures than the agitated George and the calm Benjamin.

George Blossom is a short, roly-poly sort of man. He has a shock of unruly blonde curls, vaguely reminiscent of Harpo Marx, which makes him seem too untidy to be described as dapper, even though he favours a neatly pressed white silk handkerchief in his breast pocket and often sports a sprig of flowers in his lapel that somehow gives the impression that he's ready, at a moment's notice, to appear either at a wedding or a funeral. He sports rather ostentatious spectacles with translucent plastic frames, not unlike those worn by Elton John during his Follow the Yellow Brick Road days. Everyone knows that George admires Elton with touching intensity.

"Ambrose, oh my God, what can I say? I'm so terribly sorry, are you really alright? Are you really unscathed? How is Amelia and what about poor Jocelyn? I had the most dreadful foreboding about this visit but I was assured that every precaution had been taken. Oh my God, what a mess."

Poor George, I really do have to calm him down.

"I'm fine George, a little shaken, like everyone else, but that is all. Rodney and Gloria have already spoken to me about the advice they gave Trevor and it is entirely his responsibility that he chose to ignore it."

Perhaps I should mention that Rodney Snodder, the head of MI6 and Gloria Fitzbagley, the head of MI5, are rumoured to be sleeping together. Whatever the case, (and I am not entirely comfortable with it), the alacrity with which they both contacted me, subsequent to the attack, and the seamless juxtability of their information, does leave a lingering soupçon of doubt in my mind. There was a time when getting the two services to work together seemed as remote as an Arab marrying a Jew, however, such circumstances are not without precedent. Nonetheless, I do not sit happily with extremes of behaviour; besides, Rodney is married with three children.

I shall just have to tread warily where those two are concerned.

"So what are your immediate plans, Prime Minister?" asks Benjamin, sensing that George needs a moment or two to find his composure and reading correctly the glint of action in my eye. Benjamin is nothing if not totally alert. I appreciate too the way he addresses me formally. Over familiarity is not something I encourage. It has nothing to do with my ego, I hasten to add. All the cabinet knows that I am happy to be called Ambrose on a one-to-one basis, but when there are two or more ministers present, I prefer the formal address. I feel it is more conducive to the business of government which is, after all, what we are about.

I smile at Benjamin. He remains serious, his spiral notebook open, his Parker biro poised. He is handsome, clean-cut, clean-shaven, with dark Semitic features and a lean, healthy build. What with his impeccable manners and cultured baritone voice, it is small wonder that so many women find him attractive.

"At eight o'clock sharp, tomorrow morning, I shall invite Trevor Skidmarsh to fall on his sword."

Benjamin says nothing but poor old George begins to flutter.

"But what if he doesn't?"

"I shall sack him."

George fiddles with his tie. Benjamin remains still.

"Do you have a replacement in mind?" he asks politely.

"Yes, Kevin Doppler."

George is distinctly fidgety now.

"But what about Henry?"

I open my hands in benevolent supplication.

"George, the assistant commissioner is fifty-seven and has already suffered three angina attacks, it would be an act of cruelty to appoint him. The time has come to offer him ill-health retirement, a generous pension, a public vote of thanks for his many years of faithful service and possibly a wall-mounted brass barometer or something like that."

George settles down a bit.

"Actually, I think he'll probably be rather relieved, after all, these are very trying times for all of us."

"Indeed. Benjamin, perhaps you could prepare a press statement for George to read out after the cabinet meeting tomorrow morning. George, I'm sure you'll agree that an announcement as important as this should come with the authoritative stamp of the Home Secretary, no offence Benjamin."

"None taken, I'll start right away."

"Splendid and perhaps you could also prepare a general security statement to follow afterwards, you know the sort of thing, a full investigation is under way and we shall review our procedures if considered appropriate. Might be a good idea to mention that Amelia, Jocelyn and myself are fully recovered and it's business as usual etcetera, George, I think it would make sense if you were to tag that bit on after the Kevin Doppler announcement, or at least be ready with it if there are questions."

George sinks into his chair like a pin cushion pricked with a needle too far.

"If I could have sight of your first draft as soon as possible Benjamin," he whispers, "I would be obliged."

"It'll take me ten minutes and you'll be the first to see it."

I smile in collusion. Benjamin knows how much I value George and is fully aware of his commitment and loyalty. Why he gets so anxious about things is a mystery to both of us but I am determined to nurture his talents and Benjamin appreciates this.

"There's just one more question Prime Minister, if I may?" says Benjamin.

I know what he's going to ask but I let him do so anyway.

"Who else besides the three of us knows about Kevin's appointment?"

"Only Kevin. I spoke to him earlier and he will receive the formal offer when he comes to see me tomorrow morning at eight-thirty a.m. I hope you don't think I'm treading on your toes, George?"

"No, no, not at all, not at all. . . umm, what about Henry?"

"If Scott can track him down, he will be seeing me at nine o'clock tomorrow morning."

"So, Scott knows about the situation too?"
Benjamin doesn't miss a trick.

"No, not as an actuality, nevertheless, as my personal parliamentary secretary, I daresay he has put two and two together." A little nervous tick starts to jump at the corner of George's mouth but Benjamin remains calm. "Scott Rignold is the soul of discretion and no one knows better than he does why he must remain so."
George's tick begins to expand until his cheek quivers like a fretful peach.

"Umm, I don't want to complicate matters Ambrose, but what about Rodney and Gloria?"

"I'm sure they'll be glued to the television when you make your press statement after the cabinet meeting, I shall inform the cabinet then of course."

"You don't think that will put their noses a bit out of joint?"

"I would imagine that they'll both be pleased to see the back of Trevor Skidmarsh, besides, a little bit of sweat comes with the territory."

George fiddles with his tie and then his breast pocket handkerchief and then gives me one of his funny little smiles, it's a kind of nervous acquiescence that can be very touching at times.

"Well, I think that buttons things up, for the time being," I say, after a moment's silence, "I'm going to play some Schumann and afterwards I'll probably give Amelia a back massage, it's not every day that one is compressed by Jocelyn."

There are chuckles all round as the meeting breaks up.

Through the open doorway I see George making a beeline for the toilets. Benjamin lingers in the corridor to exchange words with a tall blonde. She has her back to me but that incredibly long pony-tail is unmistakable. She is even taller than Benjamin, and he must be six foot. Such a striking figure.

I make my way upstairs to the drawing room which is dominated by a baby grand piano. Not having any children, Amelia has turned her considerable talents into maximising the rooms to their full advantage. I feel very strongly about using taxpayer's money simply to imprint one's own presence on an official residence which is, after all, only on loan. I made it quite clear to all my ministers that if they had any thoughts of Pugin wallpaper and exquisite furnishings I would come down on them like a ton of bricks. Number Ten is tastefully furnished as it is and although it may not reflect our exact tastes, it will suffice. Amelia has merely personalised it with superficial dressings and various object d'art which already belong to us. As a consequence, our farmhouse in Hertfordshire (which backs on to the estate of the late Barbara Cartland, whose copious novels neither of us have read) does look somewhat bare. Nevertheless, it hasn't prevented us from renting it out to a Japanese businessman and his family who I think quite appreciated its minimalist appearance.

I seat myself at the piano, which incidentally, is a Blochstein. No, please don't correct me, I did say Blochstein and not Bechstein. Not many people know that a Blochstein is a kind of poor relation to the Bechstein, and therefore considerably cheaper to buy. Thirty years ago, when we spotted it in Münster, en route to visit dear friends in Greven, we had very little money to throw about, but we both fell in love with it immediately. We felt a full-sized concert grand piano would be a bit ridiculous, particularly as, in those days, we were living in a two bedroomed flat in Muswell Hill with a lounge smaller than a grand piano itself. But the baby Blochstein was just the ticket. It is finished in deep cream with a beautifully embossed black nameplate on the side. Many people prefer to blend cream with brown (not unlike those elegant Pullman railway carriages in days gone by) however, I beg to differ. Cream and black is so striking but at the same time, not unsettling. I must confess that I did sanction the replacement of the existing green carpet with a nice black one. Our drawing room is really our music room and it has a sober, Zen like quality about it.

I peruse the musical score that is already open. It is Schumann's Fantasiestück, opus 12. It is way beyond my meagre pianistic talents although I have managed to master the first piece, which is not so demanding as the others. Amelia can play all of it, although sadly, these day she does not seem inclined to play anything. I don't know why. She is the talented one whereas I just fumble and bumble along with very little sense of rhythm or phrasing.

As I glance at the opening bars, I realise that my mind is still occupied with the events of the day and those still to come. I know that Kevin Doppler will be a controversial appointment but I will not be swayed from achieving my ultimate goal, namely, a society that no longer lives in fear of crime. Trevor Skidmarsh is one of those fast-tracked academics, a very nice chap who can write a splendid report at the drop of a hat but is pretty useless at catching criminals. Kevin Doppler on the other hand, is a policeman's policeman. It is unfortunate that with his pock-marked complexion and rather ugly scar tissue across his throat (the result of a knife attack whilst on the beat) he does resemble a rather unsavoury thug. Nonetheless, he's come up through the ranks and has done wonders as head of the drug squad. Most significantly, he has come to the same conclusions as I have. Drug related crime can never be totally eradicated and no amount of manipulating the statistics can hide the fact that the situation is getting worse not better. The drain on police resources is staggering and unless radical action is taken, we will never have sufficient manpower to put a bobby on every street corner in the land, which is one of my most heartfelt wishes; not to mention, a police station in every town with more than two thousand residents.

I have had many discussions with Kevin about the way ahead and he is in total agreement with my determination to put a new law on the statute books that will effectively legalise all categories of drugs. Everything from Class A heroin to Class D camphor impregnated cough mixture. We know there will be huge resistance from the usual quarters but I am absolutely determined to bring about a sea change in an area of crime that causes such devastation amongst villains and victims alike. Kevin knows, (and I have confided in him) that fundamental to any future success will be our ability to control the drug supply lines. In this respect, I have already sent the hares a-running, so to speak. Be it Colombia, Thailand, China, Pakistan or Afghanistan, indeed, anywhere in the world where a drugs route is known to exist, British agents have established contact and, possibly even as we speak, are brokering deals backed up by a purse of handsome dimension.

Naturally, for obvious reasons, I cannot declare this publicly just yet, however, take it from me, two ministers are actively involved in this endeavour. They are, Aubrey Fynch-Chilling, the Foreign Secretary, and Rashidi Mboya, the Minister for Overseas Development. Different as chalk from cheese, I grant you, but working together delightfully well and it looks as if we will have everything in place by the time it comes to declare our intentions in the Queen's Speech later this year.

Their progress (and it is very much theirs rather than mine) is probably due to a synergy that thrives on opposites.

I do not approve of nicknames, particularly as they tend to be derogatory and this, I believe, can undermine the positive qualities of the holder. Nonetheless, I am aware that Aubrey is known as LC, mainly due to his extraordinary similarity to Lord Carrington, (the ill-fated Foreign Secretary of the Falklands debacle), right down to the heavy-lensed spectacles and supercilious air. There are some who say that LC stands for liquid crystal, as it reflects Aubrey's uncanny ability to adopt a different line of argument within the blink of an eye.

And then there is dear Rashidi, whose detractors call him Idi Bang Bang, which is most uncharitable in my view. There is no disputing the fact that he does remind one of that dreadful despot Idi Amin, but only because he is so beautifully black. His nostrils are as big as the entrance to a model railway tunnel and he's got a glorious set of gleaming white teeth, always on show as he grins and laughs his way through the trials of the day. When he becomes animated, which is often, he bangs the table with extraordinary force.

Personally, I find him an absolute tonic, utterly fearless, definitely a buddy to have on your side. Above all else, he is an African fixer and for that I can forgive him certain indiscretions, such as dancing in the fountains of Trafalgar Square on New Year's Eve, clad only in his underpants and waving a Ken Dodd feather duster! Such tremendous spirit, such a lovely man.

Deep down I think Aubrey despises him but it is up to him to work through his own prejudices. For the time being they are proving to be a highly effective team. What's more, Jocelyn assures me that the revenue we shall gain through drug taxes will off-set the cost of our police and prison expansion programme within five years. These are the things that keep me going.

And so I turn to Schumann. The score is open at the beginning. Des Abends, a poignant piece, rather befitting the events of the day. I place my hands on the keyboard and softly, gently, with deep feeling, proceed to play. It is such a lovely, moving piece. I manage to play it without faltering. When I have finished, I close the lid of the piano carefully and make my way to the bedroom.

Amelia is fast asleep, face down and naked, the duvet revealing the long curve of her back. She has a beautiful body, quite remarkable for her age. I pull the duvet up to cover her and sit quietly on the bed beside her. Today, somebody, some person or persons as yet unknown, tried to murder us. In the greater scheme of things, my passing will be of little consequence. But Amelia has yet to fulfil her potential and nobody should be denied that opportunity, no matter how late in life they may rise to the occasion. If Kevin Doppler can find those responsible for the attack, I swear to all the Gods of every faith, they will be brought to trial, and, if found guilty, I will, by then, I swear it, on my mother's grave if necessary, have introduced capital punishment for terrorists.

The bastards will hang by their necks until dead.

As a politician, religious precepts must sometimes take second place.

5

After the chaos of yesterday, this morning begins with satisfying routine. As usual, I rise at six-thirty and meditate for an hour. Unfortunately, it is not an easy meditation. I find there is much anger arising. It's hardly surprising that the shock of yesterday's attack still dominates my mental horizon. I do not attempt to squash it. That would be useless and would only frustrate the clearing of the mind.
I close my eyes to aid my concentration but images and thoughts continue to shriek and jump about like a kaleidoscope in pain. I concentrate on my breathing, the regular inhalation and exhalation, the gentle expansion and contraction of my lungs, the sensation of air through my nostrils, the tempo of life itself. Gradually, oh so very, very slowly, I begin to let go, to disconnect myself from the mental jumble. I see the anger and frustration but am not part of it. Even though it remains vivid and disturbed I do not wrestle with it or try to banish it. I observe it dispassionately. I note its arising. Like all phenomena it will eventually subside. The only constant in life is change.

I do not believe in breakfast meetings, preferring instead to dine with Amelia who, like me, has always been an early riser. This morning she chooses to remain in bed reading the newspapers (you can imagine what the headlines are like) so I arrange for a poached egg on toast to be sent up to her.

I change out of my meditation robes (a simple sarong, a holiday purchase from Thailand) and put on my suit. I always wear a plain white shirt with a velvet bow tie. I like to be neither flamboyant nor dull. We exchange kisses and I descend the stairs to proceed with the business of the day.

Trevor Skidmarsh is shown into my office at exactly eight thirty. He tries to shift the blame on to Ivor Pleeth, the Head of the Anti-Terrorist Squad. I simply avail him of the information passed to me by Rodney and Gloria. He turns white and then scarlet. I push the resignation letter across the desk. He signs it with a trembling hand. Scott Rignold ushers him out the back entrance.

A few moments later, Kevin Doppler appears. He has a kind of menacing charisma that I think is entirely appropriate to his new job as Police Commissioner. Personally speaking, I think community policing is something that can be driven quite satisfactorily from further down the ranks. The top man needs to bare his teeth, not with a politically correct smile, but with a pit-bull snarl. It is the only language the criminal fraternity understands. We should not lose sight of the fact that the police exist to maintain law and order and that means, first, foremost and last, catching criminals. Shoring up the inadequacies of Social Services is not part of that agenda. Kevin understands this. Scott has already presented him with the formal job offer in writing and he's clearly delighted. We shake hands and I signal for him to sit down.

"I trust everything is in order Kevin?"

"Yes, Prime Minister, highly satisfactory, thank you very much."

"Good. Splendid. Now look, there's not much more I want to say right now that we didn't discuss last night. Scott will give you a copy of a press statement that George will make after this morning's cabinet meeting and then it's full steam ahead."

I notice that in the cold light of day, his ravaged complexion does seem particularly unpleasant. No doubt, I will become accustomed to it. His eyes are grey and steady, if a little bloodshot. "Bernard has prepared something which I would like you to include in your first press conference."

"Certainly."

"Trevor has now departed and I think the least said about him the better."

"Of course."

"Unfortunately, we have yet to locate Henry, I know that he will be philosophical, possibly even relieved that he has been passed over but I would hate him to hear about your appointment via the media."

"I understand that he was admitted to Hampstead Royal Free hospital last night with further chest pains."

"Oh dear, that is very bad news. I'd better get someone over there as soon as possible."

"Actually sir, one of my colleagues is already at his bedside, I can convey your best wishes if that would help?"

I was about to buzz for Scott but relax my hand on hearing Kevin's remark. I feel better about this man already, so focused and assured, a welcome change to the wishy-washy Trevor.

"Yes, I would appreciate that, I have a cabinet meeting very shortly and I have a feeling the rest of the day will be rather vigorous to say the least."

As I gesture, he returns my smile. It's the first time I notice a large gold filling on the lower right hand side of his jaw. Perhaps he ought to have it replaced? Then again, maybe not. As we shake hands, I hold his grasp for a while.

"Don't let me down, will you Kevin?"

"You can depend on me, Prime Minister."

I smile and pat him on the shoulder.

"Please call me Ambrose, except when there are more than two ministers or civil servants about."

Instinctively he understands where I am coming from.
I watch his large frame as he passes silently through the doorway. I glance at my watch and notice I've got time for a quick cup of tea before the cabinet meeting. Scott appears like a genie from a lamp. Sometimes I think he's got a sixth sense.

"Is there anything you require?" he asks.

"Yes please, a nice hot cuppa would go down a treat."

"I'll get on to it right away. Here's this morning's agenda, together with a list of attendees."

"Thank you Scott."

My private parliamentary secretary is nothing if not efficient. I might wish for a touch more sense of humour but you can't have everything. He's very good looking in a blonde, blue-eyed Aryan sort of way and I'm told he's ferocious on the squash court. He has a first class degree in classics, a subject which I always think makes for an interesting personality. He will go far. I never actually asked for a list of ministers attending cabinet meetings, I think it was something Scott thought I should have. At one stage there were as many as twenty-two people crammed into the room, although that included a fair sprinkling of under-secretaries and suchlike.

The key to effective government is to keep in regular one-to-one contact with ministers. This I do assiduously. They all appreciate this. Quite often, I invite them to undergo further cranial therapy, to alleviate their stress. I usually take the opportunity to reinforce the message from the far side. It's a little bonus to lift their spirits. As for the cabinet meetings themselves, well, they are for discussion and debate and to ensure that we continue to sing from the same hymn street, which as I've mentioned earlier, is so important. I do not pressurise anyone to attend because I am mindful that they have duties and responsibilities every bit as important as mine. Sometimes even a Prime Minister can get in the way! As long as I can see that the blue touch paper of my vision is still smouldering, then I am happy for cabinet meetings to ebb and flow organically. This approach does not sit happily with the civil servants who seem incapable of functioning without sub-committees and steering committees and strategic target groups and all the attendant bureaucracy they so love.

Sir Mallard Kane, the head of the civil service, is a quintessential framework and structure man but he dare not voice any adverse comments because he knows, only too well, that this administration is pursuing the most radical of policies since the partition of India. The corridors of Whitehall are galvanised with our programme of change. Civil servants everywhere, and at every level, are not only working full blast but, for once in their grey lives, are excited and energised. He senses, as they all do, a wind of change that cannot be diminished, or deflected, let alone destroyed by an Opposition that virtually suffered ritual disembowelment at the polls.

A public humiliation of such ferocity that it is all they can do to enter the chamber without exposing their bleeding entrails. Pressure groups, lobbyists and corporate fixers are still reeling in the vortex of our power. They can barely keep up with us, let alone persuade us to modify our thinking. We are the strongest, most resolute government this country has ever seen, and yet, in spite of that, some lunatic, or group of lunatics, saw fit to lob a bomb in our direction. Well, Kevin Doppler is on the case and I remain Prime Minister, totally in charge. I shall prevail.

Scott appears with my tea.

"Ah thank you Scott, most welcome. What's the weather like outside?"

"I'm afraid I haven't had time to look, I think it's quite sunny."

"We must never lose touch with nature Scott, the behaviour of the elements can be our strongest guide."

He places the tea on my desk.

"Shall I open the window?"

"Yes, that would be a very good idea."

Needless to say that wasn't quite what I was driving at but I prefer to give encouragement whenever I can. Scott fiddles with the security latch and eventually raises the lower sash. The fresh air is most pleasant and he turns to me with the faintest of smiles, pleased that his suggestion has brought me comfort.

"Everyone is present in the cabinet room, shall I join them if everything is in order here?"

"Yes, please do, I shall be along as soon as I've finished this splendid cup of tea, Assam Tips by the taste of it."

"Freshly opened this morning."

"I thought as much."

Another smile, no tea-bag philistine he. I run my eyes down the list, sipping gently as I go.

I have three women ministers in my cabinet, and each one of them is performing brilliantly. They all have demanding briefs, each one playing a pivotal role in the rejuvenation of this country. I cannot understand why some male politicians feel so threatened by the presence of women in power. Just because Maggie went off the rails towards the end does not mean their copybook is sullied forever. We have only to look at the international stage for fine examples of accomplished politicians with distinguished careers, which is not to undermine the achievements at home.

In the days when I was no more than a back bench whipper-snapper, I shall never forget Barbara Castle, with her blazing blue eyes, absolutely determined to succeed with her drink-drive legislation. A rare voice of reason in the socialist cadre. Nowadays, women are in the ascendancy and foolish is the man who attempts to turn the clock backwards where matters of emancipation are concerned.

My administration is all the more effective for having Hattie Chapelthwaite in Education, Lucy Bowens in Social Services and Susan Palmero in Arts. I am so pleased they are all here today and very touched that each one of them telephoned Amelia last night to enquire after her well being. Kindness and sensitivity, just when it was needed. George was the only male minister to express consideration in that direction; he sent Amelia a beautiful bunch of spring daffodils this morning. She was delighted.

Susan Palmero had a telephone chat with her this morning, I expect she'll pop up to see her after the meeting. They get on very well together. It is very much a meeting of the minds, of kindred spirits. Amelia worked in arts administration for a number of years and before that, when I first met her, she was dallying with the idea of a career in dancing. But, her musical talents seemed to take precedence and she entered the Royal College of Music to study the piano. Susan Palmero was an actress before turning to politics and quite a successful one too, appearing in TV soaps as well as the National Theatre. Or should I say actor? Personally I think that's another example of political correctness overtaking common sense. If ever there was a profession where a person's gender was of paramount importance, surely it is in show business? But, as Susan reminded me, it was no less a personage than Dame Edith Evans who remarked, 'well, you don't say doctress do you?' She had a point, I suppose. Whatever the case, there is no doubting Susan's gender when you meet her. A stunning brunette with sultry Italian blood coursing through her. In her mid-forties she still has the figure of a woman half her age and there's no denying the fact that, when she enters a room, there is electricity in the air. Needless to say, her communication and presentational skills are superb and she can wrap most opponents round her little finger in minutes. When she faces the opposition at the despatch box, her jet-black eyes gleam with the thrill of combat.

"The Labour government feared freedom of speech and expression as much as they tried to suppress it, this government celebrates its very existence and will nurture and encourage it from John o' Groats to Lands End."

I believe very strongly in the performing arts and we have injected massive sums into numerous schemes that will encourage creativity and talent in every discipline. A nation that cannot express itself is a nation in decline. Those were the very words in our manifesto. Our market research showed that actors, writers, dancers, musicians, artists, indeed, creative souls of every persuasion, flocked to the polling booths in their thousands to place their cross in our favour. Susan's personal dream is nothing less than a total renaissance of provincial theatre, and I am behind her one hundred percent. No more couch potatoes. Let the population fall about in the aisles with tears of joy or indignation. A nation come alive again!

Hattie Chappelthwaite is a different kind of woman altogether. Sadly, many people refer to her as a battleaxe, behind her back. They haven't the nerve to make derogatory comments to her face, because, without doubt, she is a formidable lady. I think she's the same age as me, certainly the same height, which is six foot, and she always wears sensible shoes with flat heels. I'm no expert on dress sizes but

I would hazard a guess that she must be somewhere around eighteen, or even twenty. She is not obese, just massively framed. Once, when she sat next to me on the front bench and Jocelyn was on the other side, I felt hugely protected, as if positioned between two boulder dams. She always wears the same charcoal grey suit with a feint chalk stripe, and a white blouse buttoned severely at the neck. Typically, she doesn't bother to hide the many grey streaks in her hair which is cropped short like a man's. Her gold-rimmed, half-moon spectacles sit precisely on the bridge of a dominant, bulbous nose, whose left nostril sports a large mole on the outside, from the centre of which sprout several dark hairs, not dissimilar to those of her moustache. Intellectually, her fire power is awesome and with her deep, stentorian voice, she is a sight to behold at the despatch box.

She is equally impressive in committee and many are the misguided, arrogant, self-opinionated, liberal academics whom she has swept the floor with, scattering their silly, muddle-headed, so-called progressive theories on education to the nearest skirting boards. Our radical reforms affect every level of education, from pre-school right through to university. In the latter case we have had to sort out the mess left by Labour. Hattie has imposed a system that allows universities to charge whatever fees they like. Student loans have been cancelled outright and have been replaced by means-tested grants, administered, not by the local education authority, but a specially created department of the Inland Revenue. Nobody is going to hood-wink this government.

Moreover, universities will be proper universities and not these Mickey Mouse socialist aberrations that have grown like verrucas on a foot, crippling the forward march of progress. And these proper universities will have to justify their fees by the quality and quantity of their research work, not solely their degree pass rate. Hattie has made it clear that all polytechnics, technical colleges, and establishments of a similar ilk created since 1970, will, by law, return to their former status and curricula. That will put a stop to the nonsense about national shortages of skills in the trades and industry. The opposition hated us for it but Hattie demolished them with commendable style. Her mocking tones at the despatch box remain a delicious memory for ever.

"*The Right Honourable Gentleman is of course entitled to his opinion, however, I am sure he will be as relieved as any of us that, in the event of a blocked lavatory, his call will be answered by a qualified plumber, and not some disillusioned graduate with a spurious degree in cling film wrapping.*"

The speaker called for order but to no avail.
Lucy Bowens, my Social Services Minister is neither formidable or sexy, however, she does have a phenomenal memory for facts and figures which she trots out to devasting effect. Part of her armoury, (and I suspect she is fully aware of it), is that her opponents are lulled into a false sense of security by her diffident personality. It is accentuated by her small physical appearance. She is the first to admit that her height is only four foot, eleven and three-quarter inches and she has no intention of wearing high heels to compensate for it. She has a tiny, almost inaudible voice and this forces people to listen hard when she speaks, a fact which often unsettles the bellowing bully. With her short bobbed hair and beady eyes, the mouse-like quality she exudes has a shy charm all of its own. Many are those who patronise her as if she were a little child who has just dropped a sticky lollipop, when the reality is that she's as deadly as a rattlesnake. These are my three diamonds in cabinet. Sometimes I wish their male colleagues would sparkle in the same manner but I suppose that would be asking too much? To be fair, dear George does twinkle now and again and Rashidi always behaves in full-blown Technicolour, so perhaps I shouldn't split hairs? As we progress in our second year in office, we remain as tight a ship as ever there was.

I finish my tea, gather my papers and proceed to the cabinet room. As soon as I enter, everyone rises spontaneously and applauds me.

Now that's what I call, real team spirit.

6

I await for the applause to subside. Even Clive Smeelie, the Lord Chancellor, a man of morose disposition at the best of times, cannot suppress a crooked half-smile. Clearly, the entire cabinet is pleased to see me, alive and well.

"Good morning everyone," I say, beaming genially, "please be seated."

I wait for them to settle themselves and remain standing to deliver my next line. I do so enjoy a bit of theatricality at times.

"I suppose I must be the only Prime Minister to be sat upon by his Chancellor without resenting it."

More laughter. I took a chance that Amelia would have mentioned to Susan Palmero about our somewhat undignified scrum in the back of the car, knowing that she couldn't resist spreading the story. I was right, they got the joke. A super start to the day. I take my seat.

"I trust you slept well, Jocelyn?"

Jocelyn gurgles in basso profundo merriment.

"Indeed yes, Missoo was firmly ensconced under the duvet as usual."

There are polite titters all round. Perhaps I should explain that Missoo is Jocelyn's cat and they always sleep together, nor does he hide the fact that his prodigious snoring often drives her to seek refuge under his duvet. It's all very touching really. Such a gentle giant.

"Okay, let's make a start." I catch George's eye, just long enough to give him a friendly visual, "by now you will all know what happened last night and doubtless you will have read tabloid and broadsheet alike. The first thing I want to tell you is that I accepted Trevor Skidmarsh's resignation this morning and have appointed Kevin Doppler as the new Commissioner of Police."

There are ruffles of interest around the table and I note the disdainful and somewhat exaggerated glance that Aubrey Fynch-Chilling sends in George's direction. It's unspoken message is clear to everyone, namely, isn't that something the Home Secretary should do? Aubrey can be very naughty at times. I ignore him and continue.

"You are aware, I'm sure of the Assistant Commissioner's failing health, unfortunately he was taken ill again last night and is currently hospitalised. I think early retirement is almost inevitable. George has prepared a press statement that he will give direct to camera after this morning's meeting. George, perhaps you might like to read it now?"

George reads out the statement without a single stumble or fluff. So far, so good. Aubrey clears his throat importantly.

"May one enquire as to whom Kevin Doppler's replacement will be?"

The questions hangs in the air. Naturally, cabinet members know about our intention to legalise all drugs, even though they are sworn to secrecy for the time being. Kevin's replacement will be pivotal in managing the supply chain and ensuring the safe delivery of drugs, via Customs and Excise, to licensed GP's. We anticipate the usual moans about increased workload and security of stock etcetera, but hopefully they will settle down when they hear about the financial incentives we shall be offering them. Quentin Nesbitt the Health Minister is working on that particular package and it's a pity that he's not here today. Scott tells me he telephoned earlier with his apologies for absence, (apparently his haemorrhoids are playing up again).

Needless to say, Kevin and I have discussed potential candidates and agree that such an important position must go to a determined and streetwise police officer with proven administrative abilities. Damien Chick, Kevin's assistant in the Special Drugs Unit is one such a man.

"I have asked Kevin to make some recommendations and in due course he will discuss his shortlist with George, who I am sure will steer matters competently towards a successful conclusion."

I give George a quick wink. He likes it when I shoot from the hip. Aubrey sinks into a little sulk. I know he wanted to be Chancellor of the Exchequer, but with somebody like Jocelyn on the scene, there is simply no contest. If he continues to have these little petulant fits I shall have to take him in hand, or to be precise, both of my hands with his head between them. Unfortunately, seconds later, Aubrey chooses to pipe up again.

"Prime Minister, I need hardly remind you that with the sensitive brief that the minister of international development and myself are undertaking, it is of paramount importance that the future head of the drugs squad will be someone who is not only fully cognisant with our brief but is politically adept at discussing it with a wider audience too."

He tails off with a distinctly sardonic air. I adjust my bow tie before replying.

"Aubrey, I hope you are not inferring that the Home Secretary is unaware of the significance of this appointment in relation to the current modus operandi within the foreign office?"

Sometimes, where Aubrey is concerned, it is necessary to adopt a rather pompous attitude, if only to deflate his own mounting sense of self-importance. He does not miss the subtle emphasis I place on the word *current* modus operandi.

"I am merely saying," says Aubrey, his mouth curling with displeasure, "that it would be appreciated if, in this particular instance, the wisdom of at least some basic consultation with the Foreign Office will not be overlooked."

I notice George beginning to flush. His somewhat nervous disposition is, in part, attributable to the fact that he is only too aware of the broader implications of his decisions. He is not terribly good at defending himself and since I don't want this kind of spat to dominate the meeting I step in.

"Let it be known to all concerned," I intone sternly, "that I shall be the final arbiter of any appointment and if there is anyone here today that feels I am somehow out of touch with the political sensitivity of such an appointment, then I shall be happy to discuss the matter with them, in private, after this meeting." The only sound is the rumbling of Jocelyn's stomach. "Right, let us continue."

The atmosphere eases and papers are shuffled amidst the welcoming sound of sparkling water hissing free from several bottles and glug-glugging into glasses up and down the table. George kindly offers me one. I accept.

"Thank you George, hmm, Highland Spring, my favourite, a pity the Secretary of State for Scotland isn't here to enjoy it with us."

That raises a faint titter. We all know that Hamish McToot wouldn't be seen dead with a glass of water in his hand, not when the conspicuous consumption of whisky would do the job so much better. I wait for things to settle down again.

" . . . I have given much thought as to the way ahead after yesterday's bombing. Already our opponents are demanding to know what measures we are taking in the fight against terrorism and how can we guarantee the safety of our citizens from such outrages in the future. I have little doubt that their criticism will spread from security matters to crime and policing in general. I believe the time has now come, not only to accelerate the pace of change, but also to introduce some of our feel-good measures, as a way of neutralising any feelings of anxiety that may exist amongst the community at large. George, if you would be good enough to update us on the progress of our police recruitment and prison building programme."

George and I agreed on this tactic last night, so I'm pleased to see that his hot flush has subsided and he is no longer twiddling his fingers like George Formby on a ukulele. He reads out his notes with considerable elan. There are copious facts and figures and data of all kinds at every turn. It is evident that the civil servants have been burning the midnight oil and it all sounds very impressive, which is to say, I am impressed. George finishes with a flourish.

"Based on these facts, I am confident that we can contain any foreseeable rise in crime for the duration of this parliament."

He relaxes in his chair like a schoolboy who has just delivered an error free translation of some tricky Latin.

"Thank you George, most comprehensive. Comments anyone?"

It is Lucy Bowens' mouse-like voice that pipes up.

"If the current prison population is seventy-nine thousand, and the available spaces will increase by an additional twenty-one thousand when three of the six mega-prisons become operational by the end of next year, what rise in crime are we anticipating to justify locking up so many people?"

"Well, without wishing to pre-empt anything the Prime Minister may wish to say," says George, politely, "if we bring the legalisation of drugs programme forward, then it is unlikely that drugs related crime will diminish rapidly, in fact the prognosis is that, initially, it may soar dramatically as organised drug dealers seek to sustain the black market by stealing government stocks from bonded warehouses and GP's surgeries. There is also the possibility that the figure of one in seven road accidents attributable to drugs, may rise by as much as fifty percent, as thousands of drivers take to their vehicles whilst under the influence of mind bending substances of one kind or another, albeit obtained legally through government controlled outlets. If our retributive punishment scheme becomes law, by which I mean our proposed amendments to the Criminal Justice Bill, then all those found guilty will be subject to custodial sentences ranging from six weeks for demolishing municipal property such as a street lamp, to fifteen years for manslaughter for killing a pedestrian or other motorist."

"I hear what you say George," says Lucy, piping away, "but it still sounds as if we're creating a situation simply to lock people up."

There is a distinct restlessness around the table and Aubrey cannot resist one of his stage whispers designed to be heard by all without actually appearing so.

"Oh dear God," he sighs, projecting his voice across Rashidi towards Lucy, who is sitting opposite, "there's always one, isn't there?"

Lucy maybe mouse-like in her demeanour but it's never stopped her from arguing her point. She flares up to a shrill squeak.

"Excuse me, but from where I'm sitting, the numbers simply don't stack up, and when it comes to the committee stage of the amended bill, that's precisely what the other side will capitalise on to undermine our raison d'être."

Unfortunately, for all her splendid grasp of facts and figures, Lucy still does not seem to appreciate that when you've got a whopping majority on the scale we have, the endless carping over detail, which typifies the committee procedure, need no longer be considered a threat since the combined force of the opposition parties is so weak that the government has virtually got carte blanche to do what it wants to do anyway.

I was just wondering how I might intervene without undermining Lucy when Mervyn Mallatratt, the Employment Secretary makes his customary opening moan. He's known as MM, not because of the alliteration in his name but rather because of his strange habit of preceding everything he says with a long mmm. He's a very conciliatory man, always looking for the middle ground, for the areas of agreement, of minimal confrontation. His long mmm's are like some kind of emollient poured on troubled waters.

"Mmm . . . Lucy, I think you may not have been present when we discussed the ramifications of this particular policy. Even if the prison spaces are not filled as quickly as a cost effective analysis might demand, the resultant increases in jobs for the police, prison services and ancillary positions, are so significant that I'm sure our detractors, not to mention the general public, would realise the robustness of our raison d'être."

"Have you got any figures?" she pipes back.

"Mmm . . . well, I have no doubt George will correct me if I'm wrong, but I think, on a percentage basis, we're talking something in the region of a three-hundred percent increase for police, four hundred percent for the prison services, six hundred percent for supporting services such as psychiatrists, psychologists, behavioural therapists, drug counsellors and probation officers. And then there's three hundred and fifty percent for Customs and Excise officers, and nine hundred and sixty-two percent for the National Coast Guard Service.
Mmm . . . and that excludes the job increases arising from the services infrastructure necessary to sustain such operations, and I'm talking generally about cleaning and catering contracts and general trades skills such as plumbers, electricians, carpenters, plasterers, glaziers and er, well - "

"Let us not forget the educational opportunities as well," interjects Hattie Chapelthwaite, her booming tones in stark contrast to the dreamy soliloquy that Meryvn has almost lapsed into, "there is a great deal of illiteracy amongst the criminal fraternity, to say nothing of the cessation of higher education courses due to their misdemeanours. It would be foolish to assume that the criminal mind does not possess enormous potential, if only it could be channelled in the right direction. We are, after all, not simply incarcerating them, but training them to re-engage with society in a meaningful way. It takes a special kind of teacher to do that and we shall need them to step forward in their hundreds, quite possibly in their thousands."

"Mmm . . . I do take your point."

"Nor should we ignore the role of performing arts in this equation," says Susan Palmero, visibly anxious that she may have been overlooked. A snigger gathers pace in various quarters which only serves to incense her. Back she comes, eyes blazing, shoulders braced, brandishing her elegant hands like a pair of talons. "There is enough research to demonstrate that pent up emotions benefit enormously from role playing and improvisation. Many offenders are natural actors if they did but know it, and who's to say we should not train them to express themselves in a controlled and professional manner?"

"Mmm . . . well, certainly not me."

"Did any of you watch Coronation Street last night? Well, maybe you should've because an ex-con by the name of Jack Barnes was in it and the only acting experience he had prior to that was in one of our prison theatre workshops. Who's to say we cannot do the same for others? Let's put drama teachers on the agenda shall we?"

"Mmm . . . I'd be delighted to, who knows, if the remaining three mega-prisons come on stream according to plan, we may yet be the first government to preside over a total employment situation."

"Perhaps we should train them to be ballet dancers too," mutters Aubrey cynically.

Before Susan can parry, Lucy chimes in, a lot calmer now.

"Yes, thank you Mervyn, I get the picture," she says, "if that really were to come about, then you could add another eight billion pounds savings annually in respect of benefit fraud."

At this point, all eyes return to George who, as everyone knows, is being given the run around by civil servants who seem to place every possible query and obstacle in his way when he tries to press ahead with the introduction of national identity cards. It's not George's fault, and since I don't want to seem him become rattled, I make a timely intervention.

"Ah yes, I'd like to focus our minds on my opening remarks concerning security. The fact of the matter is that such audacious terrorists acts could be severely undermined, were we to have national identity cards up and running. Originally, our plans were to introduce them by next spring, however, I intend to see them operational by the end of this year."

A gasp goes round the table. It's very much of the pigs might fly variety and is followed by more hissing of sparkling water bottles and glug-glugging of glasses being refilled.

"I am aware that the Home Secretary has done everything possible to maintain our original schedule," a silence ensues as they pick up my use of the formal nomenclature, "however,
I am also aware that our colleagues in the civil service have a different perspective concerning our implementation plans.

I have been appraised of the complexities surrounding this issue, not the least the apparent difficulties of integrating the computer systems of the National Insurance, the Inland Revenue and the Benefit Agency, not to mention the cross-referencing to the Passport Office and Police National Database, which are, of course, essential if we are to do the job properly. To this end, I shall be summoning Sir Mallard Kane to my office and will require him to make an account of his department's lethargy in this respect. After all's said and done, the civil servants are noticeably galvanised in every other endeavour, so why not this one?"

I can see that they remain sceptical. No matter, there comes a time when the Prime Minister must flex his authority for the good of the nation. Having played my authority card I seem to have little alternative but to revert to the next agenda item. At that point, Leonard Welling, the Treasury Secretary coughs politely. He has such pronounced thyroid eyes that I sometimes think that if he sneezes, they'll pop out of his head altogether. Apart from that oddity, he's a dull man with scuffed shirt collars and a fifties Brylcreem hairstyle.

"What is it Leonard?"

"Well Prime Minister, I was just thinking, if national identity cards come on stream six months early, this will surely increase all known costs significantly."

I throw a glance at Jocelyn.

"Jocelyn?"

"More than likely."

"If we have to charge more for the card itself," says Leonard drearily, "that will hardly make it any more popular."

"It's not popular now," says Jocelyn.

"Well, I don't see how we can force people to pay for if they can't afford it."

"We can always send them to prison," bellows Rashidi, "or better still, why don't we link our database to all the supermarkets, so nobody will be able to eat who doesn't have a card. Eat, die or go to prison, yeah!" he slams the table.

Maybe things do need lightening up but it's a serious issue and I'm determined to succeed.

"I know it's a political hot potato," I intone, "but I'm sure there isn't a single one of you here today that doesn't appreciate how much it remains a pivotal tool in so many of our major initiatives. I am under no illusion that the final cost will be horrendous, but we shall just have to weather the storm. If necessary, cuts will have to be made in other budgets."

Everyone falls silent.

"We can start with Defence," there is a wave of relief, "their overspending is fast reaching biblical proportions. I would imagine that our contribution to the Euro Fighter alone would be sufficient to fund the identity card project several times over."

"More than likely," chortles Jocelyn.

I am aware that Claude Napper, the Defence Minister, is absent today.

"Where is Claude by the way?" I ask.

"In Brussels, attending a Nato Strategic Planning meeting," replies Hugo Snatch, the Cabinet Secretary.

"Do we have his apologies for absence?"

"No," says Scott, beating Hugo to the mark, much to Hugo's chagrin.

I feel my temper rising. It is Claude's lack of courtesy that annoys me more than anything else. I will have to do something about it.

"Right, what's next?"

"Amendments to the Asylum Bill," says Hugo quickly.

He resents Scott's presence as he feels it undermines his position. I'm not sure whether Hugo is entirely trustworthy.

I am about to gather my thoughts when the beautiful blonde assistant principal private secretary with the incredibly long pony-tail enters. There is something about her poise, as well as her looks, that give her such presence. All eyes are on her as she hands me a typewritten note.

Jim Brigginshaw, MP for Leicester Central died at ten-thirty this morning.

Oh bugger, right now we need a by-election like a hole in the head.

7

Harold Wilson once said 'a week is a long time in politics'. What a silly billy. No wonder he didn't succeed. There is absolutely no point in trying to assess your progress in terms of survival. You can only deal with the moment. Therein lies the key to happiness. If only people would stop thinking about success and what they are going to do to achieve it, they would be so much happier. As a politician, and particularly as Prime Minister, I have to think ahead to some extent. The human race as a whole is anxious at heart and that's why we had to publish a manifesto. They needed some point of reference. Well, that's democracy for you. Load of tosh really. They were not prepared to take a leap into the dark, even though the Guardian claimed that that was precisely what they had done by voting for me. Now they are beginning to eat their words. Three months after the failed assassination attempt, we increased our majority by five thousand at the Leicester Central by-election. It was not a sympathy vote for the sad passing of dear Jim Brigginshaw either. What the constituents saw was our determination to create a life worth living. They can now see police on the streets and daily read about the villains we are putting in jail. All good stuff. Understandably, however, they were alarmed when Jocelyn increased VAT to twenty-five percent in the Spring Budget. Nonetheless, their consternation soon subsided when we caught the temple terrorists.

Shortly afterwards, George went on prime time television to announce the opening of Howardsville, the first of our six mega-prisons. During the by-election campaign, the National Front did their best to stir up racial hatred, even trying to incite violence between the various ethnic communities. It backfired when three of their thugs were caught daubing racist slogans on the garage doors of Doctor Mangal Bali Chakkar, our candidate. His Jack Russell terrier, Pandit, got kicked in the jaws in the process but, in spite of several broken teeth, returned to the attack and locked his jaws on one of the assailant's testicles. All three were jailed for six months and sent to Howardsville. Through the auspices of the Kaya Centre for Mindfulness, (of which, may I remind you, I am no longer Chairman) a gift of twenty thousand pounds was donated to the Shree Swaminarayan Temple rebuilding project, in memory of His Holiness, Shree Sahajanand Narayan Muni and all those who died in the explosion.

I was very pleased when I found the original piece of paper on which I had written the guru's name, as it saved me from the most dreadful embarrassment. Scott assured me that he had placed the official invitation to the funeral with all the other papers, including my speech of condolence. It is most unlike him to be inefficient. I chose not to make an issue of it, although, when I mentioned it in passing to Benjamin, he remarked that just prior to my leaving, he had heard Scott and Hugo engaged in some kind of argument. Apparently, Hugo accused Scott of being a Nazi. Neither of them have mentioned the incident to me, however. I'm rather concerned about their deteriorating relationship. I'm not sure about the wisdom of intervening, particularly since Hugo, as a civil servant, will go running to Sir Mallard Kane the minute I say something he doesn't like. I'm sure he does anyway.

When I spoke to Mallard about the lack of progress with the national ID programme it was evident that he was prepared for my criticism beforehand. It's not that I really mind anyone fighting their corner, it's just that when it comes to a meticulous Whitehall mandarin like Mallard, the argument becomes giddy with circumlocution. This morning, feeling that I was getting nowhere, I meditated for two hours, and then, with a much clearer mind, summoned him to my office.

"Mallard, I've been thinking about the national ID programme again."

"That does not surprise me, I am similarly occupied"

"As indeed you should be."

"I was going to say, to a vexatious degree."

"Well I'm glad you didn't. Now, as I understand it, what you're really saying is that in order to meet the revised timetable, you will need several hundred more staff, is that correct?"

"Well, three hundred and ninety-eight to be precise."

"Precision is exactly what I want Mallard, and accuracy too, but above all else, delivery on time, so, go ahead and recruit them."

Normally, Mallard is as inscrutable as a pane of frosted glass, however, in this instance, I notice a flicker of emotion across his face. A brief expression of joy before returning to his usual enigmatic self.

"That is most generous of you Ambrose . . . but may I enquire as to whether the Treasury are fully reconciled to the cost implications?"

"Please don't concern yourself on that count, Jocelyn is on the case."

He gives me the faintest of smiles.

"Then I can only say how appreciative I am of your decision and will pursue matters with all convenient speed."

"I want national identity cards fully operational by the end of the year, so may I suggest that you pursue matters with all indecent haste."

"I take your point," he says, chuckling diplomatically, "will there be anything else?"

"Just keep me posted."

As he makes his exit, I'm fascinated, as always, by the play of light on his huge, bald, dome of a head. I wonder if he polishes it? I ponder for a while on the myriad secrets that he must hold inside it, like data in an observatory. Then I ring Jocelyn.

"Hello."

"Jocelyn, I've just given Mallard the go-ahead to recruit three hundred and ninety-eight extra staff, can we afford it?"

"Shouldn't think so."

"What about the defence budget?"

"We've already raided that."

"Yes I know, but there must be something else, what about their procurement projects?"

"Still spiralling out of control."

"Ye Gods, I thought I told Claude Napper to get a grip on things."

"Well, how about axing the Nimrod MRA4 project?"

"Jocelyn, you're not thinking straight are you? You know how important I regard maritime surveillance apropos our plans to combat illegal drugs and immigration."

"Well, it could save us five hundred million."

"No, Claude tells me they've almost cracked the communications problems and then they'll be able to link directly with all the coast guard motor torpedo boats and swap computer files digitally or something clever like that."

"Rule Britannia."

"Exactly, even though it's only the English Channel, the North Sea and parts of the Atlantic. Now what else is there?"

"The Eurofighter Typhoon?"

"No, I don't want to upset Chirac and Schröder just yet."

"Well, you could always move the Gurkhas to Cyprus."

"How much would that save us?"

"Difficult to say off hand, there would be certain installation costs and may I remind you that when they're not in the jungle, these boys like to shower daily and you know what Greek plumbing is like."

"Well fiddle about with it, and maybe a few others like it and let me have the figures by lunch time. I'm putting out a call for Claude right now."

"Okay."

I ring off and buzz Scott.

"Where's the defence secretary today?"

"I think he's with his department."

"Get hold of him and tell him I want to see him at two o'clock sharp, and emphasise the word sharp."

"Yes, Prime Minister."

Scott knows that I know that Claude thinks I don't know that when he's with his department, it usually means he's planning an early liquid lunch and a quick grope with the barmaid at the Mermaid and Cutlass. Scott seems to have moles everywhere. He is my main source for information that my enemies would rather I did not know about. Alas, in politics, as in life, no matter how decently you treat people, there will always be some who despise you, often for reasons that are not immediately transparent. Even though I hand picked my cabinet, and revealed to them my vision of the future in a way that no other Prime Minister in living memory has done, I sense resentment amongst some of them.

I am most worried about Aubrey Fynch-Chilling. It is not simply that he craves to be Chancellor, I think it goes deeper than that. Perhaps it is just plain jealousy? I cannot put my finger on it. These days, whenever I invite him to join me in our special one-to-one sessions, when my motive, let me remind you, is only to refresh his memory with the life affirming message from the far side, he makes every excuse to avoid them. Naturally, I do not persist. That is not my nature. Nevertheless, I have this uneasy feeling that, if ever my position were to become compromised in some way, he would rejoice and take advantage. Scott tells me that he spends an inordinate amount of time with Gloria and Rodney. Obviously, as a Foreign Secretary, I would expect a certain level of discourse with the heads of MI5 and MI6 but I gather this often runs to lunch dates of several hours duration.

I sincerely hope a political ménage à trois is not in the making.

Perhaps I should ask Kevin to keep an eye on them? He is turning out to be a first class Police Commissioner, even better than I had expected. Scott tells me he has a network of moles that extends into the very fabric of society. Naturally, he did not say that in so many words, he is too discreet for that. I got the distinct impression however that, in his opinion, Kevin knows more about what goes on than both Gloria and Rodney put together (including when the two of them are together in more than just the intelligence gathering sense). It is a sorry state of affairs when one cannot trust a key minister or the secret service. Nevertheless, I have a country to run and will do my utmost to maintain a sense of equilibrium.

There is a tap on the door and Scott enters.

"Yes Scott?"

"The defence minister confirms he will see you at two o'clock sharp."

"How nice of him."

"May I remind you that you have an audience with the Queen at three o'clock."

"Thank you, what I have to say to Claude won't take long. Was there anything else?"

"Your wife rang to see if you were okay."

"Oh?"

" . . . She said it's usually a bad sign when you meditate for more than an hour."

"I'll pop up and see her at lunch time."

"I understand she is having sandwiches with Susan Palmero at twelve-thirty."

"Oh really, what's that all about?"

"I'm not sure, but apparently you're joining them too."

"Oh really?"

"Apparently your wife made the arrangement."

"Oh really?"

"She said she mentioned it to you this morning and you promised to include her and Susan in your meditation."

"Oh really, was there anything else?"

"Well, she did say that you ought to skip the pickled onions if you were still going to the Palace this afternoon."

"Point taken. Good Lord, is it really twelve o'clock already?"

"Seven minutes past, to be exact."

"Well, I may as well push off now."

"Before you go, Prime Minister, Benjamin would like you to see this message he's just received from the Archbishop of Canterbury's press office."

Scott passes me the paper and waits dutifully as I read it. I've noticed that these days, if there's one thing that typifies a communication from the Archbishop's press office, it's the archness of the message itself. It seems they are getting themselves into a lather over the fact that the Kaya Centre for Mindfulness have responded generously to requests for financial assistance from a Sikh temple in Neasden and a Muslim one in Leeds, *'even though such places of worship have not suffered terrorist attacks as was the case in Leicester'*.

How churlish can one get? I return the note to Scott.

"Tell Benjamin that perhaps we should remind them that,
a) I am no longer chairman of Kaya, and b) the church of England owns more land than the M.o.D. and we are still looking for a suitable site for our sixth mega-prison."

I leave Scott to his own devices and make my way upstairs. I have little doubt that Amelia did mention the lunch arrangements but clearly I had forgotten about it. Sometimes I worry about my absent mindedness. I have never been in any doubt that the pressures of high office can, on occasions, reach intolerable levels, but that's part of the territory and all things come to pass. Besides, I am sustained by my spiritual practice. Having said that, there was a fleeting moment during meditation this morning, when I thought I saw the grim reaper. Worrying enough in itself, but, when the image includes a woman's brassiere, strung, somewhat insouciantly, across the blade of the scythe, there is cause for greater concern. Is there scandal afoot?

Claude Napper is a bounder, that's for sure.

8

Shrieks of laughter greet my ears. Amelia and Susan are facing each other from either end of the settee. What a picture they are. Both beautiful and vivacious women, Susan the more demonstrative in this instance, waving her arms about in grand theatrical gesture. I can only assume that she's just cracked the punch line of a big joke, for there is Amelia, hugging herself with both arms in humorous convulsion, her eyes welling with tears of mirth. I savour the moment before entering. The level of hysteria is such that it's difficult to become part of it. I just grin and help myself to a glass of Marquieres, already uncorked on the coffee table; a vin de pays of modest distinction but pleasantly chilled for all that.

"Well cheers," I remark, somewhat lamely.
Somehow this seems to precipitate further hilarity and I can do no more than sip away and watch in fascination as the pair of them roll about like giggly schoolgirls. Naturally I'm delighted that they get on so well together, it's the kindred spirit kicking in.

It was Amelia who drew my attention to an article that Susan had written for the Guardian Arts section, not long after she had entered parliament, concerning what she had referred to as the dumbing down of television and the duffing up of theatre. It was an impassioned plea to all the creative movers and shakers, not to jeopardise their artistic integrity for the lure of short term lucrative gains and instant celebrity. Considering that she had once turned down the offer of a regular part in Casualty to play Racine for three weeks at the Donmar Warehouse, one could not accuse her of hypocrisy. Apparently, when one of her local party activists, (the association treasurer, in fact), had rather snidely pointed out, in a letter to the editor, that she owed much of her current popularity to her stint in Coronation Street, as opposed to being MP for Newport and Norbury East, she confronted him at a Queen's jubilee constituency party, and threatened to engage his face with a plate of tiramisu unless he publicly withdrew his remarks. A feisty lady not to be trifled with.

I settle myself into an armchair and wait for them to compose themselves.

Eventually, when some semblance of normality is achieved, Amelia says, "Oh God, that's the best shaggy dog story I've heard for years . . . I'm going to get the sandwiches."
And off she goes.

"You seem to be enjoying yourselves," I remark to Susan, hoping to indicate that I'm game for a laugh too. Being Prime Minister is not always that much fun.

"Oh, we always have a laugh, Meely and me."
I wince at the nick name. I know they're chummy but why bastardise such a pretty name as Amelia? I shan't say anything. Yesterday, Amelia accused me of being a censorious fuddy-duddy because I disapproved of people who drank straight from the bottle instead of a glass. Young people think it's hip, she said. I think it's vulgar and American, I replied, and then she accused me of being stuck in a time warp. I must admit that did sting a bit, after all, I've spent most of my life following a philosophy that examines the reality of the here and now. We didn't argue about it. Amelia has always been a

dedicated follower of fashion, and more so, it seems, since the blossoming of her friendship with Susan.

I remember now why I'm supposed to be here. Susan wants Amelia to become a non-executive director of the controversial Sutchworth Arts Centre which is due to open in September with much ballyhoo and banging of drums. When Lord Cranley Sutchworth's stately pile in Shropshire burnt to the ground five years ago, with himself and Lady Sutchworth tragically reduced to toast in the great banqueting hall, a huge battle took place between the heirs and English Heritage, and the local planning authority, as to what should replace it. When the insurance claim was finally settled and inheritance tax had taken its customary spirit-crushing toll, they turned to Susan, as their local MP, for help and advice. She was instrumental in securing a huge lottery grant and seeing off bids to transform the site into a grotesque range of options, including, amongst others, a Tesco's superstore, a dry-run synthetic ski slope, and an EC approved state-of-the-art abattoir.

The creation of the arts centre is a personal triumph for Susan and a super shot in the arm for Amelia . When she heard that it was to have a resident dance company, she was for ever zooming down the motorway, at Susan's invitation, to immerse herself in whatever was going on. I see no reason why she shouldn't become a non-executive director, after all,
I hold a similar position with the Kaya Centre for Mindfulness.

"Well, how's everything going - at Sutchworth, I mean?"

"Amazingly, everything's on target, I can hardly believe it."

"The credit's all yours, you've led from the front and inspired people."

I can almost detect the beginning of a faint blush. Natural modesty is such a beguiling quality. I shall embarrass her no further.

"Well, fingers crossed all the same," she replies, the colour still discernible in her cheeks, "we're not over the last hurdle yet."

I'm about to ask what that is when Amelia returns with a huge platter of sandwiches.

"I decided we should make pigs of ourselves," she says, "but you'll have to go easy Ambrose, it won't do to belch in the presence of our Maj."

"If it was accidental, I don't think she'd mine too much. According to Philip, she only becomes interested in something if it's got four legs and farts."

"All the same, best not to take any chances. Help yourself to a smoked salmon and gravlux."

I do as I'm told. We all munch away merrily until Susan, being the first to finish, licks her fingers and says, rather matter-of-factly, almost as if she visits the Queen as frequently as I do, "So how do you find our Maj, these days?"

"She does not seem to be as optimistic as she usually is but I don't think that's because of anything to do with this government."

"So what's her beef then?"

"I think she's finally realised that she's surrounded by a bunch of stuffed poltroons."

"Oh for God's sake Ambrose," interjects Amelia, "you're not going to ride that hobby horse again, are you?"

"Well it's true, she's always been ill-advised. If ever there was a reason to bring back the guillotine, then it's the behaviour of those bloody elitist bunch of snobs that call themselves courtiers, that would justify it."

"I had no idea you felt so protective towards her," says Susan, "but surely, we never touched the guillotine, that was an exclusively frog thing, wasn't it?"

"Yes, but what I'm saying is that nothing ever changes at the Palace," (for some reason I can feel myself getting steamed up), "God, I can remember the time when I was a junior whip and Maggie Thatcher was Prime Minister - "

"Oh not that one again Ambrose," says Amelia.

"No tell me," says Susan, "I'm interested in your experiences."

(As well you might be, I think to myself, you are not without ambition)

"Well, it's not a major issue but it does illustrate the point I'm trying to make. It happened during some big banquet or other, I can't remember exactly what, but unfortunately

Maggie and the Queen turned up wearing virtually identical dresses. Subsequently, Maggie wrote a letter to the Palace suggesting that in order to avoid any embarrassment in the future, perhaps they should co-ordinate their wardrobes, or words to that effect. Rather a sensible suggestion, I would've thought. Needless to say, nothing was heard for ages until, eventually, this snotty letter arrived, proclaiming that, 'Her Majesty does not notice what other people are wearing'.
I mean for God's sake, what's the matter with them?"

Maybe I've got the wrong end of the stick because Susan is now falling about, coughing and spluttering. Amelia gets the giggles again and starts to thump Susan's back, as if regurgitating her lunch is a good idea. I think perhaps I should withdraw before I too become frivolous and unable to carry out my duties in a responsible manner, (my imminent meeting with Claude Napper will not be an agreeable one). When things calm down a bit I empty my glass and make ready to go.

Susan says, "Oh dear, what a classic, still, at least that's one problem you won't have to contend with, unless there's something we don't know about." And then the two of them start giggling again. Definitely time for the off.

"Well, if you'll excuse me, I've got to study some figures before seeing the Secretary of State for Defence."

"I bet they won't be the same figures as he's been studying," says Susan, "did you know he actually put his hand up my dress during a cabinet meeting?"

"No, I did not, had you brought it to my attention at the time, I can assure you I would've done something about it."

"It's alright I sorted it out myself."

"Ooh, how long ago was this?" says Amelia, "you never told me, the old letch."

"I can't remember, it's a long time ago, anyway, I got him with a stapler, so he won't go there again."
More hoots of laughter.

"Shall we open another bottle?" says Amelia. I pretend the remark falls on deaf ears as I head for the door.

Downstairs in the lobby, I can hear a fair bit of chit-chat coming from the private secretaries office. This is not surprising as I have six private secretaries. Sir Mallard Kane loves to remind me that it's the highest level of secretarial support afforded to any Prime Minister in history. And in response, I love to remind *him* that so was my parliamentary majority. It's a touching kind of touché situation although I daresay it was at the back of my mind when I decided to grant him additional staff to deal with the national ID card programme. However, I am the first to admit that my organic approach to administration does create a rather heavy workload that might otherwise not exist.

Now and again, and it's usually when I emerge from a particularly deep meditation, I have the feeling that we are not all singing from the same hymn sheet, or at least, some of the junior ministers think it is acceptable just to mouth the words silently. To me this signals a lack of commitment. A fissure in the foundation of team work which, if ignored, will gradually undermine the very structure on which we have built our success. On such occasions, I issue instructions for everyone to attend, and I do mean everyone. Cabinet ministers, junior ministers, departmental assistant under-secretaries, the whole cat and caboodle. I insist we all cram into the cabinet office too, even if it means double and triple seating, which it usually does. It is so important that everyone gets a taste of number ten, the power house, the nucleus from which all energy radiates. Needless to say, such activity arouses intense interest from the media and press. What is going on? they all chorus. What is about to happen? Is it somebody's birthday? A surprise general election?

Benjamin handles such occasions brilliantly. He faces the cameras and turns on his wonderful charm, his glowing black eyes, his winning smile, his deep mellifluous voice, his magazine sexy five o'clock shadow, slinky as a Jack Vettriano painting. He is always careful never to stray from the basic message, the raison d'être for the gathering, namely, to capitalise on the benefits of team working. The punters love it and the party ratings always go up a notch. Usually, he will announce details of some event that has already been mentioned in the House, a little puff for the government.

For example, next month, George will stand on the steps of Plymouth Hooe to wave at a special ceremonial by-pass of our recently commissioned fleet of Coast Guard motor torpedo boats. The timing should be perfect, as I took quite a pasting at Prime Minister's question time over the incident of thirty Albanian refugees, disguised as local fisherman, who ran aground off The Needles, near the Isle of Wight.

As I have explained, my team meetings are usually semi-spontaneous and I appreciate that getting everyone together at a moment's notice does take some doing, especially as most people's diaries are pretty choc-a-block. But in these matters, when I have received enlightenment from the far side, the matter is non-negotiable. Whatever my critics may say (and I know they are about) I remain absolutely convinced that it's fatal for a Prime Minister to get bogged down in the detail of any situation. Let the civil servants deal with it, after all, that's what they are there for, and most of the time they are very good at it.

The one exception is Andrew, my principal private secretary. He is a rather anxious sort of man and does not seem capable of dealing with more than one task at a time. When I voiced my concerns to Mallard about this, he became rather defensive and said that Andrew had gained a first class degree in logistical ergonoptrics at Keele University. I accepted his explanation rather than show my ignorance of contemporary studies. When his performance became less than satisfactory I tried to counsel him. I invited him to attend one of my individual healing sessions but unfortunately that seemed to induce some kind of panic attack. He said it was inappropriate behaviour for a civil servant and in any event he was only permitted to attend officially approved training courses. And then he spent the rest of the day hiding under his desk. Shortly afterwards he suffered a nervous breakdown and has been on extended sick leave ever since.

However, one positive outcome was the subsequent promotion of the assistant principal private secretary, albeit in a temporary acting capacity. And this was Helga Vine.

German on her mother's side and definitely of good Aryan stock. A truly stunning blonde. Tall, confident, poised, and with the grace and dignity of a statue. She is always immaculately groomed, right down to the tip of an extraordinary long tightly plaited pony tail that hangs down her back like a sleeping python. She is very much in command, little wonder that some people refer to her as the valkyrie. Rumour has it that she is dating Scott and I wouldn't be at all surprised. I am aware of a special ambience between them, a kind of blonde on blonde, chemical symmetry. I try to distance myself from these personal alliances, although, as a politician, I cannot ignore the possible outcome of such intrigues. A close personal bond between a member of the civil service and the government may not be appropriate but it's certainly very useful.

As I approach the office, Helga appears at the doorway to greet me. I don't know if somebody has installed CCTV cameras without my knowledge but she always seems to anticipate my coming, it's quite uncanny.

"Good morning, Prime Minister, I have some papers for you, I have just received them from the Chancellor's office."

She smiles and hands me the papers. She has a knack of being friendly yet formal. I've noticed that whenever we interact, she never invades my personal space but positions herself immediately outside it, as if standing to attention.

I am rather attracted to her and I think she knows it.

"Ah, thank you very much Helga, I've been expecting these. I shall take them at once to my office."

She smiles again. "The Secretary of State for Defence is in the building."

"Oh really, it's unlike him to be early, where exactly is he?"

"I have asked him to wait in the blue room."

"I wonder if he will remain there."

"I expect so, I promised to bring him a cup of tea."

"Good move . . . um, I think my watch must've stopped, or is it really only one thirty three?"

"I make it one forty-seven precisely."

"Gosh, I'd better get a move on and read these."

I wave the papers about importantly but seem unable to disengage. She smiles again. There is something extraordinarily hypnotic about her.

"I'm sure the Minister can wait a bit longer, I haven't yet made his tea." She is right of course. I am the one who is calling the shots. Claude Napper is clearly trying to ingratiate himself by arriving early, but I'm not falling for that one. "Perhaps you might fancy a cup of tea too?" she adds.

There is something very soothing about the whole premise, besides, we can't stand around like this forever.

"I would prefer a cup of coffee, if that's not too much bother."

"Strong, black, arabica, with one sugar?" Now it's my turn to smile. "I'll be with you in five minutes," she replies.

As she turns to go, I feel as if some kind of spell has been broken. The hairs on the back of my neck are tingling.

A definite frisson, if I'm not mistaken.

9

Jocelyn's recommendations for cuts in the defence budget are straightforward and to the point. He has even highlighted certain sections and scribbled a little note at the foot of the page saying, *these are the one's I'd go for.* It doesn't take long for me to arrive at the same conclusion. Five minutes, to be exact.

At this point, there is a tap on the door and Helga enters with a tray of coffee. She glides towards my desk with the slow, languorous movements of a Sibelius swan, and smiles, oh so beguilingly, as she reaches shore. I try to avert my eyes as she bends over, but to no avail. Half a second's glimpse of her cleavage tells me all I need to know. I'm sexually aroused. Sod it. I must be at least thirty years her senior. I thought, by now, I had such feelings under control. Double sod it. If only Scott were to appear, there would be order and balance, his guiding hand would bring everything back to an even keel. Unless, of course, he became instantly jealous! Ye Gods, what am I thinking? What am I doing? Wait a second, just a minute, I am doing nothing. Absolutely nothing. I'm just receiving a most welcome cup of coffee. A beautiful Turkish pot of it, to be precise, with a small, exquisite shaped cup, terracotta with delicate, hand-painted blue flowers, and a little matching plate with two ginger nut biscuits. How does she know they're my favourites? Scott must have told her.

"Thank you, that's lovely."

"Let me know if you want a second cup, and I'll bring the sugar."

"I'm sure one will be just fine."

We exchange smiles.

"I'll leave you alone then."

Somehow I stop myself from saying 'alas'. She remains standing there, so still, so calm, so erect. I fight off this incredible urge to leap over the desk, sweep her up in my arms, kiss her passionately and say, sod this, let's run away to Rio. But instead, I find myself saying, "Have you seen Scott?" I'm not sure if I detect a momentary flicker of disappointment, I'm probably just imagining it. I must get a grip of myself.

"He's at the dentist's," she replies.

"Oh." I notice she has perfect teeth.

"I'm covering for him until he returns in about half an hour."

"Okay, fine."

"Is there something else I can do for you?"

In this life, there are pregnant pauses, dramatic pauses and tragic pauses, and sometime they are all rolled into one to produce an embarrassing stutter. Such as now.

"I-I-I'll buzz you when I'm ready to receive the Secretary of State for Defence."

She demurs and glides silently away. Somewhere in the ether, a foreboding Wagnerian refrain arises then subsides in the minor mode.

I really must concentrate. These figures are important. According to last month's National Audit Office report on twenty defence projects, the cost of over-runs had doubled last year to at least three point one billion pounds! It's scandalous. We've been in office for nearly eighteen months and right from the start I made it quite clear to Claude that this kind of profligacy had to be knocked on the head. But what has he done about it? Nothing, as far as I can see, apart from swanning off to Brussels at the drop of a hat, to hob-nob with a bunch of cheese-eating, surrender monkeys and muesli-munching, tree hugging, tuba players. No wonder I'm taking so much flak at Prime Minister's question time. I hate to admit it, but it looks as if one of my ministers is out of control. There are degrees of final solutions and I feel a preliminary one is upon me. I press the buzzer. Helga answers.

"Yes, sir?"

"Please ask the Secretary of State for Defence to come to my office, at once, thank you."

I ring off. I hope she will not think I'm being abrupt with her. More than likely she will have glanced at Jocelyn's figures before handing them over and will have come to her own conclusions. Civil servants who make it to the Prime Minister's private office are as opportunistic as stoats on the run. And Helga has a knowingness about her that has not gone amiss. At least not to me.

There is an assertive rap on the door and Claude Napper enters without invitation. I pretend not to be rattled by his lack of manners or subsequent over familiarity.

"Ambrose, hello, what's cooking, anything interesting?"

"Sit down please and pay attention to what I am about to say."

"Of course, my eyes and ears are open, as ever."

I fix him with a beady look and wait until he settles himself in the chair. And then I wait some more. And then a little bit more on top of that, until he is manifestly uncomfortable. Then I transform my beady look into a steely look. Unless I'm not mistaken, I think I spot a slight nervous tick breaking out underneath his left eye. It is time to begin.

"Please will you tell me," I intone, with a coldness bereft of any rubato, "why the defence budget has a deficit of three point one billion pounds and rising?"

"I wasn't aware that it was rising," he parries instantly, "I thought it had been contained."

"It has not," I lie, (Jocelyn has stopped short of prognostical data), "and I want to know why you allowed it to reach such levels in the first place."

"I did not allow it, I issued instructions to the effect that monthly audits should be carried out on all major projects and the results made known to me accordingly."

"And were they?"

"Yes."

"And what did they reveal?"

"That project over-spend was rampant."

"And what did you do to stop it?"

"I replaced all the project managers."

"And?"

"It had no beneficial effect whatsoever."

"So what conclusions did you come to?"

"I concluded that either the Services personnel selection procedure or the accounting procedures were deficient, or a combination of both."

"And which of those conclusions was correct?"

"It is too early to say."

"Why?"

"In order to obtain reliable and verifiable information, it was necessary to establish a working party to establish the parameters under which a formal assessment could take place without detrimental effect to the on-going operations of the various projects."

"And?"

"I was advised that there were insufficient funds to sustain the aforementioned working parties."

"Who advised you?"

"The Parliamentary Under Secretary of State for Defence."

"Did you challenge his findings?"

"Yes."

"And?"

"I found his report to be correct."

"So what action did you take?"

"I issued a strongly worded memorandum to the Minister of Defence Procurement pointing out that the current level of over-spend could not be allowed to continue."

"And did he respond?"

"Yes,"

"And what did he say?"

"He said that he was under the impression that project overspend had been contained."

"Well, clearly it has not," (Claude slumps in his chair, a defeated man) "and it is causing me a good deal of political embarrassment."

"I am aware of that, Prime Minister, and regret that my actions thus far have not been adequate."

Too late to start ingratiating yourself now, I say to myself, and if you are half the man you purport to be, you'd better take what I am about to dish out, firmly on the chin.

"Adequate is not the word I would use, in fact your actions seem barely plausible."

"At least I sent a warning shot across the bow."

"A direct hit is what was needed and I am about to make one." I clear my throat and rustle my papers. A bit of theatricality never hurt anyone, or in this case, heighten the expectation of pain. "You will summon the heads of defence immediately and inform them that the following cuts in the overall defence budget will now be applied. ONE - two infantry battalions will be cut, I do not care which ones, but two whole battalions must go. TWO - half the Gurkha troops will be moved to Cyprus until further notice. THREE - The Jaguar base at RAF Coltishall will be decommissioned next April, we cannot afford to wait until the planned date of two thousand and eight. This naturally includes the early retirement of all sixty-two combat jets. FOUR - The proposed decommissioning of four Type 42 destroyers is now confirmed."

I pause to see how all this being received. Claude has gone completely white. His nervous tick has escalated into a kind of St Vitus dance and I fear that if it doesn't subside it may very well damage his facial muscles permanently, or even induce a stroke. As I have no wish to be cruel, I decide a modicum of compassion would be timely.

I set my papers aside and remove my spectacles in a deliberately wearisome manner. I notice that Claude's white-knuckled hands, which have been gripping the arms of his chair like a griffin's talons on a cast-iron bathtub, relax sufficiently to allow normal blood circulation to be restored.

"If there is such a thing as good news in this depressing scenario then it is this," I place the tips of my fingers gently together in as benign a posture as possible, without loss of authority, "you will be pleased to know that certain decisions, equally far-reaching, are held in abeyance. I refer to the upgrading of two Type 23 frigates that have not yet taken place, and confirmation of the retirement date of the Ark Royal."

"The Navy will appreciate that," croaks Claude.

"Indeed, and I hope that the RAF will be equally appreciative of my decision not to axe the Nimrod MRA 4 project, even though, to do so, would realise savings in the order of five hundred million pounds."

"I'm sure the RAF will breathe a sigh of relief," says Claude, weakly, "they have invested so much money in it."

"One point five billion of government money to be exact."

"Yes, that was the figure I had in mind, but they are so near to technical break through."

"I know that. The point is, if you bothered to attend cabinet meetings more frequently, you would know how much importance I place on marine surveillance in our battle against terrorism and the influx of undesirable persons generally."

"I always read the minutes."

"Good. Then you will know exactly what to say to the heads of defence when you inform them of these cuts." I notice a small bead of sweat begin to trickle down his left temple, accompanied by a rather sheepish grin. "Alright Claude, let me spell it out. The new enemy is terrorism. Unfortunately, the buggers won't come out and fight in the open. They prefer to hide in council flats making bombs and claiming social security benefits, not to mention legal aid to fund their asylum appeals. The only way to get a half-way decent grip on things is to introduce national identity cards, utilising the very latest cutting edge technology such as electronic iris recognition and automatic DNA identification. I insist that this will be up and running by the end of this year and that will cost a bomb, if you'll pardon the pun. The money has to come from somewhere."

Claude has now gained a little composure.

"Yes, of course, I understand, but what about our contribution to the European Union Rapid Reaction Force?"

"We'll cobble something together"

"What about the Americans?"

"If we can stop the NATO generals getting any more big ideas Congress might just swing a few billion dollars our way on the understanding that we buy more of their hi-tech security stuff like the laser portcullis system at Dover."

The colour has returned to Claude's cheeks and I must confess that I'm somewhat relieved that our meeting has not degenerated into total acrimony. I know he likes to play it flashy in Brussels, but alas, in purely military terms, his mind-set hasn't developed much beyond Trafalgar.

"Claude," I continue, "sickening though it may be, especially to patriots like you and me, you must understand that today we are fighting the enemy within, as much as the enemy without."

I watch him closely as he mentally disseminates my statement. I would like to think I have given him a little bit more backbone where it was needed. His expression does not give anything away. When I signal that our meeting is at an end and he rises to go, there is this nagging doubt in my mind that he harbours another agenda, but as yet, I have no idea what that may be.

"I appreciate your frankness," he says, "I will carry out your instructions to the letter and report back."

He offers his hand, which slightly catches me off guard, but I respond in good cheer, feeling that some kind of understanding has now been established.

"Good. Splendid. I'm so glad we see eye to eye."

When he is gone, I am left in silence. I sit quietly, pondering my actions until there is a polite tap on the door and Helga enters. After the relative tension of the past twenty minutes, I find her serene bearing most pleasing. The early summer sunshine streams through the window accentuating everything in brilliance, especially Helga's eyes, which are stunningly blue at the best of times. As she moves gracefully towards me, the sunlight plays directly on to her face, giving her eyes an extraordinary, vivid translucency. They have a strange, hypnotic quality about them which I cannot resist . . . . and neither do I want to.

"That wasn't so difficult, was it?" she says, dreamingly.

"No."

"I watched him leave the building, like a dog with its tail between its legs."

"I hope I wasn't too harsh."

"I'm sure you weren't, it is not in your nature."

"That's kind of you to say so."

Usually, at this hour of the day, there is always the hustle and bustle of activity somewhere or other, but today is different. Everything is quiet. Just Helga and me. Or so it seems.

"The palace telephoned a short while ago," she speaks so softly, with gentle undulating tones, "Her Majesty is indisposed and will be unable to receive you this afternoon as planned."

"Oh dear, that's the third week in a row, perhaps she's caught another chill whilst riding?"

"They didn't say."

"They never do."

"I have also been speaking with the Police Commissioner."

"That's funny, I was about to telephone him myself."

"I thought so."

I am momentarily lost for words. Her reply does not startle me. I cannot quite put my finger on why her knowingness does not disturb me.

"Well, now that the Palace has cancelled, I'm suppose I'm free to see him."

"Yes, your diary is clear until five o'clock."

"In that case, perhaps you would be good enough to invite him over."

She smiles one of her long, lingering, beautiful smiles.

"He is already on his way."

In the garden, two birds engage in some chattering dispute. Helga notices them too. Her smile is now radiant. I feel we are in sync with nature and much more besides. Suddenly, with much fluttering and circling, the birds disappear over the wall to heaven knows where.

"I don't think they were spying on us," I say.

"No chance."

I am very sensitive to auras, and as she removes the coffee tray from my desk, I am aware of a barely imperceptible shift in the atmosphere, as if a spell has been broken. She turns at the door.

"By the way, Scott also rang in. He's had a rather painful time at the dentist's and asked to be excused for the rest of the day. I took the liberty of saying that I'm sure you wouldn't mind."

"No, of course not, thank you very much."

"I am covering for him anyway."

"Yes, I'm delighted, um, er, I hope he recovers soon."

"I'm sure he will. It's just a nasty bout of neuralgia by the sound of it, I advised him to take a couple of Nurofen and lie down in the dark."

"That's most considerate of you."

"I call it teamwork."

She grins and is gone.

Once again, I am left alone to my ponder the reality of now. After eighteen months of unremitting hard slog, I sense a certain lightness in the air. Perhaps it's just the summer sunshine? Who cares? The point is, unless I have totally misinterpreted the events of the past hour, I think a true convert to my master plan has just stepped into the limelight.

Helga, the civil servant from the far side.

10

When Kevin Doppler enters my office, I am surprised that he is not in uniform. I thought that was de rigueur for all senior policemen on duty. Instead, he is wearing a badly tailored suit of indeterminate patina, with a dark blue shirt and greasy tie that's got some kind of brown moose embroidered on the front of it. I know it sounds uncharitable, but he looks like a meths drinker who has spruced himself up for an appearance before the local magistrate. Nevertheless, I give him a friendly welcome.

"Hello Kevin, do have a seat."

"Thank you Prime Minister."

"Oh please, do call me Ambrose."

He nods and we settle ourselves down. He can tell that I'm rather bemused by his casual attire.

"I entered by the back door, so as not to attract attention whilst I'm off duty."

"I see, well what I have to say is . . . " and I tail off because the penny is just beginning to drop that what I'm about to say is about as far from being official as Downing Street is from

Mars. I wonder if he senses this, and if so, how? There is something strangely omnipotent in his blood-shot gaze.

I continue, all the same. "well, um, I'm not entirely sure how to begin . . . um . . . this is strictly off the record by the way."

"Of course."

His reassurance doesn't facilitate my temporary inability to express myself. I realise that what is at the back of my mind has been worrying me considerably, and that is a gross understatement to put it mildly. The truth is that for the past six months, what has been knawing away at my subconscious, like a rat in a garbage bin, has finally burst forth into the open, into my absolute conscious like a festering boil that has finally been lanced. I have meditated on the issues many, many times, almost to the point of distraction, but they simply won't go away. It is only now, and I literally do mean now, when I find myself alone with Kevin Doppler that I realise the course of action I am about to take, (given the conviction of my feelings) is virtually pre-ordained. Virtually inexorable. And yet, I can't help feeling how odious it is that political reality dictates that I must sink or swim in a sea of pus. So be it.

"Well, the point is Kevin that unless I'm becoming totally paranoid, I regret to say that there are certain people whom I can no longer trust."

He does not bat an eyelid. "For a person in your position, that is not surprising."

He is right, of course. All the same, it doesn't make me feel any better. Nor does the silence that follows.

'This is most uncomfortable," I finally manage to say, "I could be so wrong."

"You could also be right, so, who are we talking about, Ambrose?"

His directness is quite disarming. Oh dear, too late to change my mind now, I suppose. So I take the plunge, knowing that from now on, things will never be the same again. "Well, to begin with, I have my doubts about the Secretary of State for Defence."

"Claude Napper."

"Indeed."

I'm pleased that Kevin knows who I am talking about, which is more than can be said for his supposedly big-brained predecessor Trevor Skidmarsh.

"Why do you suspect him?"

I flinch at the word. If there is one thing I thought would never arise in my cabinet, it is suspicion. It is the rough track down to the stony beach and the unwelcome sea of pus.

"Well, I'm not sure that I suspect him of anything, it's just that I feel rather uneasy about the way he's conducting himself." Kevin doesn't say a word. He remains disconcertingly mute. I feel obliged to continue. "He's always been a bit of a law unto himself and maybe I'm to blame because I've always given him a long leash, so to speak."

"Why?" says Kevin, bluntly, "isn't he as accountable as any other minister?"

"Yes, of course, but defence is a complex brief, very political, I feel I must give him as much space as possible."

"Has he done anything wrong?"

"Well, not exactly, but his procurement budget is drastically over-spent and until this morning, he did not seem particularly concerned about it."

"Is he now?"

"Oh yes, I have instructed him to summon the heads of defence and inform them of specific cuts."

"Will he carry out your instructions?"

"I sincerely hope so. Yes."

"But you have your doubts?"

I am not finding this meeting particularly easy. It's almost as if I am the guilty party and am being interrogated to establish the truth. I suppose the truth is that I *am* suspicious of Claude but don't want to admit it.

"Look, God forbid if any of this reached the tabloids, but there's something of the second-hand car salesman about him."

"You mean he's bent?"

"Well, the potential to be less than economical with the truth is always there."

Kevin lets out a sigh of breath through pursed lips. It's all very well for him, he only has to police the country whereas I have to run it. From the expression on his face I can tell he expects me to reveal more and I know that I've started something that it will be very difficult not to finish.

"And are there others?" he enquires.

I was right. I've started so I must finish.

"Yes, I'm afraid so." He settles back in his seat and fixes me with a dull, passionless stare. "Er, look, would you like a cup of tea? I should've offered you one ages ago, I'm so sorry."

"Maybe afterwards. Let's get the cards on the table first, shall we?"

"Oh righto then," I do not relish the moment although I believe that ultimately it will prove to be cathartic and will therefore lighten my burden. "I have grave concerns about my foreign secretary, Aubrey Fynch-Chilling."

"So what's he been up to?"

"Well, nothing as such, in fact he's handling his brief very well, it's just that of late, he's become a bit of a wooden spoon merchant, if you follow me."

"I do. We have them in the police force too. Eventually we get them on some kind of disciplinary."

"Politics are not always as straight forward as that. I can't fault him on any professional basis, it's just that he's so ambitious and cannot resist criticising others for their failings without offering any kind of solution."

"A right pain in the arse, by the sound of it."

"Well, I wouldn't put it in quite those terms but I'm becoming increasingly concerned about the frequency of his meetings with the heads of MI5 and MI6."

"Oh really?"

"Yes, he often lunches with Gloria Fitzbagley and Rodney Snodder and their sessions usually last for more than three hours. Last month he dined with them every week."

"How do you know this?"

Without thinking beyond the immediate dynamic of the conversation, (which I must admit I'm rather warming too), I blurt out a name.

"Through Scott Rignold, my personal parliamentary secretary, he's an avid networker and very well informed."

Kevin's expression gives nothing away. He eases himself in the chair, crossing his legs and running his thumb and forefinger along an ill-defined trouser crease. I sense a question in the offing.

"And has he told you anything about Mr Rashidi Mboya, your extremely industrious minister for international development?"

I'm sure my heart just missed a beat. The question seems to hang in the air before landing on the blotting pad like an unwelcome bluebottle. I resist the impulse to swat it, as I know it is far from harmless. It has a sting like a wasp. A hornet even.

"In what context?" I reply, rather feebly.

Kevin's face finally takes on an expression. It is one of contrived patronage. Clearly, he does not wish me to play games. I remain silent, if only because I am fearful of what he may know that I do not.

"Ambrose," he begins slowly and quietly, "do you seriously think that anyone could attempt to control the UK's drug supplies without our own anti-drug squad knowing something about it?"

He has a point, of course, but I was under the impression that Rashidi and Aubrey had concentrated their operations much further afield and with the utmost secrecy. At least, that's what they told me. When I shared this with Kevin he became droll almost to the point of buffoonery. Indeed, at one stage I almost felt he was mocking me. He was becoming tiresome but I could not escape the fact that my position as Prime Minister was now totally compromised. Kevin Doppler may only be the Commissioner of Police but I can hardly replace him without creating a formidable enemy. How silly of me not think strategically. Never mind, I am not unfamiliar with the twists and turns of political life and I did not get where I am today through a paucity of ideas. More accurately through a fecundity of them.

"Alright Kevin," I said, asserting my authority, "you asked for cards on the table, let me begin with the ace of spades."

And so I told him everything. Clearly he was impressed as he did not utter a word as I unfolded before him my grand vision. Naturally I did not reveal the source of my inspiration or how I had introduced my ministers to the wisdom of the teachings from the far side. That would be going too far.

Besides, it would not look good if I had to admit that on that particular point, Claude Napper and Aubrey Fynch-Chilling had recently displayed a marked reluctance to take the trip again. When I had finished, I sat back in my chair, cathartically irrigated. What I had not bargained for was his response.

Apparently, he had been wised up from the very beginning and when Damien Chick took over from him, the pace of their investigations had increased ten fold. Even Ivor Pleeth, head of the anti-terrorist squad had become involved. My heart sank lower and lower as I was informed that huge sums of money were being paid to mercenaries world wide to stop Al Qaeda operatives and other fundamentalist cells from taking over the drug supply lines with the intention of poisoning everything within their grasp. Whether the nation would be better off with a generation of dead junkies instead of live ones, is not the point. What was breath taking in its audacity was the fact that Claude had been siphoning off defence procurement money to fund it! And it did not stop there.

"But this is outrageous," I stammered, "I instructed the Chancellor of the Exchequer to allocate huge sums of money, albeit covertly, for this operation and Aubrey Fynch-Chilling and Rashidi Mboya never once complained of a lack of finances."

"Which brings me to my next point," said Kevin, matter of factly, "we have information that would suggest certain off-shore accounts are being credited with large amounts of money, circuitously linked to your government's supposedly secret operation. Moreover, a certain trio of ministers, whose names I shall not put in writing but, suffice to say, have featured prominently in our investigations, are all complicit with the mechanics of servicing said accounts."

I do not like the term gobsmacked. It is too vulgar and facile for my tastes. Nonetheless, I will admit to being totally flabbergasted. After the lengths I have gone to, to ensure that the lines of communication between myself and all my ministers, not to mention the very foundations on which our relationship is built, are as pure and transparent as it is humanely possible to be, I find that greed and evil has infiltrated the very core of my administration. Is human nature always so bedevilled? Will there ever come a time when those in power will seek only to inhabit the higher worlds of existence, leaving behind forever the lower worlds of animality and desire? Is it really impossible not to inspire a nation by recognising and fuelling the fundamental dignity of life itself?

I realise I must not sink into despair. What has occurred is a direct challenge to my resolve. Now is not the time to wobble. I must be strong. Obviously, it would be political suicide to arrest Claude, Aubrey and Rashidi and throw them in jail, much as though I would like to teach them a harsh lesson. No, my first priority is to find a way of keeping the lid on things. I shudder to think what further incriminations may yet be revealed.

I can see that Kevin is waiting for me to exercise my executive responsibility and I shall not falter in this.

"Right Kevin," I say assertively, "I want the entire cabinet put under twenty-four seven surveillance. Can you manage that without arousing suspicion?"

"Yes, of course."

"Good. Right. Next thing, where do Rodney and Gloria feature in all this?"

"Unfortunately, their motives are not clear at present, but I do not trust them."

Our eyes meet across the desk. Kevin's are rather bloodshot and hazy, whereas mine are on fire. We may not see eye to eye in the strictest interpretation or the word but there is a definite meeting of minds.

"Neither do I."

He smiles. I press the intercom. Helga's svelte tones are a blessed tonic.

"Yes Prime Minister?"

"Tea for two, if you would be so kind."

11

After Kevin Doppler's revelations, I decide that the next best thing to do is meditate. Although I had tried to put on a brave face by suggesting a cup of tea to round things off, I must confess that after Kevin had left, a kind of delayed shock set in.

Helga enters the room just as I am trying to get a grip of myself. It probably shows.

"Is everything alright, Prime Minister?" she enquires, gently.

I do not know what to say. I feel betrayed. Devastated. Emotional.

"You may call me Ambrose, if you wish," is all I can manage to say.

Rather pointless, perhaps, but I think she senses my mood of disarray.

She moves closer and stands in front of my desk, as still as a nun at prayer.

"I can cancel your five o'clock meeting, if you wish."

"What's it about?"

"Human Rights legislation with the Lord Chancellor."

"I'll definitely give that a miss. Tell him I haven't had time to read his brief, which is a statement of fact, just in case he gets stroppy, which he probably will."

"Morose men do not intimidate me."

And with that, she presses the telephone key pad on my desk and waits patiently. I can hear Clive Smeelie's gruff voice answer. She responds by announcing the cancellation of the meeting for the reason given. Her manner is clear, direct and courteous. I cannot catch the words that follow but she replies, in concise terms, that he will be informed of an alternative date when my appointments diary has been rearranged. I hear a grunt of disapproval and then she rings off. I remain seated, simultaneously impressed by her authority and charm. We exchange mildly conspiratorial smiles.

"Thank you," I say, "but don't be surprised if my direct line rings in a few moments."

"Then I shall answer it, " she replies.

A simple statement of fact. Sure enough, the telephone chirrups and she takes the call.

"The Prime Minister's office."

She offers no more than that. I have never approved of all that 'how may I help you' school of nonsense, and am rather tickled to imagine Clive's look of indignation at the other end of the line. I can hear the irritation in his voice but not the actual words. He is a bully and I know that he using his authority to try and brow-beat her into submission. But Helga's response is clear and firm.

"The Prime Minister is temporarily unavailable, he has asked me to re-schedule his diary and I will contact you as soon as that is done . . . . . this is Helga Vine, acting principal private secretary speaking . . . . . I'm afraid that the principal private secretary is still on sick leave . . . . . yes, six months, and twenty-three days to be precise . . . . . . I am sure Sir Mallard Kane is aware of his responsibilities but I will pass on your comments to him . . . . . I'm afraid Mr Rignold is recovering from a painful session at the dentist's . . . . . . yes, in my current capacity I report directly to the Cabinet Secretary, Mr Snatch . . . . . I am afraid he is on annual leave until next week . . . . . the Prime Minister is perfectly happy with the arrangements . . . . . I note your comments, good afternoon, sir."

This time we exchange fulsome conspiratorial grins. I'm beginning to feel better already.

Outside, the clouds are scudding across the sky. There is a break and the sun streams through the window. It's probably a daft thing to say but somehow it always seems sunny when Helga is about, and especially when she smiles.

"Well, it looks like the affairs of state are buttoned up for the next few hours," I quip.

"You have control," she replies.

I feel myself becoming intoxicated by her presence yet again, but this time I am not so flustered, in fact I am not flustered at all. I have control.I push the chair back and move away from behind the desk. There is no longer any physical barrier between us and it feels good. This time it's my turn for a simple statement of fact.

"I'm pleased you see it that way."

She draws closer, just to the edge of my personal space. The sunshine is now streaming steadily through the window, lighting up her face with a radiant glow. Her complexion is near perfect.

"I have always seen it that way, Ambrose. Right from the moment you took office, I could tell you were unlike any other Prime Minister that has gone before. You have a sense of mission that is breathtaking in its boldness and scope. I know, as a civil servant, I should not be expressing any political view but I cannot help myself. Somehow, I sense that only you can make this country great again. I am proud and privileged to serve you, Ambrose."

She is much closer to me now. Close enough to sense her perfume, close enough to feel the heat of her body, close enough to see the gentle rise and fall of her breasts.

"I was just going upstairs for a spot of meditation, would you care to join me?"

Her eyes are steady, their colour of the purest hypnotic blue.

"You lead, I will follow."

En route up stairs she leaves me briefly to issue some kind of instruction to the other secretaries. When she re-emerges she is carrying a small sports bag. We enter the meditation room. I leave her to change and retire to my bedroom to do likewise.

A few minutes later we are back together again. She has changed into loose cotton slacks and a simple top; I am wearing my Thai robes. We say nothing. There is no need to. The aura is so good. So peaceful. So powerful.

She slips into a full lotus position with sublime agility. I yearn for the lost suppleness of youth. I light candles and incense and then settle myself in a half-lotus position supported by two small cushions. In meditation, comfort and correct posture must go hand in hand. We settle ourselves.

I am not surprised that Helga meditates. It is evident in her stillness and general composure.

The room is bathed in sunlight. The gold of the Buddha statue shines beautifully, the dark leaves of the greenery in their golden pots are lush and shiny. I concentrate on my breathing. The ebb and flow of life itself. I strike the bell three times, close my eyes and we begin our journey to the far side.

Time loses all meaning. Meaning itself is no longer important or relevant. I am no longer part of the sentient world. That is but an illusion that we humans have constructed to satisfy our intellectuality. But I know that the reality of everyday life requires us to live inside that construct because, for the vast majority of us, that is all that we can comprehend.

Although my eyes are closed, I can see a huge panoply of intense white light. Gradually, I open my eyes and there, right in front of me, bathed in glorious luminosity is Helga. Huge shafts of brilliant while light emanate from her body. She appears to be floating, motionless in the air. It is the most incredible vision I have ever seen. Her beauty is breathtaking. Awesome. Slowly, she opens her eyes. All knowingness is contained within.

She smiles, gently, gently, oh so gently. Our deepest consciousness is joined. Our dominion is of one. The message is clear. My courage and determination will not falter.

I am reminded that I have the biggest parliamentary majority in British political history.

I have control. I will use it. No matter what.

12

The fact that I have unofficially authorised Kevin Doppler, my Commissioner of Police, to mount a round-the-clock covert surveillance of all members of the Cabinet, not to mention the heads of MI5 and MI6 (I included them during our final cup of tea), no longer fazes me. I am convinced that my nearest and dearest of colleagues, Jocelyn and George, to name but two, will prove themselves to be as loyal and trustworthy as ever before. If Gloria Fitzbagley and Rodney Snodder are in cahoots with Aubrey, Rashidi and Claude then I have no doubt that Kevin will eventually root them out. I have always striven to create a culture of openness and trust, deliberately spurning the political machinations that I am now forced to implement. It is quite possible that Rodney and Gloria are stringing Aubrey along and will present their evidence to me in due course, and in the proper manner, but I cannot understand why they are taking so long. I realise that one false move and everything could blow up in my face. I would be hounded from office. A national disgrace. Reviled and ridiculed. But that will never happen because I have access to a higher power. I am in control.

I have also let it slip that I may reshuffle my cabinet in the not too distant future (an innocent rumour I let slip in the corridors of the Palace of Westminster). Before long, the political hacks got wind of it and started writing their silly opinions about who was in and out of favour. Everybody was very on edge after that, except me, of course. I had toyed with the idea of taking every single cabinet member through another special one-to-one session to the far side but decided against that in the end. Recent events have provided a certain shift in emphasis. It will not be long before we celebrate two years in office and I feel I have done enough supporting, nurturing and encouraging. It is pay-back time. My ministers must show me what they are made of. I intend to forge ahead relentlessly. It is time to apply some pressure and it is up to them to keep up with me, or drop by the wayside. Or, to be more precise, be dropped by me.

Naturally, I revealed my change of tactics to Helga. I say naturally because, since that momentous day when we first meditated together, there have been other sessions, and each time we emerge with a stronger bond between us. Meditation can teach one humility. When we are together, I no longer feel the burden of high office with its pressure to make a decision on every issue. I feel free to share my doubts and anxieties as much as my convictions and enthusiasm. She is so attentive (which is more than can be said for some) and I value her opinion tremendously and will often seek it. Her respect and admiration for me is beyond question, but of course, we are discreet in our conduct. These days I feel we have entered a special phase in our relationship. She has become so much more than just a loyal civil servant. She is my guiding hand from the far side.

Purely administrative matters have also played their part in bringing us closer together. Unfortunately, since his visit to the dentist's, for what was apparently a routine filling, poor Scott has now contracted septicaemia and is confined to his bed with huge doses of anti-biotics. I have been too busy to see him myself although I understand from Helga that he is hardly in a state to appreciate any visitor. She does not say much more about him and I do not think they are quite the item that I had previously imagined.

Hugo Snatch is making the most of his absence and has clawed back many of the responsibilities that he felt were rightfully his. Although there was no love lost between the two men, I'm pleased to say that my discussions with Hugo and Helga have clarified the dividing line between parliamentary and cabinet administration. This was always somewhat vague to me although I never bothered much about it since my organic approach to administration tended to transcend functional barriers and the like. Having said that, I must admit that nowadays the three of us are working together so much more efficiently.

Helga has taken over responsibility for my day to day appointments diary and I must say it has been like a breath of fresh air. 'A Prime Minister needs time to think', was all she said, as she cut my appointments by half with one purposeful swipe of her 3B pencil. I did query whether some people might react to this practice by bombarding me with lengthy memorandums. 'What's to stop you insisting that all internal correspondence requiring your personal attention must be contained on one side of A4 paper, otherwise you will refuse to read it?', was her only response. Hugo was present at the time and remarked that Churchill applied this rule during the war years to remarkable effect. I decided to give it a go.

Needless to say, this newly found tripartite harmony has greatly pleased Sir Mallard Kane, so much so, that the fusty old dome (as he is popularly known) has urged his forces to make even greater progress on the national ID card project. And that pleases me more than greatly.

Political life is never predicable though. Just as I was preparing to implement my new thrust, Benjamin came to see me with a stern look on his face.

"What is it Benjamin?"

"Prime Minister, I'm afraid to say that according to The Guardian, the party has dropped three percent in the opinion polls and your personal rating appears to have plateaued."

"Oh dear, what have we done wrong?"

"Nothing as such, I think it's more a case of what the opposition are doing right."

"But the opposition are so small they've hardly worth bothering about."

Benjamin gives me one of his careful looks. I've noticed it's a habit of his and is usually the precursor to something I suspect he thinks I should already have been aware of.

"With respect Prime Minister, I think, like most underdogs, they realise they cannot beat you on the main battlefield, so they are attempting to move it elsewhere."

"And where is that precisely?"

He places a copy of The Guardian in front of me. These days it is an action that seems to becoming ever more frequent. The liberal press have never been slow to pick holes in my policies and I've always assumed that the insidious drip drip of leftish tosh was no more than just that. As my eye catches the front page headline - *The corpses of human dignity* - I realise they have chosen to become more virulent in their attack. A bleak picture of an elderly woman on an ambulance stretcher alongside another picture of the bodies of three children, laid side by side on the pavement with their heads covered, extends across the whole width of the page. The text is equally bleak:

84-year old Elsie Donohue lies battered and traumatised following an attack by 18-year old Danny Briggs who robbed her of her pension before crashing a stolen Mercedes Benz into a bus shelter and killing three young children, ages six, seven and ten. Briggs, who was arrested by police following a high speed chase, was found to have three times the legal amount of alcohol in his blood. He is already wanted by the police for a string of offences including car theft, criminal damage and drug dealing, and has broken bail three times.

"This bloody newspaper gets more like a tabloid every day," I snarl, as Benjamin remains passive, "they can't even write a decent introduction."

"It's the remainder of the story that I'm most concerned about, Prime Minister."

I have already started to glance down the page and can see that at every opportunity they are ridiculing our manifesto pledge to put the dignity of human beings above all else. I can feel my temper rising and since I do not wish others to see how sensitive I am to attack, I ask him to leave on the pretext that I wish to read the article fully before commenting further.
I detect a certain archness in his eyebrow as he turns.

"I'm sure you can find other statistics that will contradict this so-called opinion poll."

"I'll look into it, Prime Minister."

I was about to remind him that I prefer to be called Ambrose on a one-to-one basis, (if only to demonstrate that I was not as riled as I actually was) but he had gone. I continued reading the story, including several related articles that, as far as I could see, were hell bent on taunting the government at every opportunity. In some cases it was downright personal:

The only significant changes that our resident dandy Prime Minister has achieved, is to discard his awful pea-green cardigan in favour of a beige one. He also appears to have swapped his floppy bow tie for a stiffer one, presumably to indicate some kind of authority. Unfortunately, since it more closely resembles the propeller of a Spitfire, the nation can only wonder how long it will be before he takes off to tally-ho in the great blue yonder with his so-called 'humanitarian policies', only to discover that they, like pigs, do not fly.

As if to add credence to the column, there's a picture of the cutting edge journalist himself, sporting, somewhat predictably, unkempt designer stubble and one of those short, spiky, perpendicular fringes that give the impression of being in constant battle with a minor gale. A stupid, blithering, inept, ill-educated young hack, who doesn't even know that Spitfire propellers were always configured with three blades, never two, a significant blow to his snide attempt at sartorial mockery. God help us if slap-dash fools like this ever run the country.

I am still fuming when George enters, all happy and sprightly.

"Good morning Ambrose, lovely day isn't it?" His jauntiness falters when he takes in The Guardian and my expression.

"Oh dear, what have those scallywags said now?"

I appreciate his attempt at lightness but somehow, today, in spite of the summery weather, I need more than that to cheer me up.

"George, do you realise we have been in power for almost two years?"

"Goodness, how time flies."

"And already we have put more laws on the statute book than any other administration."

"Everybody has been working extremely hard."

I can tell it's going to be one of those days. Hard going.

"My point is George, in spite everything, Benjamin tells me we are trailing in the opinion polls by three percent, now why is that?"

George ponders my question. There are times when the seriousness of a situation does not dawn on George and he just sits there with a silly grin. He's like that now. It's as if I've asked him to name the number of Elton John songs that don't have the word baby in them, and he's slightly embarrassed that he doesn't know.

"Perhaps we're not getting our message across," he finally offers.

I bury my head in despair. It prompts another response.

"Well, I've got some good news, if you're interested?"

George is too kind to be sarcastic so I take his remark at face value.

"Yes, make my day."

I try not to sound too weary, knowing only too well that good news to George can often be nothing more significant than the successful removal of tomato ketchup from his favourite suit.

"We won't have to stop immigration outright because the numbers have dropped to their lowest level in fifteen years - AND - although the number of asylum seekers have increased by twelve point seven percent compared with last year, the number of refusals have risen by twenty-two point two percent"

"And what percentage of refusals have been returned to their country of origin?"

"Unfortunately, less than one percent."

"And we both know why, don't we?"

Fortunately, George recognises my rhetorical question. Ever since the Lord Chief Justice ruled that it was illegal, under the Human Rights Act to limit an asylum seeker's right of appeal, the numbers living in limbo, at immense cost to the state, have spiralled out of control.

Poor George, he tries so hard but I fear I may have burst his temporary bubble of happiness. I know I said I was going to push forward relentlessly but on some issues it's still a case of two steps forward and six back.

"I suppose I must congratulate you for getting the front end of the queue right but it's still the back end that gets buggered, if you'll pardon my turn of phrase."

George fidgets uncomfortably, he doesn't like it when I use crude language. I have no wish to detain asylum seekers in special camps, particularly as that would only highlight our failure to get to grips with the situation and, worst still, empirical evidence would suggest that they will burn the place down in pent-up anger and frustration. I push The Guardian across the desk. George gives me a sheepish look.

"Actually Ambrose, I was discussing it with Benjamin, just before he came to see you."

"Was that why you tried to cheer me up?"

"Yes, sort of." There's an awkward silence. "The thing is, Ambrose, quite a few ministers have noticed how moody you are these days, we feel as if something is getting to you and we'd much rather you confide in us than bottle it up . . . . er, we could be wrong of course."

We both know he's right. The trouble is, being spied on is unlikely to foster the bonds of loyalty.

"I know that I haven't been as communicative in Cabinet as I used to be, and I certainly don't want to blame others for being moody. The fact is George, when you're trying to change the culture of an entire nation, it only needs one negative headline like The Corpses of Human Dignity to blow hope and optimism into oblivion."

"I share your frustration Ambrose. However, notwithstanding the immigration situation, we are making good progress on the crime front. The conviction rate has risen by thirty three percent overall and our second mega-prison is bang on target to open next month. It's too early to say how effective our rehabilitation programme is but it does sadden me that yobs like Danny Briggs are still granted bail. It must be very demoralising for the police too."

We sit facing each other, knowing that a problem shared is not a problem halved but still a bloody big problem.

"Well, best snap out of it," I say, clapping my hands and trying to sound hale and hearty, "p'raps we both need a holiday."

"P'raps we both need a new judiciary," he quips.

Now there's a thought.

13

When Lord Justice Selwyn-Smythe, an Appeal Court judge, was mugged whilst walking his dog in Kensington Gore on a sunny Saturday afternoon, I was as appalled as everyone else. Perhaps the most wretched aspect of the attack was that nobody went to help him; he was, after all, an obviously elderly gentleman. Two male joggers, who went to his assistance afterwards, when questioned by the police as to why they had not felt able to intervene sooner, replied, quite unashamedly, that the assailant would probably sue them for common assault, and they did not think a criminal offence would do them any favours on their CV. However, they did give an accurate description and an arrest was made shortly afterwards. The culprit was named as John Firls, a twenty-year-old crack addict with a string of offences including breaking and entry and grievous bodily harm. He was granted bail but failed to turn up in court which was not surprising given his previous record of non-attendance on five occasions. A warrant was issued for his re-arrest. Lord Selwyn-Smythe declined to comment publicly beyond the somewhat terse remark that it would be some while before he could wield a gavel due to a broken thumb and forefinger. The incident was soon forgotten.

Some while later, another judicial attack occurred. This time it was inflicted on Sir Roland Quince, a High Court judge, and his wife Lady Margaret Quince, as they were partaking of tea in their caravan, somewhere near the Brecon Beacons. The assailant tied them up with a length of tow rope, relieved them of their wallet and purse, then disconnected the caravan and drove off in their Range Rover, subsequently crashing it in Merthyr Tydfil where an arrest was promptly made. Alun Morgan, a twenty-five-year-old decorator from Cardiff, with six previous convictions, was charged with robbery and assault, car theft and drunken driving. He was granted bail but failed to appear on the due date which, according to PC Davies, the arresting officer, was 'par for the course round here'. The incident made it to the front page of the local rag but was soon forgotten.

A few days later, Mr Samuel Packer, a Crown Court judge, and his companion, Ms Selina Sheen, a fashion model, were attacked whilst eating strawberries and cream on his boat, Impecunious Party, at its mooring on the river Thames near Cookham The incident happened during a Sunday afternoon when the popular riverside location was crowded with other boat owners and dog walkers. There were many witnesses who claimed that Mr Packer and Ms Sheen both defended themselves vigorously (he with a Calor gas spanner, she with an ice pick) but to no avail. Fortunately, the police arrived just in time to prevent the assailant from realigning Mr Packer's back teeth with a mooring spike. An arrest was made and wordy statements were taken. The assailant, who was identified as Paul Challis, a thirty-year-old unemployed labourer from Slough, claimed that he had asked Mr Packer if he could spare him some bread for his dog but Mr Packer had become abusive and Ms Sheen had pelted him with mussel shells. Several witnesses said that although there were a lot of dogs about at the time, none of them appeared to belong to Mr Challis. Subsequently, Mr Challis was charged with assault and battery and bailed to appear before Slough Magistrates Court later that month. Needless to say, he did not turn up and a warrant was issued for his re-arrest.

Like most people, I tut-tutted, and then largely forgot about it, or to be more precise, tried to push it out of my mind completely. It annoyed and depressed me to think that all over the country, the police were arresting social deviants like Paul Challis, Alun Morgan and John Firls, every day of the week, and not one of them was ever remanded in custody. They put two fingers up to their bail conditions in the sure knowledge that the same process would be repeated next time. If and when they finally appeared in court, the chances were that a custodial sentence would not be applied and they would be given some paltry community service order which they would treat with as much contempt as their bail conditions. Why? WHY?

The old excuse of overcrowded jails can no longer apply, particularly as Needle Point, our second mega-prison, had just become operational with six thousand available places and a fully staffed rehabilitation centre. When all six mega-prisons finally come on stream, we shall have increased our custodial capacity by nearly forty thousand and will have created nearly twenty thousand prisoner related new jobs. And yet, in spite of this, the judiciary bulk at sending anyone to prison. Why? WHY? I have created a golden template for a retributive penal system and they treat it like some latter day leper colony. It is enough to make one spit in the gutter.

The tricky aspect of politics is to maintain your vision whilst effectively managing reality. The latter is more often than not the trickier of the two. You can imagine my surprise, when, as time went by, yet more attacks took place on members of the judiciary. Every judge from the Appeal Court to the Crown Court appeared to be the target of a concerted wave of violence, often directed at them personally as much as their property. Even magistrates began to suffer the same fate. Beyond a generalised hate of the establishment, the motive was unclear.

I'm pleased to say that the police reaction was highly successful and in the vast majority of cases, arrests were made and the Crown Prosecution Service put the offenders in court. Unfortunately, as is the way of the world these days, at least in this country, bail was granted in virtually every instance, but alas, (although not surprisingly) was broken in the majority of cases. The press were on the case right from the start, but what really bought matters to a head was an armed attack on Lord Justice Buntock as he was alighting from his car at the Old Bailey.

Although police protection for the judiciary had been increased soon after the troubles began, no one was prepared for the high speed hit and run motorbike that vaulted the barricades like Steve McQueen in The Great Escape. A hooded pillion rider let rip with some kind of stutter machine gun that fired a lethal hail of bullets in a matter of seconds, six of which found their target, two in the chest and one direct hit to the head.

Lord Buntock, or Old Buttocks, as he was popularly known, was an endearing character, admired as much for his wit as his erudition. The contents of his brain were splattered in a grisly arc across the walls of the Old Bailey, a gruesome sight that the tabloids could not resist. Such was the ensuing furore that Kevin himself had to appear on television to defend the police operation. Given his customary bluntness, he was most diplomatic.

"I am as appalled as anyone at the spate of mindless attacks on members of the judiciary, and utterly sickened by the murder of Lord Justice Buntock today. The motorbike used by the assailant has been found abandoned behind Kings Cross railway station and is now undergoing extensive forensic tests."

"Have you any idea who the killer was?"

"No, not as yet, but we are pursuing all lines of enquiry vigorously."

"Do you accept that the police are losing the battle against crime?"

"Absolutely not. Since achieving our optimum level of manpower, apprehensions for all categories of crime are up by forty-three percent and in respect of the recent wave of attacks against the judiciary, I would remind you that arrests were made within twenty-four hours and in ninety-eight percent of the reported cases."

"Is it also true that ninety percent of those arrested were released on bail and nearly all of them have since absconded?"

"Regrettably, police officers throughout the United Kingdom are all too familiar with this scenario, however, I would remind you that it is not our duty to interpret the law, that is a matter entirely for the judiciary."

"Do you think more offenders should be remanded in custody?"

"That is a matter for the courts to decide."

"Is it true that morale in the police force is low because of soft sentencing?"

"Police morale is higher today than it ever was."

"Do you accept that the police have failed to provide adequate protection for members of the judiciary?"

"No. "

"Will you be resigning as a result of Lord Buntock's murder."

"No."

"Do you favour a return of capital punishment?"

"I fail to see what relevance that question has to the current situation. The fundamental role of the police is to apprehend law breakers, determining the nature of their sentencing is a matter for the judiciary and parliament. Thank you."

I thought the addition of the word parliament in his final comment was quite a masterstroke. Kevin and I have had quite a few one to one sessions (both in and out of uniform) and he knows only too well my frustration at the blocking tactics employed by the judiciary to maintain what I perceive as their archaic status quo in the face of much needed legal reform. Whatever my opinion, there is no knowing what prompted their learned lordships to reconsider their position, nevertheless, after Old Buttocks' funeral, no sooner had their tear ducts dried, than Lord Sackbut-Slid, the Lord Chief Justice himself, requested an urgent meeting at Number Ten. Naturally, I palmed him off with Clive Smeelie, the Lord Chancellor. Well, I always thought that Sackbut-Slid was too big for his own boots and since he was in the habit of channelling most of his obstinate rebuttals through Clive's office, I thought it only appropriate that his blue sky thinking should occur there.

"Smacks of a Versailles railway carriage, if you ask me," muttered Clive in his usual morose manner, but inwardly I knew he was delighted to have the Lord Chief Justice on the ropes.

"Just listen to what he has to say and report back," I counselled, being mindful that Clive could be rather brutish when sensing victory, "I want no hint of triumphalism."

Having said as much, I was so excited at the prospect of change, that I found myself pounding the Blochstein at the earliest opportunity, and I do mean pound. This was not an occasion for the melancholy of Schumann but the frenzied exaltation of Liszt. I literally threw myself into his transcendental study, number 4 in D-minor, known as Mazeppa.

Somehow I identified closely with the Polish Cossack count of the same name, whose enemies bound him to the back of a horse and sent it stampeding across the Ukrainian steppes. It wasn't that my radical administration had anything to do with galloping Poles or the Russian landscape, it was more a feeling that my massive parliamentary majority had mounted me on a great stallion and, instead of thundering from one victorious battle to another, the forces of negativity, those snivelling hordes who resented change, had fettered me to the horse, whipping its buttocks with the venomous flails of jealously and fear, causing it to bolt into the valley of oblivion and me with it. But I had freed myself from their evil bonds and now, and now, the Great Race was on!

Pianistically speaking, my performance left much to be desired since most of the mighty chords and rampant tempi were lost in a befuddled and befisted mess. I was hopelessly out of my depth, but that wasn't the point. I was enjoying myself. And if you cannot enjoy life, then what is the point of living it?

When the tumult ceased and my emotions calmed down, I remained seated on the piano stool, lost in my thoughts until I became aware of another presence in the room. I was about to turn when I felt a gentle touch on my shoulders. It did not startle me as there was something extraordinarily comforting about it. All the same, I let out a little gasp when I realised it was Helga. The hairs on the back of my neck stood up in a frisson of delight as she slid her hands over my shoulders and held me in her arms. I smelt the sweetness of her breath as she whispered in my ear.

"All will be well, Ambrose."

"Yes," I replied, turning slowly to face her, "fate works in many mysterious ways."

Physically, we were closer now than we had ever been before, our faces almost touching. I was entranced by the beauty of her eyes as they glistened like pools of the most wonderful iridescent blue. I marvelled yet again at the delicacy of her skin, as pale and smooth as porcelain, and oh, how I craved to taste the fullness and sensuality of her lips.

"It is not fate Ambrose . . . you have made it happen."

"I have?"

"Do not seek to unravel that which is best left alone."

I was lost for words as she began to loosen my tie and unbutton my shirt. Everything was so still and silent.

"What time is it? Where is Amelia?"

"Amelia is with Susan in Shropshire, she is staying overnight, she left a message earlier."

I felt a strange mixture of relief and excitement. All my senses were crystal clear, yet I knew I was intoxicated in some peculiar and beguiling manner.

"Helga," I whispered.

She put a finger to my lips to silence me.

"Everything will be alright Ambrose, you are a great statesman and destined to become even greater."

That was certainly no understatement as she began to unzip my trousers. I offered no resistance. Then, she took my hand and placed it gently on her breast. It was a temptation I had resisted for so long.

But no longer.

14

I was in a cabinet meeting when Amelia returned home which probably explained the late arrival of the Arts Minister too. Susan Palmero was very seldom late, a product of theatre discipline as she was wont to remind the serial stragglers. However, this morning, she looked rather sheepish, muttering a quick apology about the bloody traffic or something before settling herself in the chair and faffing about with a sheaf of papers all over the table. I assumed this was some kind of ploy to minimise her embarrassment or possibly elicit some kind of sympathy. I chose to ignore it.

More than a week had elapsed since the last cabinet meeting in which I informed everyone of my new approach. I was as available as ever but would no longer be as accommodating to their shortcomings as before. Naturally, I did not let slip that whilst this stern edict would be applied rigorously across the table, I would still take into account individual personalities. George, for example, broke into a visible sweat when I first mentioned The Great Thrust Forward. I had to take him aside afterwards to assure him that he was doing a splendid job (which he was) and how much I was looking forward to surging ahead with him on all the exciting Home Office initiatives that we had both worked so hard on. Proclamation of the GTF (Great Thrust Forward) had an immediate effect, a certain tension in the air being one of them.

Having emphasised that I still believed in the importance of one-to-one communication, I was not surprised that nearly every minister made an appointment to see me shortly afterwards. Later, I would confide to Helga that the meetings were revealing as well as interesting. Everyone was aware that I had taken George to one side and there was much speculation about his future as a result. I was pleased that my little crack of the cossack's horse whip had put them on their toes.

Susan was the first minister to see me and I was intrigued to learn that one of her main concerns was the amount of time that Amelia was spending at the Sutchworth Arts Centre in Shropshire.

"But I'm delighted that she finds it so absorbing," I say "it's given her a new lease of life. I'm sure you're only too aware that she finds life at number ten rather boring."

"Well, yes, she did say that she doesn't get to see an awful lot of you these days."

"I do try to make a connection as often as possible, even if it is last thing at night or first thing in the morning."

"I know it must be very difficult trying to fit everything in, it's bad enough dashing all over the place as the Arts Minister, so God know's what it must be like for you, Ambrose."

I shrug my shoulders. It's not like Susan to ingratiate herself. I feel as if we are fencing about, or at least she is.
I decide to be mildly provocative.

"I had hoped that my ministers, of all people, would recognise how much more uncluttered my official diary is these days. I am not half so frazzled as I was six months ago. I feel more balanced, more centred, and consequently, I hope, more able to give clearer direction than before."

I watch closely for her reaction and detect a glint of fire in her eyes. I press forward.

"I'm not necessarily referring to the Great Thrust Forward which is of course a party initiative, but more along the lines of personal communication. I still put great stead in one-to-one cards on the table stuff."

"Yes, and quite frankly I miss that."

I am somewhat taken aback by her remark. Nothing has changed as far as I am concerned, I am simply demonstrating more personal resolve.

"My direct line remains open Susan, it is up to you to use it."

"Ambrose, on the last three occasions when I have, I've been more or less batted off by that bloody valkyrie of yours!"

I practically drop my spectacles in surprise. I knew something was bothering her but I certainly wasn't ready for that. I cannot believe that someone as charming, patient and correct as Helga could brush any government minister up the wrong way. Only yesterday George said what an absolute petal she was and Jocelyn described her as a very straight bat.

"Susan, please! Such a malicious remark is quite inappropriate for someone in your position."

I can feel my temper rising. Knowing it is fuelled by my passion for Helga does not make it any easier to control. Susan is looking at me intently. I fear I may have over reacted. Have I given something away? The atmosphere remains charged for a while until Susan, realising she has been soundly ticked off, attempts to make amends.

"I'm sorry Ambrose, I didn't mean to be offensive, it's just that people are beginning to talk, and I think you should be aware of it."

"What people? What talk?"

"Most of the cabinet plus quite a few others who feel their access to you has become unacceptably restricted. The general feeling is that as a civil service secretary she has far too much authority and something should be done about it."

"Is that why you're here? Are you the elected spokesperson?"

"No - on both counts . . . and it wasn't my intention to blurt things out like this."

"Well, maybe it's better to get it off your chest and have done with it."

That seems to do the trick. We both relax a bit. The last thing I want is to start getting overly defensive about Helga. Like most women, in fact more so, Susan is extremely intuitive and I do not want to give her any cause for suspicion. For that reason, I do not attempt to change the subject but take it on board in a quiet and measured manner. I explain how Helga had been the natural choice to fill the breach after Andrew, the Principal Private Secretary had suffered a nervous breakdown. I am careful to point out that the decision was taken by none other than Sir Mallard Kane and was whole-heartedly supported by Hugo Snatch, the Cabinet Secretary, who spoke highly of her abilities. When it came to the issue of my internal appointments diary and availability, Susan said that since Helga had taken over, getting to see me was referred to as breaching the blonde wall. When Scott had been in charge, there was no difficulty whatsoever. I chose my words carefully when it came to Scott Rignold. Most people were aware of his clashes with Hugo and that the source of their arguments were always about influence and responsibilities and their perceived power base. Susan cut in at this point.

"Yes, most of us were aware of that but at least you were more accessible then."

"Possibly too accessible. As a Prime Minister I had very little quality thinking time, sometimes I didn't even have enough time to read my briefs properly. Did you know that I started to read them in bed until Amelia remarked that I was on the slippery slope to becoming a workaholic."

"Yes, she did."

"Oh?"

My surprise seems to fluster Susan. Perhaps she thinks she has betrayed a confidence? Whatever the case, she is quick to make amends.

"Well, actually it came up in the context of literature. We were discussing favourite authors and Amelia said how you always used to have a novel by the bedside but you hadn't read one for months and she was so sick of the sight of red boxes in the bedroom that she decided to buy you Robert Harris's Pompei because you were fascinated with Roman emperors and their political intrigue."

I nod in an ah-yes sort of way. I am beginning to wonder how much more Amelia might have said and whether Susan is holding any aces up her sleeve that might prove to be uncomfortable at some stage in the future. Amelia is often indiscreet, particularly after a few gin and tonics. My recollection of events wasn't quite so straightforward.

I remember all too clearly the argument we had late one night when she was drunk. Tempers were frayed and I accused her of drinking her life away. She responded by telling me to piss off, preferably in an aqueduct because, in her opinion, I had enough piss and wind to fill one, and then she promptly threw Harris's book at me. It struck me in the groin and was most painful. I hobbled downstairs to meditate and slept the night on the futon. Things have never been the same since then. Perhaps that's why Amelia spends so much time away? But why should Susan be concerned? The Sutchworth Arts Centre is her flagship project and she needs every bit of help she can get to make it succeed. A direct link to Downing Street must surely be an advantage? I decide to tackle it head on.

"Well Susan, red boxes and literary thrillers notwithstanding, I do not share your concerns about Amelia's absence from number ten, nor do I understand them."

"Oh, I wasn't complaining or anything," she says quickly, "I was just anxious that I wasn't placing too many demands on her."

"Has she complained?"

"No, not once."

"And have you ever known her to hold back when something is bothering her?"

"No, quite the contrary."

"Well there you are then."

Susan eyeballs me. I don't think she can quite believe that I'm raising no objections whatsoever to Amelia virtually decamping to Shropshire. What would be the point anyway? Amelia has always been something of a free spirit and for all I know, perhaps our marriage has reached the stage where a bit of absence might make the heart grow fonder. Susan smiles.

"You're very understanding Ambrose."

"I try to be. Now, what have you got to tell me about matters artistic?"

Susan takes my prompt and we get stuck in to an animated discussion about street theatre and how so many of the troupes seem to be plying a political message rather than the traditional stuff of clowns and jugglers and silly acts. Some of them are really quite subversive, so much so that regional television stations are beginning to fill their early evening news bulletins with the most provocative bits.

"Benjamin thinks we should curb some of them," I say.

"Obviously he's forgotten what spin did for Tony Blair," replies Susan.

"That's exactly what I told him. As soon as you start to gag the press then you're really heading down the slippery slope.
I really don't mind if a group of actors and writers accuse me of creating a police state because I know it's not true. Eventually they will realise that they have more freedom than ever before to voice their opinions. Besides, it makes for some great theatre too, talking of which, how's your prison drama project coming along?"

"Oh yes, I was just about to tell you, Howardsville did Waiting for Godot last week to a packed audience of fellow inmates and there wasn't a hint of violence from anyone."

"Why should there be?"

"Well all the performers were paedophiles."

"I see." It takes me a while to absorb the significance of that.

"Does that mean our rehabilitation programme is succeeding?"

"I guess so. A year ago they would've probably been torn to shreds."

"Good Lord, what a terrible thought."

"I think it's amazing that an audience of hard bitten cons can actually remain seated through several hours of Beckett without hurling abuse."

"Quite. It's a pity that the number of performers was so small, shouldn't we be looking at something bigger, more inclusive?"

"Well I was considering approaching Andrew Lloyd-Webber and Ben Elton with a special commission."

"That's a good idea, but could we afford them?"

"Probably not, but what if we were to offer some kind of tax incentive?"

"Such as?"

"I don't know exactly, maybe something along the lines of ten percent flat rate if you write for H.M. Prison Service but still retain full copyright."

"You'd better have a word with Jocelyn, I rather like the concept though, highly innovative Susan."

She flashes me a brilliant smile. We are friends again. Mind you, I can hardly wait to hear what Kevin may have to say about her.

One mustn't forget, she's half Italian.

15

So this is it then. The Great Thrust Forward has been launched amidst mounting criticism in the press and media. The Guardian, in typical style, chose to ridicule it as The Grand Theatrical Farce. Who cares? Not I, for I have long since ceased to be disturbed by their silly jibes, much to the relief of my Communications Director, the super-cool Benjamin Finkel. To be truthful, I am more concerned that the Opposition are beginning to get their act together and that three of my cabinet ministers are creaming off government money into illicit offshore accounts. Damn greedy fools.

I have placed my entire administration under covert twenty-four hour surveillance, including the spymasters themselves, MI5 and MI6, whose respective directors, to use the unsavoury language of Kevin Doppler, are shagging each other silly most Friday nights. Amelia has more or less decamped to Shropshire and sometimes does not even bother coming home for the weekends. This does not bother me unduly because, I must confess, my liaison with Helga has developed beyond the purely spiritual. Heady times indeed but let me remind you of one very important fact. I remain in control. For evidence of this fact, I point to my decision to have a cabinet re-shuffle. It comes as a surprise to many people but it is clearly necessary in the light of Kevin's first surveillance report.

Having remarked that I remain in control I will admit to being utterly flabbergasted at the contents of Kevin's first report. Jocelyn consorts with prostitutes! To make matters worse, he picks them up during kerb crawling excursions around Kings Cross using his ministerial car for said purposes! It beggars belief. I had difficulty in believing it until Kevin passed me the photographs. Quite how he acquired such intimate and revealing material I shudder to think but the evidence is unmistakable. How a man of such towering intelligence could flirt with political suicide so recklessly is beyond me. It's not as if there haven't been salutary examples in previous administrations. Why do supposedly sane men resort to such lower depths? The only crumb of relief in the entire revelation is the fact that his misdemeanours haven't become public. However, I cannot risk that being otherwise.

And so it was with sinking heart that I summoned Jocelyn to my private office and confronted him with the evidence.

"But why Jocelyn, why?"

"I don't know, just a need, I suppose."

"But why kerb crawling? There are high class agencies with beautiful hostesses who service most of the heads of state and their respective governments with the utmost discretion. What's more, I'm told they're well within our, or rather your, budget."

"Beautiful women find me repulsive, only the lowliest of whores can stomach me."

It is such a pitiful remark that I find it difficult to tell him that I can no longer risk his continuing presence in office. I feel even worse when he puts up no resistance.

"I understand Ambrose. I'm sorry. I'll resign."

He remains seated, humbly awaiting instruction.

"You realise we'll have to work out some kind of exit strategy."

"Yes. Perhaps Benjamin can come up with something?"

"I'll talk to him."

"Okay. I'd better start clearing my desk."

And with that matter of fact remark, the most trusted, reliable and competent member of my cabinet shambles from centre stage into the wings of oblivion.

Benjamin suggests that ill-health retirement is the most plausible exit, particularly as Joceyln's unprepossessing appearance is capable of sustaining a myriad of health disorder problems. A period of fake hospitalisation in a private colonic irrigation clinic in Switzerland is organised to lend political verisimilitude to an otherwise bald and unconvincing narrative.

Not surprisingly it doesn't prevent the press hounds from sniffing away. They catch Amelia off guard, with a gin and tonic in the squash bar of the Sutchworth Arts Centre.

"I'm not surprised he's got intestinal trouble, he farts like a blue whale."

We have a big row over the telephone about that one.

"Just because you spend more time in Shropshire than Downing Street doesn't mean that you're no longer the Prime Minister's wife."

"I'm perfectly happy being just Amelia."

"What's that supposed to mean?"

"Nothing, nothing."

"For God's sake Amelia, I've got a cabinet reshuffle on my hands, I can do without that sort of nonsense."

"Well shuffle away, they're all a bunch of wankers anyway."

"Presumably that includes the current Arts Minister?"

"Oh piss off."

And thus I start my cabinet reshuffle in earnest.

Sometimes the solution to a problem lies within the problem itself. Just as I was beginning to wonder how I would ever replace poor Jocelyn, another set of issues crossed my mind and with them the answer to both. It is possible that my administration could weather the storm of a sex scandal without serious debilitating effect but not so the case of three cabinet ministers stealing government funds. At the very point when the corrupt activities of messrs Fynch-Chilling, Mboya and Napper were about to send me into a black hole of despair, I realised, in one of those glorious eureka moments, that they were actually my salvation. Yes indeed.

In spite of the fact that they all had widely differing personalities, they shared one thing in common. They were all ambitious. So I would promote all three of them! God alone only knows why they thought they could ever get away with their misdemeanours because it would only be a matter of time before Treasury officials uncovered the budget deficit and, needless to say, Jocelyn would be implicated too. Dereliction of duties I think the term is. Well, Jocelyn has gone and his departure has neatly precipitated my intended cabinet reshuffle.

So, this is the game plan. Aubrey will become Chancellor of the Exchequer, and Claude will become Foreign Secretary. Both men covet the posts so there is not the slightest possibility that they will not accept.

In Rashidi's case it is not quite so straightforward. However, two elements come into play, namely, his ego and my vision for a future administration. I intend to create a new position, namely, Deputy Prime Minister. Rashidi will love the title and equally the remit that goes with it.

For some while now, I have been concerned at the size of George's burgeoning workload and his ability to keep abreast of all the issues, not that he hasn't given of his utmost. He is such a lovely chap but prone to self-doubt and nerves. Rashidi will have special responsibility to oversee the introduction of national identity cards. It will relieve George of some of the pressure and I know he will not feel sleighted in any way. Fortunately, they both get on very well together being fans of the Buena Vista Social Club.

There is, of course, one very important condition attached to these appointments. The immediate return of all government funds and the closure of the offshore accounts.

When I interviewed each man and calmly handed him a photocopy of his personal offshore account, his shock and incredulity was almost palpable. My magnanimity, not to mention my covert intelligence operation was not lost on any them. They realised that the game was up, and if I went down, so would they, along with the entire government at the next general election which would be upon us faster than a

West Indian bowler. Not only was I offering them forgiveness and salvation but a chance to fulfil their dreams.

If they were in any doubt as to my resolve to return to an honourable status quo, then the appointment of Hattie Chapelthwaite as Defence Minister clarified the matter. Only on hearing that news did each man behave differently.

"I wouldn't be surprised if she demands that budget negotiations take place on board a naval frigate," sneered Aubrey Fynch-Chilling, Chancellor of the Exchequer to be.

"Bloody hell, not that rottweiller," snorted Claude Napper, Foreign Secretary to be, "we'll have an emergency UN Security Council meeting every other damn week."

"Great lady," boomed Rashidi Eaglescliffe Mboya, Deputy Prime Minister to be, "I'm looking forward to working with her, who's taking over from me?"

"I'm still working on that one," I smiled.

Needless to say, each minister accepted his promotion on the spot.

The remainder of the reshuffle was not without its occasional blips. I have decided to combine the Department of Health with the Department of Social Security and ask Lucy Bowens to take on the increased responsibility.

"Will I receive a salary increase?" she squeaked back immediately.

"Yes, I'm sure we can sort something out with Jocelyn, er sorry, Aubrey."

"Thank you."

She remained silent. No doubt she was mentally formulating a fence mending approach, I just hope that Aubrey will respond positively to the gesture.

"Now Lucy I want you to concentrate on finalising the GP's special remuneration package vis-à-vis our national drugs programme which Quentin seemed incapable of completing."

Lucy did not fail to pick up on my use of the past tense in relation to Quentin. His dismissal came as no surprise. Well, dam it all, the man has piles and hardly ever turns up to cabinet meetings. He's not exactly a good example of health and efficiency.

Hattie accepted her appointment with dignity and patriotism.

"Thank you Prime Minister, I shall look forward to fighting the corner for Great Britain."

"Oh please Hattie, do call me Ambrose."

Naturally, I had to take her into my confidence, knowing full well that within hours of her appointment she would be scrutinising the Defence Procurement Budget.

Not surprisingly, being a woman of steadfast principle, she was shocked at what I had to say. Thankfully, she was astute enough to understand that my options were limited and that the survival of the government and everyone in it was the only real consideration. Even so, under her steely gaze, I did succumb to a confession.

"I was almost on the point of resigning."

"Thank God you did not Ambrose."

"We still have so much to do, I couldn't bear the thought of how history would judge us."

"The Great Thrust Forward has started and is inexorable."

"Quite so. Your wholehearted support is most gratifying."

We smiled as allies. I was relieved that we had got off to a good start as I knew that she would not be entirely pleased at my choice of her replacement. She had worked her way steadily up through the ranks, gaining friends and enemies in equal measure but in so doing, amassed a wealth of political experience.

On the other hand, Doctor Mangal Bali Chakkar, MP for Leicester Central, had never held office. Nevertheless, he had been instrumental in writing the controversial white paper on educational reform which had propelled her so dramatically into the spotlight. She was fairly guarded in her remarks.

"He's an intellectual and a stickler for detail, he'll certainly keep the civil servants on their toes. Let's hope they don't resent it."

My reason for appointing Dr Chakkar as Education Secretary is entirely political. Ever since 9/11, the Asian community have become increasingly agitated over just about everything.

I can't say as I blame them but I'm also aware that nothing we have said so far appears to alleviate their fears of a racially motivated backlash. With a manifesto centred on humanistic ideals the last thing I want to see is race riots. It was bad enough during the Leicester by-election but at least we saw off the thugs and increased our majority by two thousand.

The fact that Dr Chakkar is an academic, and a former university lecturer in anthropology (a bona fide university somewhere in India, I hasten to add) not to mention being a worldwide authority on the behaviour of elephants, is merely a bonus in the wider context of my cabinet re-shuffle.

When he entered my office I was reminded immediately of his rather unfortunate speech impediment, the result of a slack jaw and over-active saliva glands.

"Nice to see you again Mangal, do take a seat."

"Thank you, shall I shit here?"

He hobbled to the chair in the corner. I say hobble because he has a prosthetic foot. That's another thing I like about the dear doctor. I don't mean his disability but the fact that he tells the story against himself; humility is such a rare quality in a politician. Apparently he was conducting behavioural field studies in Kandy, Sri Lanka, during the parade of the sacred tooth of Buddha, and a rather disagreeable fully tusked matriarch took objection to his cross-examination of her offspring and trod on his toe to make her point. It wasn't until he discovered the UK National Health Service, conveniently staffed by medical practitioners from the Indian sub-continent, that he eventually found relief and a brand new foot. Naturally, being a man of enterprise with much to offer, he stayed on with our blessing. And now look where he is.

"The shecretary of shtate for educashun, a great honour indeed, I accshept with gratitude, Prime Minishter."

"Oh please, do call me Ambrose."

"Ambroshe it is, shertainly."

"Right, well, jolly good Mangal, we'll have an in depth discussion later, meanwhile I'll notify Sir Mallard Kane of your appointment and no doubt his civil servant chappies will pave the way for your entrance, so to speak."

"How shplendid, I can hardly wait. May I be permitted to display Shariputra in my office?"

"I beg your pardon?"

"Shariputra, the old matriarch who crushed my foot, we had to put her down for her anti-soshial behaviour but she's a very fine shpecimen of Indian elephant."

"Er. . . I'll talk to Mallard about it, but I doubt if your office will be big enough."

"Shplendid, thank you."

He departs in a sea of shpittle (I'm sorry, I shouldn't mock), a happy man indeed. I have little doubt, however, that both he and I will be pilloried for quite a while to come.

No matter, as Hattie so succinctly put it - the Great Thrust Forward has started and is inexorable.

16

Events, dear boy, events, is what that old Tory grandee Harold Macmillan once said caused governments their problems. I think he was probably right. The heat of summer was upon us and I thought it would be nice to enjoy the sunshine. So there I was, happily sitting in the garden of number ten, reading official papers. Naturally, I had taken precautions with the application of a high-density sun block and a nice big coolie hat. Helga had thoughtfully presented me with a large silk Japanese fan which, when fully opened, displayed a beautiful print of Mount Fuji surrounded by cherry blossom. I sat there in a state of gently fluttering concentration, totally unaware that a press photographer was taking a long-lensed shot of me. After all the security measures we had undertaken as well, it could so easily have been a terrorist sniper! To make matters worse, it transpired that the snapper had acquired a special security forces police uniform to infiltrate the cordon sanitaire that Kevin had assured me was fool proof. Well, more fool him. I was not amused and would have seriously considered sacking him were it not for the fact that he was within minutes of apprehending the intruder. There's no denying either that his ruthless efficiency in every other respect is so impressive. I was also mindful of the fact that he was privy to more political secrets than any other police commissioner in living memory. I was not so much on the horns of a dilemma, as strapped naked across a barrel. Fortunately, Helga has a way of dealing with him that I can only describe as uncanny. It's almost as if she controls him. There's an element of spookiness in their relationship. Unfortunately, seconds before his forces pounced on the slippery snapper, a photographic image bounced off a satellite dish somewhere in space and onto a tabloid editor's desk. A scoop too far, in my view. *Ambrose the Fluttering Fandee* crowed The Guardian. In contrast, The News of the World placed a marksman's telescopic gun sight on my head with the typically inane headline, *A FAN-tastic shot!* Poor Benjamin had a tough time defending that one.

Things didn't cool down until Kevin went live on television with details of the capture and a video of a police raid on a clothing manufacturer in Neasden. Forty sets of fake police uniforms were seized together with half a dozen fully dressed mannequins, including two kitted out as women officers with unusually muscular legs. Achmed al Zawazzi, the owner, had a forged passport, three stolen credit cards, sixty rounds of ammunition and an AK-47 in his office. He was denied bail and held in custody under the provisions of our recently amended Anti-Terrorism Bill. This meant he was banned from using the Human Rights legislation as part of his defence. Clive Smeelie, my morose but Machiavellian Lord Chancellor was the architect of that. One mention of human rights and he launches into a gloating reverie about his meeting with Cyril Sackbut-Slid, the Lord Chief Justice.

"Poor old Cyril didn't like it one bit," says Clive, "but I just sat there and let him whine away, 'the whole of Stuttgart will come down on us like a ton of bricks' he whinges, 'we'll become the pariahs of Europe overnight'. The poor sod was really getting his breaches in twist. I think you need to consider it in the context of our Great Thrust Forward, I says, knowing how much he hates being drawn into political arguments. 'But the presumption of innocence is at the cornerstone of English law,' he twitters on. Of course, Cyril, I know that as well as you do, I says, but like it or not, you and I, and every other mortal in the land, are living in a dangerous new world. 'But Clive,' he squeals, practically jettisoning the immaculately brewed Darjeeling that I'd so graciously served him in my best bone china, onto the carpet, 'maintenance of the law underwrites the very existence of democracy'. Cyril, dear Cyril, I says, placing my hand on his knee, knowing how much the old fart views such intimacy as an affront to his precious dignity, you are the embodiment of the law, whereas I am merely its servant. And then I sock him with my killer line. Cyril, the awful reality of the situation is that in spite of giving the Commissioner of Police every resource he asked for, nobody can guarantee that you won't suffer the same fate as the dearly departed Old Buttocks, whose disintegrated brains still bloody the walls of the Old Bailey. Naturally I tried not to laugh, but the old coot was still shaking when he tottered out of my office."

Clive in full flood can become a bit wearisome at times but it's difficult to stop him once he gets going. However, I need hardly say that the upside to his triumph was that the amendments to the Anti-Terrorism Bill were not opposed in the House of Lords and entered the statute book shortly afterwards. This event was something of a watershed in respect of the government's relationship with the judiciary.

It was widely acknowledged, but never publicly articulated, that moody old Clive had clobbered pedantic old Cyril for six. From a legislative standpoint, and from that day on, supporters of my Great Thrust Forward cracked open the champers and popped the balloons. If the sight of party pooping MP's were anything to go by, I think it would be safe to say that opponents of my GTF were restricted to the opposition parties and their ideologically aligned hacks in the press and media.

And so the summer break beckons. My critics made much of what they perceived to be an ill-timed cabinet reshuffle but they seem to have overlooked the logic of common sense. What better way to allow a newly appointed minister to get their feet under the table than to study their briefs whilst relaxing on holiday? A glass of plonk and a prawn salad sandwich does wonders for the concentration. Nor does the pressure of constant scrutiny apply, or the punishing schedules that civil servants insist upon. In short, they can absorb their new responsibilities at their leisure and return to parliament refreshed, invigorated and raring to go.

The summer holiday itself did present a few personal problems however. We had planned to spend the whole of August in a lovely lakeside cottage in Finland, courtesy of Tapani Ikonen, a very rich record producer who had made a generous donation to the Sutchworth Arts Centre's musical education programme. I was really looking forward to smoking my own fish and dunking barbecued sausages in that funny sweet Finnish mustard. And then Susan Palmero threw a spanner in the works by inviting us to join her for two weeks in her old farmhouse in the south of France. Needless to say Amelia wanted to go south, whereas I wanted to go north.
I tried to reason with her.

"Accepting hospitality on this scale from a member of my own cabinet does put me in a rather compromising situation for the future."

"Why, are you planning to sack her?"

"No, she's doing a splendid job."

"Well there you are then."

"You refuse to understand my position, don't you?"

"And you refuse to acknowledge that sitting by some isolated lake for four weeks being bitten to death by mosquitoes whilst listening to you drone on about the far side, is boredom personified when compared to the alternative."

In the end we reached a compromise. Amelia would stay for two weeks in Finland and then depart south. I would remain put. It would not be without its problems.

"Can you imagine what the press speculation will be like if they get wind of it?" I said.

"Get Benjamin to fix it, after all, we can't be the only couple of our age who don't want to behave like young lovers any more."

"We are, however, the only couple who happen to live at number ten Downing Street."

"Not for much longer if the opinion polls are to be believed."

Well, to be perfectly frank with you, when the time came for Amelia to depart I was more than a little relieved. It had been tense fortnight. We spent most of the time trying to avoid having an argument but failing miserably. Matters weren't helped when Tapani Ikonen dropped by to entertain us, with his very young and very pretty girlfriend. Tapani is married with seven children I hasten to add. The Korskankova vodka flowed and the conversation became more indiscreet as the evening wore on.

"Too much work and no play make Jack dull boy," said Tapani, "I know so."

"He play with me," giggled Minna, "I know so too."

"He never plays with me," said Amelia, casting me a dismissive look.

"Play with other man," said Tapani, putting his arm around her.

"Or play with other woman," said Minna, grabbing her hand and shoving it roughly against her breasts.

They all collapsed across the table laughing. I drank straight from the bottle.

Fortunately, by the time Helga arrived, the mosquito attacks had somewhat abated.

"Did anyone recognise you?" I enquired anxiously, as she discarded her sunglasses and wig.

"Only the security guys."

"Thank God for that."

"Ambrose, we are ever so slightly off the beaten track, okay?"

I did not reply. The last thing I wanted was another argument. I left her alone and walked to the small wooden jetty by the lakeside.

Although it was nearly eleven p.m. the northern summer sun still cast a gentle light across the lushness of the forest pines. The surface of the lake shimmered with a magical translucency. There was hardly a ripple as Helga entered the water naked and swam languorously to an area that seemed to possess its own luminosity.

"It's lovely, why don't you join me?"

"I'm okay, I'll just watch you."

I'm not really a water person at the best of times. Somehow it doesn't seem to be my medium. I don't know why. The human race spent thousands of years hauling itself out of the primordial swamp and the ones that couldn't face the prospect of evolving from slack bellied amoeba into Neanderthal beings in search of a Tesco store open 24/7, chose to sneak back as fishes and suchlike. Maybe I'll be a water spirit next time round? For the time being, I'm happy to sit with a can of Olaf III and contemplate the beauty of nature and Helga within it.

We meditated for two hours, sitting outside the log cabin in front of a small fire whose glowing embers lent a quiet calm all of their own. We ate supper in the small hours of the morning. Freshly smoked salmon with a creamy dill sauce and new potatoes. Then we pigged out with lashings of smelly cheese, spread liberally on those huge, chunky, Kunto rye biscuits that look like the soles of open toed sandals. I was grateful that I'd still got my own teeth. As I cracked open another bottle of wine, Helga fashioned a spliff as big as a Churchill cigar. The sweet pungency of best Lebanese soon permeated the air. What the hell, I thought, as she passed it over, I can't be a martyr to constraint all the time.

As we sat in silence, reflecting on the nature of existence, I thought what a wonderful place Great Britain would be, if I finally managed to legalise all drugs. The sun was just beginning to rise when we went inside. We made love deeply and slowly and slept for hours afterwards.

I cannot remember when we surfaced again; the hour of the day no longer seemed relevant. At long last I was beginning to enjoy my holiday. It certainly hadn't been planned this way, but then, we both agreed, it would have been daft not to take advantage of the situation. So we did, and what delights awaited us I hardly dared imagine.

You will appreciate then, how taken aback I was when Helga suddenly launched into a criticism of my cabinet reshuffle, or to be precise, my appointment of Rashidi to the newly created post of Deputy Prime Minister. It was bad enough not being able to escape those bloody red ministerial boxes with their turgid workload, but as a piece of holiday conversation, that really took the biscuit. And I said so in no uncertain way. Helga responded with rising temper and when things eventually calmed down there was an unspoken acknowledgement that we'd just had our first lover's argument. As can so often be the case, (although for me, such occurrences lie so far back in my memory that it was almost like experiencing it for the first time) our argument brought us closer together.

We spent the remainder of the day walking through the forest, listening to the sounds of nature and becoming at one with the beauty of the environment. Mutual feelings of tenderness and harmony were in the air when the subject of Rashidi's appointment arose again, rather unexpectedly as we snuggled up in bed.

"It's not because he's black," said Helga, gently nestling her head on my chest, "it's just that I think he gives out the wrong kind of signals at a time when the public needs reassuring that they are in a safe pair of hands and will remain so for the foreseeable future. Stability and security are so important right now. We live in such an anxious world."

I kissed her forehead before replying.

"I understand what you're saying, but I'm not going to fall into the trap of previous prime ministers by believing that I'm immortal. If I cannot achieve what I want to during one term of office, then it will be time to move on and let someone else have a go."

I could feel her body tense even before I had finished speaking. She abruptly turned over, our faces so close that I could feel the pulse of her breath.

"Ambrose, I don't believe it, what are you saying?"

I swallowed hard, hoping that what I was about to say would not sound like a cod version of Hamlet's soliloquy.

"Helga, my love, if we walk the middle way with courage and honesty, then we should not become deluded. The wisdom of an old sage is one thing, but finding the moral landscape of today's younger voters both frightening and incomprehensible, is entirely another. I was sixty-four when I took office and I'm not becoming any younger."

A certain mistiness crept into her eyes. She was so beautiful I could not bare the thought of losing her.

"There's no need to doubt yourself," she whispered, "you have been working so hard, you just need a rest."

"I wish it were as simple as that."

"It is Ambrose, it is."

I did not seek to challenge the premise as I felt the warmth of her hand on my penis.

17

Those two weeks in Finland were the happiest days of my life. Perhaps such an absolute state of contentment could only serve to contrast with the dire feelings of betrayal I experienced only days before we were due to depart.

Helga had taken herself off for some personal shopping and I was not expecting her return for several hours. I was most surprised therefore to hear a loud rap on the door within ten minutes of her leaving. Assuming it to be one of the security guards, I opened the door and was amazed to find none other than Rashidi Eaglescliffe Mboya standing on the threshold, grinning from ear to ear. He was wearing a Ladysmith Black Mambazo T-shirt and a pair of riotous Bermuda shorts. His bare feet were shoved inside a huge pair of Nike trainers whose heels had long since been crushed into submission. One foot rested like a log on top of a plastic crate of supermarket beer.

"Ambrose!" he boomed, as if I were twenty feet away.

"But – I don't understand - I mean, how did you? – where are the security guards?"

"Back in the trees, smoking the ganja," he grinned, "shall I come in?"

I hesitated for no good reason and then ushered him in. It was equally pointless snatching a quick glance to see if Helga was about, but I did so all the same.

"Helga's on her way to Tampere," said Rashidi, his big frame heaving with laughter, "but don't worry, your secret is safe with me."

I was too flabbergasted to reply. A myriad tortuous thoughts raced through my mind but they all boiled down to the same thing. Once again, I was strapped naked across that barrel.

I watched Rashidi stride about the room as if he owned the place. Somehow his swagger seemed more mischievous than arrogant. Eventually, I told him to sit down as his constant pacing was making me feel nervous.

"Nothing to be nervous about, Ambrose," he boomed, "I am simply your deputy prime minister reporting for service."

I wondered how long it would be before the terms of blackmail were stated.

"I admire your enthusiasm Rashidi, but I'm still on holiday and I'm not aware of any crisis."

It was rather a lame attempt to try and regain my composure.

"No worries, I'm here to chill out too, hey, d'you want a beer? They're still cold."

Without waiting for me to reply he scooped out a can of Olav IV from the crate and plonked it in my lap. Cold wasn't the word for it, I felt as if my genitals were being cryogenically treated. I quickly unclipped the can and took a fast slug; I didn't think this was the occasion to look for a glass. I tried to sound nonchalant but the tension wracked up my voice by a good few semi-tones.

"Well, Rashidi, what's on your mind?"

He kicked off his trainers and stretched out his legs.

"Okay, so now that I've got used to the idea of being deputy prime minister," he said, still grinning away, "I wanted the opportunity to discuss, uninterrupted and in private, my personal vision of the great thrust forward." I gripped the edge of my chair and said nothing. "I mean, when all's said and done Ambrose, these sure are great thrusting times," he broke into a big chortle.

I was beginning to wonder just what his angle was. Rashidi could certainly be a devious bugger but I'd never considered him to be malicious. Mischievous yes, but nasty no.
I decided to take the plunge.

"Alright Rashidi, let's cut to the chase. Amelia is in Provence with Susan and I am here with Helga, now what are you here for?"

If it was possible to break into a grin bigger than the one he already had, he did so. And then he broke into a big-throated giggle, rather like a schoolboy who suddenly produces the biggest conker of all time. Still chortling gleefully, he strode across the room, opened the door and let rip with a loud wolf whistle.

"Ambrose, I want you to meet my new soul mate, we're on holiday too!"

And before I could register any emotion, I heard brisk footsteps creaking on the wooden veranda and suddenly, there she was, standing in the doorway – Gloria Fitzbagley, Head of MI5! That was when I registered emotion.

"Good morning, Prime Minister, mind you don't spill your beer."

I was so taken aback by surprise that I just gaped like a fish and then quickly brought the Olav IV to my open lips and glugged furiously.

Having never seen Gloria in anything but a formal business suit it was a double shock to see her now in a pair of raunchy cut-away designer shorts and a figure hugging cotton top. In spite of her short, chunky frame, I was surprised how athletic she was. I found her quite sexy in a butch kind of way.
I noticed Rashidi was ogling her too.

"Please call me Ambrose," I said tartly, "since we are all on holiday."

Rashidi slumped back in his chair while Gloria settled herself next to me on the rattan sofa. Although I felt the ball was in their court, I did not relish my disadvantage at the state of play. I decided to serve.

"Well?" I said, trying to muster authority.

Gloria pulled out an A4 sized brown envelope from a gaily covered cloth bag and handed it over.

"I don't think you'll like what you'll see but it's our reason for being here."

I tried hard to believe her even though Rashidi's grin remained as big as a melon. My hands trembled as I extracted a set of photos. Black and white. Eight inches by ten. Six in total. I gasped at the images.

There was Helga, captured in a state of total déshabillé, indulging in some remarkable sexual gymnastics with an equally exposed Kevin Doppler! Clearly, they were both at the height of their innovation when the photographs were taken.

It was sickening and I felt sick. Sick, numb and betrayed. How could she do this to me? And with that pockmarked brute of a man, with his gold fillings, bloodshot eyes and, revoltingly, a pale posterior peppered with pimples. For once in my life, words failed me. The look on my face must have said it all. Gloria spoke politely.

"I'm sure you understand, Ambrose, why we had to reach you quickly."

"Yes."

"The situation has presented us with an enormous security risk."

"Yes, but why is he laughing about it?"

Gloria shot Rashidi an admonishing glance but to no avail.

"We have more information that you need to know."

"More photographs?"

"Yes."

I took another can from the crate. Guzzling cold beer was fast becoming a habit. Gloria handed me another brown envelope. I removed its contents and mentally prepared myself for another shock. It wasn't long coming. For some strange reason the photos were in colour. I could not contain my gasp.

Helga was on form again and this time with Rodney Snodder the Head of MI6. Their naked contortions were equally inventive. I suppose the only observation worth noting was that Rodney's bare flesh was remarkably smooth and free of blemishes. It was obvious he used a sunbed.

I don't know whether it was the cold of the beer can but my hands were no longer trembling. I drank the remainder. It was a therapy of sorts. I moved to the window and looked out. It no longer felt like a blissful holiday location.

"Don't worry about Helga," said Rashidi, "we have arranged for her car to break down."

"We?"

"My partner and I," he indicated Gloria, "we are an item too."

She began fussing with her bag and for one awful moment I thought she was going to produce another set of salacious photographs but fortunately it was merely to facilitate the return of the envelopes.

"I wish you every happiness," I replied wearily, and helped myself to another beer.

As a husband, I had been unfaithful. As a lover, I had been betrayed.

As a Prime Minister, my power had evaporated.

18

When events shift dramatically, some folks often refer to the results as a sea change. I think that would be an appropriate description in my case. Naturally I saw no reason not to forge ahead with the Great Thrust Forward and yet the sea of pus that I mentioned earlier had somehow polluted the very atmosphere. No one actually said anything but there was no denying the fact that something poisonous had seeped through the portals of Number Ten. I found it very difficult to trust anyone. It wasn't that my fundamental attitude had changed in any significant way, it was more a case of holding a little something back. A caution born of pain.

I was very pleased to see Amelia again. She sported a healthy tan and a radiant smile. Susan Palmero looked equally relaxed and happy at the first cabinet meeting of the autumn session.

A quick glance round the table and it was easy to see who had enjoyed the break and who had not. All those with new appointments were positive and upbeat and it showed in their body language as much as their behaviour.

I had agreed with Rashidi that he would sit next to me on my right, a position traditionally reserved for the Chancellor of the Exchequer. It did not seem to bother Aubrey Fynch-Chilling however, which was a sure indication that he was a very happy man. Already he has acquired the nickname Mr Smug. As for Rashidi himself, he seems to have acquired a permanent grin. It's not that he looks like the cat who has got the cream so much as the cat who has just become the majority shareholder of the National Milk Marketing Board.

On my return from Finland, we got straight down to the brass tacks of Helga's treachery and the ramifications thereof. As far as our on-going relationship is concerned, I will deal with that later. What I had to come to terms with quickly and completely was my responsibility in the whole affair.

I suppose love really is blind after all, but my naivety in believing that she genuinely supported me in my political ambition is almost too embarrassing to admit. But I do. Even Rashidi looked grim as Gloria presented me with information that would not only put Helga behind bars for the rest of her life as a serial murderer, but Kevin Doppler as well! Those dreadful attacks on the judiciary, culminating in the bloody slaughter of Old Buttocks was all part of her evil master plan to manoeuvre me into a position where, through me, she would begin to undermine the very fabric of democracy. Equally chilling was her manipulation of Kevin and Rodney Snodder to further her ends.

I sat aghast as Gloria talked me through a number of intelligence reports that revealed Helga as the prime instigator in a whole series of criminal activities. She was even responsible for the bombing of the Shree Swaminarayan temple in Leicester which killed His Holiness, Shree Sahajanand Narayan Muni and Jim Brigginshaw. Not forgetting the near misses of the recently departed Jocelyn, my dear Amelia and, of course, yours truly! Surely she did not want to get rid of me too? And to think that we had travelled to the far side together where she had shone like a benevolent deity.

I am devastated, mortified, and, more to the point, feel unfit for office. But I cannot resign without bringing the whole ghastly edifice crashing down around me. It would signal the annihilation of the Conservative party as we know it. I have no option other than to groom Rashidi to take over at a time of my choosing. He knows this only too well and all I can say is that I'm grateful he's not rubbing my nose in it.

We have already decided that changes need to be made to the administration of the cabinet office. Scott Rignold has at long last recovered from his bout of acute septicaemia. I feel guilty that I never went to visit him, choosing instead to rely on Helga's reports. In the light of her horrendous machinations, I'm not so sure that she didn't have a hand in prolonging his illness. It sounds incredible but only now am I beginning to grasp the scale of her plotting.

Scott is fully recovered and I have appointed him as the new Minister for Overseas Development. He will report to Rashidi who maintains special responsibility for international matters, by which I mean, the drugs portfolio, although we cannot refer to it as such publicly; officially it does not exist. I was delighted at the warm reception the cabinet gave Scott. He was always a popular figure and I think the appointment gave the cabinet a little feel-good factor.

The poisonous atmosphere I perceive inside Number Ten may very well be the result of my own paranoia but there is no doubting the ferocious attack the government is facing everywhere else. Fortunately, the cabinet presents a united front, even though Dr Chakkar is still sulking because we can't find him an office big enough to mount his Shariputra elephant on the wall. And of course, I had to deal with Helga's reaction too.

Needless to say she did not like it when I told her that I was appointing a new Parliamentary Private Secretary to replace Scott.

Angela Basoutar was a smart, sassy, young black with a Masters Degree in Philosophy and a constituency that included most of New Cross and Catford. I had discussed her appointment with Gloria from a security point of view. We both agreed that a streetwise female who could legitimately follow Helga into the loo and maybe even keep her on edge to the point where she would make a mistake, was a tactic worth trying. However, we could not take Angela into our confidence, the stakes were simply too high for that.

We also concluded that, dangerous as it was, Helga would remain as my Principal Private Secretary, the rationale being that if she was beyond my reach , I could not control her or, significantly, entrap her. Unfortunately, we have yet to formulate an entrapment strategy which does rather bother me. Nevertheless, whatever form that may ultimately take, it is agreed that I will maintain as close a relationship as possible. We don't want to set any alarm bells ringing prematurely. Easier said than done. I am a sufficiently skilled politician to feign a friendly alliance but quite how I will cope with the intimate aspect of our relationship has yet to be tested.

For obvious reasons we had to return from Finland as completely separate entities. During our final days together I pretended to be absorbed by the contents of those dratted red ministerial boxes that until then I had completely ignored. By the time we climbed into bed, the events of the past forty-eight hours had left me in a state of utter confusion.

"Ambrose, you're so tense, would you like a muscle relaxing massage?"

"Yes."

The aromatic oils were beautiful and I gradually succumbed to the gentle circling and pressuring of her hands on my back. It was her manipulation of my mind that still bothered me. How had it happened? They say that the devil is always closest to you, sometimes as close as the perspiration on your skin. Is Helga really the devil incarnate and if so, how has she got under my skin?

The bedroom is bathed in candlelight and the perfume from the oil is wonderfully intoxicating. Helga is naked and sits astride me as I lay face downwards. I can feel the soft sheen of her vulva as she moves gently back and forth.

Can these really be sensations I must resist?

19

This morning I received great insight during meditation.

I am responsible for everything. Yes. The emergence of Helga as an awesome force of evil is a direct result of causes I have made in this life and the past. For the time being I'll skip the past since I've got enough on my plate coping with the present.

Precisely what the causes were I have no idea but somehow the message from the far side was infected just like a malicious virus in a computer. I am not entirely happy with that analogy because when computers go wrong I have to call on the expertise of others and since I am responsible for everything then only I can sort it out. Or is this arrogance?

I am the leader of the party and therefore I must lead; what else is a Prime Minister supposed to do? I have speech writers, spin doctors, advisers, researchers and the huge resources of the civil service at my disposal and yet, in spite of that, I have still managed to create an unholy mess. Perhaps it was wrong of me to force the message on my ministers in the manner I did? Something tells me that the seeds of evil were sown then. And yet, if they saw the same message as I did and took action accordingly, surely there ought to be a different outcome to the one we have now? The trouble is, not every minister acted honestly and when that became evident, I took swift and decisive action.

I mentioned earlier that I felt I could no longer trust anyone but the truth is I never trusted them in the first place. Well some of them but not all. I trusted Jocelyn but he fell prey to the lower worlds. And I have too. Acknowledging that fact is part of my insight. I was granted office on the basis of a humanistic manifesto but now I can see that political pragmatism and base urges swept those ideals aside like so much chaff in the wind.

How difficult it is to be human. Finding the answer to that most fundamental question is the focus of my meditation. It is one thing to clear one's mind of delusion in order to see the absolute truth, but it is another entirely to react to that knowledge as a politician, let alone as a Prime Minister. Confronting these issues has led to lengthier periods of meditation. This has not gone unnoticed and in some cases has given cause for concern.

The other day I overheard a conversation between George and Angela.

Angela: "Has he always been like this?"

George: "Not exactly."

Angela: "Is it true he started meditating at five o'clock this morning?"

George: "I'm afraid so."

Angela: "Can you see any benefits?"

George: "Well, not so far, at least, not for the cabinet."

Angela: "Shouldn't somebody be doing something about it?"

George: "Well, the deputy prime minister spends most time with him."

Angela: "I suppose that's a start."

George: "Probably the wrong one, most of us think Rashidi Mboya is a total lunatic."

Angela: "Oh dear, that's how the opposition see Ambrose too."

George: "Yes, I know, a double whammy, it's very worrying."

I can hardly believe what I'm hearing. Have I now become the laughing stock of everybody? More to the point, do I really care? I do not. I hold this point of view because I have attained enlightenment and, unlike some, have returned from the far side to promulgate the timeless message. Those who jeer and taunt me, those who despise me, (in fact those who also admire me) have only their own perceptions by which to judge me. If they have not seen what is on the far side then they cannot know that everything, everything, absolutely everything is an illusion. I will tell you this much. You may not like it, nor even believe me, but I will say it all the same.

Nirvana is nothingness. When you get to the far side there is nothing except your self. Granted, your self is sort of suspended in a timeless nothingness but your self is still there all the same. If you don't like your self then you have a problem. Conversely, if you do like yourself, or even love your self, the problem is still there. Until you can completely let go of your self, you have not really touched base at the far side.

I now realise why enlightenment is so difficult to attain. People don't like to leave themselves behind in a state of timeless nothingness. They think that if they do, they will become some kind of empty shell, a simultaneous non-living and non-dead illusion. That's why so many choose to return with their self intact, alive and kicking and ready to party. Those who resist this and simply go with the non-flow of eternal nothingness are never seen or heard of again. They remain in a state of utter bliss, free from the pain of birth and death and all the stuff that goes in between.

The only problem I haven't yet solved is why Helga appeared with me on the far side as a radiant, shining, benevolent deity? Perhaps she is an illusion after all? Perhaps she is a figment of my imagination? Well, if that is so, then I must draw your attention to the fact that there's one helluver lot of other people also suffering a similar delusion. In the case of Kevin Doppler and Rodney Snodder, they have actually climbed into bed with it! It no longer beggars belief so much as buggers it.

I think I am fast coming to the conclusion that there is no such thing as good or evil. There is what there is and however it appears to be is a matter entirely for the individual. I am not going to do anything about Helga. In fact, I'm not going to do anything about Kevin or Rodney, either. Even more illuminating is the fact that I'm not going to do anything about anything. What will be will be. From now on, everything just is. And I have to tell you, I feel incredibly relieved by all this. I am certainly not going to take any credit for it. That would be pointless. The point being, if there is a point, is that there is no point in anything.

I offer the nation a manifesto of nothingness. I'm sure it was some Roman philosopher who said: *into nothing, nothing can go, out of nothing, nothing can come.* By adopting a policy of nothingness, nothing can go wrong.

Things being what they are, I have no doubt that whatever is judged to be right one day, will be seen to be wrong the next. I have found true happiness in nothingness. I can do nothing about what has gone before. I shall not waste a second of my energy on what I do not know is yet to come. If the present is full of nothingness, then so be it. If others choose to live a life of delusion, then so be it for them.

I accept that others may not agree with what I am saying. Please believe me when I say that I have no wish to appear rude or dismissive, but when it comes to the opinion of others, I am not exercised by their thinking.

I'm just so absolutely happy about being right about nothing.

20

When Amelia came home for the weekend, a rare occasion I hasten to add, it was for a specific reason. A few weeks before the opening of the Sutchworth Arts Centre, a grand gala of a show including dancing, singing and just about every other type of act ever devised, the technical staff threatened to go on strike.

"Bloody bastards," snorted Amelia, "they sit on their arses most of the time, occasionally condescending to flick a switch or shift a bit of scenery, and now they're demanding better pay and conditions."

"From what Susan's been telling me, everyone has been working incredibly hard and have been incredibly supportive."

Even though I say so myself, I find it very easy to inject a bi-partisan tone into my comments. I really do not care whether events prove to be a storm in a teacup or a maelstrom at the heart of British industry. People will behave in the manner they think fit and that's that.

"They just don't know which side their bloody bread is buttered on," snarled Amelia, "and their bloody shop steward drives a bloody great BMW four by four and he never gets a bloody parking ticket like the rest of us. It's obvious he's a bloody racketeer with half the bloody district counsellors in his bloody back pocket."

"I hope you haven't been saying that in the squash bar, my sweet."

"Squash bar, Jesus Christ, you can't get into *any* bloody bar without being told some bloody trade union has been given permission to hold some bloody meeting or other."

"We live in a democracy, people do have rights."

"Ambrose, if this bloody dispute escalates Susan will be blamed for everything, you know what this means to her, her reputation is on the line. The poor darling was in floods of tears last night."

"Oh dear, I am sorry to hear that."

"Well for Christ's sake why don't you bloody well do something about it?"

And there you have her reason for returning to number ten. I am neither surprised nor disappointed. This is how it is for the time being. Whether anything will happen to change it, I have no idea. It is not so much a question of sitting tight as sitting open. As far as resolving the threatened strike is concerned, that is a side issue, at least in the context of Amelia's long-term happiness. I have no doubt that if the Sutchworth inaugural concert opens as planned there will be much delight in many quarters but, like all things, the event will come to pass and eventually be no more than another memory, albeit, one must assume, a pleasant one. I try to explain things.

"Bringing the Prime Minister into a local dispute is utter madness, it is entirely a matter for the management and trade union to resolve."

"I knew you'd wash your hands of it, bloody typical."

"If they cannot reach agreement they can refer the matter to ACAS, that is what they are there for."

"ACAS, my arse, another bloody anachronism that should've been consigned to the dustbin years ago."

"Actually, they've got a splendid record of success."

"Success! Hah, you don't even know the meaning of the word."

"I know that I won office with the biggest electoral landslide in British political history, surely you're not going to tell me that that wasn't a success?"

I think my calm rebuttal may have hit home. Amelia flounces to the drinks trolley and pours herself another gin and tonic. I flick through an old colour supplement pretending to be absorbed in the feature story about some young, unkempt, heavily tattoo'd Hollywood actor who had inexplicably found his inner self by rendering seven different women pregnant, three of whom were married, two allegedly infertile and one a devout Roman Catholic. I think it best to remain silent and let her work through her anger state.

"No bloody ice again, no wonder the country's going to the dogs, I've seen better service in a youth hostel in Peru."

I somehow doubt that such institutions exist in South America; nevertheless, I do not rise to the bait, choosing instead to offer an olive branch.

"I saw a full tray of cubes in the kitchen this morning, I'll fetch those, if you like."

"Oh please don't bother yourself, I wouldn't want to divert your energies from the great thrust forward, or whatever name you call that stupid bloody initiative."

"Great thrust forward is correct, my sweet, or GTF for short, only the Guardian calls it something else."

"Hah, don't bloody kid yourself. D'you know what they're calling it down at the Sutchworth Arts Centre? Gone to fuck, that's what."

"That is most uncharitable."

"Uncharitable! Jesus bloody Christ Ambrose, at times you're so pathetic it's untrue. Why don't you get a grip of things and bloody well DO SOMETHING?"

I must admit, after all the months of planning and discussion that the entire cabinet had put into formulating the GTF, such a dismissive remark does rather wrankle. I can see there is no point in pursuing a constructive conversation since Amelia was drunk even before we started. So I choose my words carefully.

"There are no less than forty-eight separate proposals in the forthcoming Queen's speech, it is the most comprehensive legislative programme put before parliament by any administration."

"Well, unless it includes a law to ban all strikes, then as far as I'm concerned the whole bloody lot of you can go to fuck."

How amazing it is that at that moment of greatest insult, I hit upon a wizard idea. Understandably, this is not the best time to bring it up. In fact, from a strategic point of view, it would be better to create an immediate diversion. So I do.

"I think I'll get that ice, my sweet, I fancy a drink myself."
And with that, I proceed to the kitchen, leaving Amelia alone and sozzled on the sofa.

The following morning I started to energise my wizard idea. When I say idea, what I really mean is the timing of it because that was the bit that suddenly clicked during Amelia's insulting tirade. The idea itself is actually one of the boldest policies within our ground breaking GTF initiative and is included in the forthcoming Queen's speech. It won't be long before word leaks out so I have to move fast to capture the element of surprise. And surprise it will be. I can hardly contain my excitement. We are going to re-nationalise the railways! Yes! And the trades unions will love us for it and forever be in our debt. And so will every man, woman and child in the land. Rail travel misery will be a thing of the past.

And talking of the past, I must mention that I nearly sacked Christopher Meelybean, the Transport Minister during the last reshuffle. I relented when he showed huge enthusiasm for an idea put forward by Dr Mangal Bali Chakkar for a National Train Driver's School.

Apparently they are both steam engine enthusiasts and even go chasing them together along the cuttings and viaducts of the Settle and Carlisle railway; how they find the time I shall never know. Nevertheless, it was Mangal who inspired the cabinet when I first tabled the re-nationalisation proposal.

Yes, no false modesty here, for it was I who longed for a return to those great railway companies of yore. Mangal knew instinctively where I was coming from and splattered across the cabinet table in splendid rhetoric.

"Oh yesh, Prime Minishter, what an exshiting shuggeshton, the London, Midland and Shcottish, the Great Weshtern, I can shee the appeal immediately, yesh, noshtalgia and history all rolled into one, a potent pill that the populashion will surely shwallow."

I think some cabinet members were surprised that a man who has lived most of his life in India could know so much about the golden age of British steam, not to mention the ins and outs of the unquestionably successful TGV trains of modern France. At one point, when he was in the middle of what I can only describe as a eulogy about driver training - "shafety musht be uppermosht in every fashet of our operashons' - I wondered whether I shouldn't transfer him from Education to Transport!

Eventually, Christopher Meelybean stepped in and outlined his plans on the management of the newly created companies which I insisted should retain their old regional names and livery.

"I heartily agree Prime Minister, we can still be streamlined and efficient whilst indulging in the beautiful chocolate and cream coaches of the Great Western."

"Or the imposhing maroon of London, Midland and Shcottish," interjected Mangal.

"Or the apple green of LNER," piped up little Lucy Bowens.

"Or the blood and custard of Southern," boomed Hattie Chapelthwaite.

"Or that lovely blue of the locomotives of, er, um . . ." struggled George Blossom.

"Thomas the Tank Engine, perhaps?" sneered Aubrey Fynch-Chilling.

All of a sudden, I had a cabinet full of train enthusiasts. Choosh-a-puffa, choosh-a-puffa, toot, toot, toot. Lovely stuff.

The next move was to contact the Trades Union Congress and invite as many of their lads and lassies as possible over to number ten for smoke salmon sandwiches and a glass of bubbly.

"Sorry it's such short notice but timing is everything, you'll appreciate why, when you get here."

"We're very busy too you know, what's it about, is there an agenda?"

"Sorry, but it's an absolute lip-seal job until the day, we're serving real ale as well though."

The room was jam-packed and the sense of anticipation was palpable. I racked up the tension a bit more with a deliberately tantalising introduction.

"I know that traditionally we are not the party normally associated with your movement, however, I am confident that what I am about to say will bring the two of us closer together than at any time in either of our respective histories."

By now, one of them was actually drooling. I thought it was a splendid sign until Christopher Meelybean whispered in my ear to stop staring because the poor chap had suffered a stroke six months ago and never fully recovered. Naturally I averted my eyes from the saliva sodden napkin to deliver another kind of stroke, a masterstroke.

"Ladies and gentlemen, it is our intention to re-nationalise the railways!"

For half a second it pole-axed the lot them and then a great burst of applause broke out. There was nothing debilitating about this masterstroke, I can assure you. In fact, as Christopher took over, to put flesh on the bones (his words not mine) the effect was one of rejuvenation and joy. By the time Mangal stood up to announce the creation of the National Train Driver's School, with the fervent wish that two of their members would serve on its board of governors, the entire proceedings were verging on ecstasy. Twenty minutes after the meeting broke up it was still difficult to tell the difference between Mangal's shpittle and the sparkle of champagne bubbles. I grabbed a moment to buttonhole Benjamin.

"Where's the chappie from BECTU?" I asked, having been careful to ensure that an invitation was issued to the Broadcasting, Entertainment, Cinematograph and Theatre Union, even though nobody could understand what earthly connection they had with the railways.

"Justin de Rose, he's over there," said Benjamin, indicating a suave looking man with a black velvet waistcoat and an ill-fitting toupee, "he only gets prickly if you confuse his members with those of Equity, the actors' union, their general secretary couldn't make it due to a stomach ulcer."

"Oh dear, how unfortunate. Well, trust me, I shan't say a word about luvvees."

I edge my way towards him, smiling and acknowledging hand shakes en route. I proffer my own as I reach him.

"Good morning Justin, how nice to see you."

"The pleasure's all mine, a lovely speech, if I may so, although I still don't know why I'm here."

"Inclusivity," I murmur, "inclusivity."

"Ah yes," he replies, somewhat inconclusively, "the more the merrier, I guess?"

"Well, it's certainly merry at the moment."

"Isn't it just?"

Fortunately for both of us, a wine waiter appears and we seize the opportunity to refresh our glasses. Taking advantage of the general air of conviviality, I steer him away from the immediate melee and lower my voice.

"Justin, I wonder if I could take you into my confidence for a moment?"

"Of course you may."

I can see he is enjoying the attention and I must admit I am rather warming to my little piece of play-acting; I even hold him gently by the elbow.

"Um, Justin, it's come to my attention that there's some sort of industrial relations kerfuffle at the Sutchworth Arts Centre, I maybe wrong of course."

"Nothing has reached my ears as yet."

"I see, I see, well that's probably all to the good isn't it?"

"I can always make enquiries."

"Oh I'm not suggesting for one moment that you haven't got your finger on the pulse of things, so to speak, besides, I have no wish to interfere where I have no right to do so but, well, as you know, Sutchworth is something of a flagship enterprise and if we get it right there, well, I mean, what can I say without over-egging the cake?"

"Just give it one last stir perhaps?"

"Ha ha, quite, quite. The thing is, the entertainment industry is so dear to my heart and let's face it, we can't all be luv –ah - well what I'm actually saying is that I understand how vital the technical infrastructure is to the overall success of any production, not just the opening of the Sutchworth Arts Centre and er, um . . ."

"Let me assure you Prime Minister, there are no Luddites in our organisation, and if there are, I shall root them out personally."

"Oh splendid, splendid, that's truly excellent. If I may say so Justin, a number of my colleagues have remarked on your forward looking mindset."

"Oh really?"

"Oh yes, yes indeed . . . by the way, I've been admiring your bow tie, if only I could be so adventurous, where did you get it from, if you don't mind my asking?"

"Not at all, I always shop at Costello and Eve in Little Argyle Street."

"I don't believe I know them."

"Actually my brother works there, I could put you in touch, if you like."

"Splendid, splendid. I think there are some prawn vol-au-vents knocking about somewhere."

Whatever one may say about politics, when it comes to achievement, it teaches you that the shortest distance between two points is often circumlocution.

21

And talking of circumlocution, I expect you're wondering what has happened to Helga? Well, nothing has happened to her yet and she is still around on the scene. Understandably, it was a shock for her to learn that I would not be seeking another term of office if my Great Thrust Forward failed. When we parted company in Finland I was still reeling from the effects of her horrendous duplicity. I tried to disguise my dismay by feigning a wave of guilt about my infidelity but I knew, even then, that I was kidding myself if I thought she was taken in by it; women are far too intuitive for that. Nevertheless, she could see I was troubled, and, trusting in the stealth and efficiency of Gloria Fitzbagley's surveillance operation, I felt confident that she was unaware that her cover had been blown; at least as confident as one could be in the circumstances. Quite what she would be up to on her return was anybody's guess.

Gloria had assured me that her agents were tailing Kevin Doppler's every move, and practically every plain clothes officer in the Metropolitan Police as well, not to mention a fair gathering in the sticks. As for Rodney Snodder and MI6, well,

MI5 never trusted them anyway, so it was business as usual. Logistically speaking, I was doubtful that such an operation was feasible, however, Gloria assured me that ever since George had extended free mortgages to the intelligence services, their recruitment campaign had been as successful as Kevin's. I would rather have not known that they had placed their advertisements in the Guardian, but I have long since given up thinking that we live in a perfect world.

Before my insightful meditation that I mentioned earlier, I did my best to act the part of a satiated lover, albeit a distracted one. On the day of our parting, Helga and I held each other close in our arms. Incredibly, in spite of everything, I was still intoxicated by her beauty and dangerously lured by the magnetism of her aura. For a fleeting moment, in the depths of our embrace, which I must confess, I enjoyed with as much passion as before, I wondered if I was the unwitting victim of some perverted scam? The tricks that can be performed with digital photography are mind-boggling. And how would I ever know if Gloria's covert reports were true or false? Thinking back on things, the sheer enthusiasm with which Rashidi accepted the deputy premiership was almost as if he had been expecting it. But surely that was my idea and my idea alone?

Whatever my misgivings, they all fell into perspective during that insightful meditation and from which, as you will recall, I emerged knowing that nothing was the answer to everything. This does not mean that from now on my government will act as if in a vacuum. Far be it (witness the nationalisation of the railways for starters). It simply means that I will no longer attempt to control it. I shall apply my mind to the here and now as it really is, the actualité, as political pundits are wont to say. I live in the hope and expectation that others will also discover the truth. All things will come to pass. I shall not attach myself to the process. As the Prime Minister, I shall, inevitably, be part of it, but I shall observe all comings and goings from a state of nothingness. Best way to beat a stomach ulcer, if you ask me.

And now back to Helga. On the first day of work, Hugo came scurrying up to tell me that Helga had phoned in sick. Sick! She'd never had a single day off ever. I smelt a rat.

"What seems to be the problem, Hugh?"

"Holiday stomach bug."

"A common occurrence, where did she go?"

"Somewhere in Africa, I believe."

"Silly girl."

"Quite. Personally, I can't see what's wrong with Walton-on-the-Naze."

"The weather perhaps?"

"Anyway, I hope she recovers soon, our workload is getting ridiculous."

I left Hugh to grapple with the problem and immediately put in a call to Gloria. Considering that I have a secure direct private line, I was amazed when a switchboard operator asked me who was calling! I immediately rang off. A few seconds later my phone rang. It was Gloria.

"I believe you wanted me?"

"What's wrong with our secure line?"

"It drops out occasionally, but don't worry, our boys are on to it."

I was in half a mind to ask her what boys she was referring to; the twenty-first Hendon Scout Group perhaps? But then I let my irritation subside. There were more important issues at stake.

"Gloria, Hugo Snatch has just informed me that Helga has reported in sick. Can you check her whereabouts for me, please?"

"We're already on the case, she was spotted an hour ago with Kevin entering Akbar's, an Iranian restaurant in Earls Court."

"Oh my God, I hope we're not about to be drawn into some Middle Eastern debacle."

"Unfortunately, Rodney's mob are also on the case."

"I share your concern."

"We think there's a Mossad double agent working there as a barman."

"What makes you think that?"

"We're bugging MI6 twenty-four seven, remember?"
I was on the point of burying my head in my hands when something prompted me to let go of my anxiety. If people wanted to walk into a dry tinder box with a lit sparkler, that was up to them. I composed myself.

"Okay Gloria, keep me posted. The sooner she returns to work the better, Hugo is working himself up into a right little tantrum."

I rang off. I suppose I shouldn't really voice personal opinions about senior civil servants to the Director of MI5. On the other hand, since I was now in bed with both Gloria and Rashidi, (metaphorically speaking), whilst simultaneously attempting to stay *out* of bed with Helga, (as an actualité), it's only fair that I should be forgiven the occasional minor indiscretion.

When Helga did not appear for work the following day, I resisted the temptation to ring Gloria and find out what was going on. I had anticipated this possibility during morning meditation and concluded that whilst it remained very much my business (in a collaborative sense), the desire to grab or hook myself into the situation would merely increase the chances of frustration. Far better to do nothing. Doing nothing does not of course mean that everything grinds to a halt. Stuff happens all the same, to coin a phrase much favoured by Angela Besoutar, of whom, by the way, I am very impressed. Just like Rashidi, she has high energy levels although, thankfully, is less demonstrative.

Our paths crossed this morning as we were heading for the general office. We exchanged greetings. As we neared the doorway, it was evident that Mallard Kane and Hugo Snatch were having a heated discussion about workload. Hugo was being quite petulant.

"It's all very well for you, but I haven't been granted several hundred extra staff, in fact one of my small team is still off sick."

"Are you telling me you can't manage with five secretaries?"

"This bloody GTF has created an enormous workload."

"I am not immune from its effects either."

"Maybe, but you don't have the deputy prime minister on your back, like I do."

"No, I deal with the Prime Minister."

"Well, you're the head of the civil service aren't you?"

"Precisely, and may I remind you that I have only allowed you to be the cabinet secretary as part of your job development."

"Oh I get it, the next thing you'll be telling me is that I can't sign my own memoranda."

"Well, certainly not with that fountain pen."

"I beg your pardon?"

"That's my fountain pen, Snatch, give it back at once."

"I shall do no such thing, Kane, it's mine, it was a present from my wife."

"Fuck your wife, you're a bloody liar, give it back."

"Piss off you bald headed old cunt."

Angela and I stood transfixed as the two most senior civil servants began to fight like alley cats over a discarded fish-head. Papers, pencils, staplers and all sorts of desk-top paraphernalia went flying as the two men struggled for supremacy. Suddenly, Hugo lunged at Mallard, puncturing his cheek with the nib of the pen

"Aaah! You bastard! You've stabbed me!" screamed Mallard.

"Good! I hope you die of blood poisoning!"

Just then, the door opposite flung open. It was Helga. The look on her face was contemptuous. The two men froze.

"What's it to be then, blotting paper or bandages?"

Her words were as icy as her look. Mallard picked himself up off the floor, his cheek a mess of blood and ink dripping onto his collar.

"This is the end of you Snatch," he hissed, "the bloody end."

And so saying, he turned and headed for the nearest exit, which, to our consternation, was where we were standing. Instinctively, both of us turned and ran for cover behind another door.

Talk about Whitehall farce.

22

Well, I've never seen anything like that in all my life. I always thought that civil servants were thus named because their overriding behaviour, no matter what the circumstances, was always, civil. What is the country coming to when civil servants of such pre-eminence, resort to violence? Thank God I was not involved in the fracas. I intend to make sure it stays that way too. I said as much to Angela when we found ourselves back in my private office.

"Let me say right here and now that I'm staying right out of this one."

"I don't blame you."

"Rashidi can handle the fall out."

"Just the man I was thinking of."

"I'm in a state of shock Angela."

"Me too, fancy a cup of tea?"

"Good idea."

"Right, you smoke the tea leaves and I'll electrify the kettle." That's what I like about Angela, she doesn't stand on ceremony and just gets on with it. I'm impressed that she's mindful of my dislike of tea bags although I've no idea what she means by smoking the tea leaves. Perhaps that's something her father did in Jamaica? On the other hand she was born and bred in South London which might go some way to explaining certain eccentricities.

As we drink our tea I am almost tempted to tell Angela the truth about Helga but stop short. What would be the point? It will only complicate matters. I reason that it will be more interesting to see what she makes of events as they have actually been revealed. It is impossible not to acknowledge that Helga holds some kind of daemonic sway over Mallard and Hugh – both of them had been reduced to fearful cowering at the mere sight of her. What does Angela make of that? And is it a relationship that Rashidi and Gloria are aware of?

Thinking all this through as I sip my tea, I begin to wonder if there isn't something in the virtual reality conspiracy that scientists and philosophers are now debating? I have never been drawn to the big bang concept and must confess that Darwin's theory of evolution has limited interest. I have a restless mind which is why I seek to stabilise it through meditation and contemplation. Not easy when you're the Prime Minister. There are so many interruptions and demands on one's time. Whatever may or may not be the case with Helga, it is a fact that she tried and succeeded in giving me more personal space to think. So who is manipulating who and for what? Even if there is some kind of matrix super controller in some galaxy a million aeons of light years away and I am but a character in the great cosmic game, at least I remain a principal; for the time being. Who is to say that what I experienced on the far side is nothing more than an alternative programme? Precisely. One load of tosh versus another. So, I will continue to disassociate myself from the machinations of the day and let the truth reveal itself in the manner to which I am accustomed. Eventually, all plotters will be hoisted by their own petard. Period. Perhaps.

"Shall I give Rashidi a ring?" says Angela.

"Why not?"

"What shall I say?"

"Whatever you like, I do not wish to become involved. Nice cuppa tea, thanks."

I don't think Angela was perturbed by my response, if anything she was galvanised by it. She was dialling up Rashidi even as I left. Not surprisingly, I received a call from Rashidi whilst I was being chauffeured to the Home Office to see George (he's fretting again).

"Mallard's cheek is the size of a balloon," says Rashidi, trying not to laugh, "he wants to sack Hugo."

"That's his decision."

"Yes, that's what I said but he also wants to appoint Helga as acting Cabinet Secretary on a secondment job development basis."

"That's also his decision."

"Yes I know that too, but I told him to discuss it with you first as a matter of courtesy."

"Thank you."

"What will you say?"

"Go ahead, it's none of my business."

"You mean you won't block it?"

"No."

There was a long silence, long enough for the car to cross a set of traffic lights without blocking the yellow quadrangle.
I could almost hear Rashid's brain ticking over.

"Ambrose, I think we need to talk about this."

"Well, I'm going to be with George for the next hour, so I'll catch you later."

"Ambrose, this is serious."

"Yes I know. I want to discuss it with Helga first."

"What!"

"Do you realise I haven't spoken to her since she went off sick?"

"Christ almighty Ambrose, she wasn't sick, she was spotted entering an Iranian restaurant in Earls Court."

"So what, all civil servants cheat with sickness leave."

"I don't believe what I'm hearing."

"Do we know what MI6 are up to?"

"No."

"Well, you'd better ring Gloria pronto and tell her I am not amused. Catch you later Rashidi." And then I ring off.

Well, that set the cat amongst the pigeons, didn't it? I thought it would make a change to be a little mischievous. And why shouldn't I? There is so much in-fighting and tension in politics that it needs a bit of light relief to put things in their true perspective. The true perspective, let me remind you, is that nothing really matters a great deal since life itself is but an illusion. We put ourselves through hoops of extraordinary mental convolutions simply because we cannot slow down enough to train the mind to see the true nature of all phenomena. And even when we do, we still think that life should be free of friction. I'm as guilty as everyone else in this respect.

Of course, at first I was deeply hurt by Helga's behaviour, which I perceived as an act of gross betrayal. Only when I meditated and found that plane of calmness where even reason itself is no longer necessary did I move towards peace. I am not yet indifferent to earthly desires but gradually I am learning to take them on board, to investigate them to see how and from where they arise. It is the same with all my moods (Amelia always accuses me of being moody). I no longer ignore them but contemplate and see how they work against me. Only this way can I see them clearly and understand the difficulties I cause myself by believing and following them.

And so it is that I have come to forgive Helga for her transgression. It was not really a transgression at all. She was caught up in a course of action that happened to involve me and still does. How can I legitimise a judgemental attitude when I am part and parcel of that action? You know the answer as well as I do. I cannot. And so I will examine the unfolding nature of the action dispassionately. However, not being naturally inclined to such a state I feel it will be quite a wheeze to give it a little bit of mischievous spin. A sort of roulette wheel that only stops when I say so.

Well dam it all, I am the Prime Minister.

23

To say that life imitates art might be to assume that there is something in art worth imitating in the first place. Amelia says I am an old fuddy-duddy went it comes to taste. Certainly I would not wish anyone's life to be as pointless as a fluorescent light flashing on and off. Equally, I would rather avoid a miscalculation of one's shopping list to the extent that surplus French sticks had nowhere else to go except in the sky, amusing though that may be. On the other hand, if my life could acquire the wonderful isolation of a New England lighthouse, or the tantalising unknown of a lonely mid-western gas station, I might even become smug. At the moment it looks like a can of beans. The intriguing thing is that I alone hold the can opener. Others may conspire to wrestle it from my grasp but they do not understand the nature of my grip.

The other day I heard that Aubrey Fynch-Chilling, my devious Chancellor, was telling people that my Great Thrust Forward was idealistic crap. Such blind arrogance. Clearly, he does not appreciate that he has a major part to play in it. Very soon he will realise that unless he can keep public expenditure under control without jeopardising its published goals, he may very well become its first casualty (if casualties there are to be). His ego is fast becoming insufferable. Oh, how I miss the dry modesty of dearly departed Jocelyn.

Incidentally, he has now become the Financial Director of the Kaya Centre for Mindfulness. I will not deny that I was instrumental in his appointment, even though I remain a non-executive director. The executive committee was quick to realise that the huge profits the centre was accumulating as a result of it's spiritual and psychological work for H.M. Prison Services required more than just a competent accountant to manage its investment portfolio. Flawed human being though he is, Jocelyn remains a financial genius and the Treasury won't let Aubrey forget it. There are days when his chagrin practically consumes him. He takes it out on others, usually in the form of bullying. Poor George is one of his victims. His usually fragrant pocket-handkerchief is practically sodden as he unfolds his woes.

"He's told me there's not enough money for the national ID project and it's your fault because you allowed Mallard to recruit hundreds of additional civil servants but I will get the blame for mis-managing it."

"Nonsense, take no notice George. All you've got to remember is that I've given Rashidi overall responsibility, just refer the matter to him."

"Really, do you mean that, honestly?"

"Of course I do, now what else is bothering you George, come on dear chap, I can't have my home secretary in such a state."

I watch as he fiddles with his tie and adjusts the flower in his buttonhole. Poor George, he really does take matters to heart and I determine there and then to pay more attention to his sensitivity. He has a huge brief but I think it would crush him if I were to move him to a smaller department. He remains popular with the public too, probably due to his transparent honesty and daisy-dapper appearance; a benefit not to be sneezed at.

"Well, I'm not getting on very well with the police commissioner," he admits, dolefully.

"I can understand that, Kevin is a tough man."

"Well the thing is, ever since we offered free child care to women police officers, the female ranks have been swelling out of all proportion."

An alarm bell rings. Is this yet another example of human nature prostituting the hand of benevolence? I try not to sound too stern.

"I don't think we can afford to make changes to the existing maternity agreement."

George laughs. It's an unexpected titter but welcome nonetheless.

"Oh no Ambrose, you've got the wrong end of the stick completely. What I mean is that female *recruitment* has mushroomed beyond our wildest expectations."

"But surely that's good news?"

"Yes it is, it is."

"So what's the problem?"

"Well, a large number of recruits are fashion conscious women who are highly critical of our uniform which they find staid and boring."

"So what's to stop us changing it?"

George groans with exasperation and runs his hands through his blonde mop of Harpo Marx curls.

"Who else but Kevin?"

"I am not surprised," I reply, as sympathetically as I can. As he begins to doodle on his blotter in frantic Vivienne Westwood squircles, I recall Kevin's awful greasy tie with its embroidered deer. Clearly, this is a man with no sense of style whatsoever.

"It's such a shame," says George, "I've got quite a few ideas myself and I would so like to chair a uniform design steering committee."

He is visibly disappointed. I take pity on him.

"Leave it with me George, I'll have a word with him."

Privately, I doubt that I will be able to make Kevin change his mind but I know a woman who can, and there are many things other than frilly furbelows on truncheon holders that I need to talk to her about.

How smoothly the days progress with nothing more than the odd touch here and there. Indeed, how my Great Thrust Forward progresses now that I have offered it to my ministers in the manner of a gift, rather than a burden. When I said that I would no longer accept procrastination or failure, the clever ones realised that I was not pushing them out on a raft to drown in the high seas, but inviting them to prove their potential, to fulfil their dreams and become happy in the process. In this respect I am simply reinforcing my personal belief that all my ministers are human beings first and politicians second. The ball is in their court but I shall not tell them how to hit it. It is interesting to see how the results are manifesting themselves.

Take law and order as one example. In spite of worrying himself silly at every opportunity, George is incredibly loyal and hardworking and yet he is no slave driver. He'll happily talk for hours about the stitching on Elton John's fiftieth birthday costume and his staff love him for it. As a consequence, the Home Office is a very happy place and everyone delivers in spades. We now have more police on the streets than ever before and better still it looks as if women are flocking to the call. Gone are the days of the thin blue line replaced perhaps by a brave new hemline. Perhaps Great Britain will become a maternal land in the very best sense of the word and how wonderful is that?

George has convinced the Archbishop of Canterbury of the short-sightedness of carping to the Guardian about donations to temples of other faiths and instead, the wisdom of selling deserted cathedrals and the rolling fields wherein they stand, for the socially acceptable purposes of building new prisons. Implicit in such agreements is the Criminal Offenders Rehabilitation Programme, or CORP, as it is popularly referred to by its principle provider, the Kaya Centre for Mindfulness, (under competitive tender I hasten to add).

There was much ballyhoo when Guildford Cathedral came under the hammer but this soon abated when an independent market research company with impeccable ecumenical connections, published the results of a survey that showed that the South East of England was the most heathen place in the

British Isles. It revealed that forty percent on the electoral register were too busy earning an honest crumb in the city to attend Sunday services. Out of those who were available for spiritual sustenance, forty-five percent said they were too exhausted to get out of bed, eight percent said they were committed to family access arrangements, five percent claimed it was the best time for internet shopping and the remaining two percent attended car boot sales. Efforts to establish the preferences of those who did not respond to the survey subsequently revealed that they went to the pub although this was disputed by Alcoholics Anonymous who nevertheless could not provide accurate records of attendance to support their claim.

Even more difficulties arose with house dwellers from the private rented sector. Some folks disdained to mark the tick boxes, preferring instead to scrawl rude or semi-literate comments on the back of the buff coloured card. A Muslim gentleman (who shall remain nameless) said his son was already being detained on terrorist charges without trial for the fifth consecutive year and therefore saw no reason to comment on the viability of building yet another prison, notwithstanding the fact that the demolition of a cathedral was further manifestation, if any was needed, of the moral decay inherent in all infidels (the Archbishop of Canterbury included).

Another response simply said, 'I am on incapacity benefit and cannot afford the taxi fare.' On hearing this, a local support group known as Christians on Wheels, sent a Ford Transit van equipped with an electrical wheelchair platform the following Sunday. However, when the door was answered by a woman in curlers, smelling heavily of nicotine and coughing dangerously, she said 'you're wasting you're time, Maurice always goes hare coursing on Sundays.' Shortly after that, Guildford Cathedral was purchased as our next mega-prison development site. I thought it would be nice to call it Hubbard House, after dear Jocelyn.

Our progress in the Arts is very revealing too. Unfortunately, Aubrey Fynch-Chilling does not see how the social infrastructure is being cultivated by our manifesto pledge. The other day he got very uppity.

"It's absolutely ridiculous the millions we spend on the arts, most of the recipients are dysfunctional layabouts incapable of holding down a proper job."

"Aubrey, do I really have to remind you that a nation that cannot express itself is a nation in decline?"

"The only expressions I'm aware of are seditious drivel daubed across motorway bridges by semi-literate anarchists."

It is true that the government had to endure a spate of insulting slogans painted on no less than fifty bridges across the M1, including one that said 'AFC = A Fucking Cunt'. On that occasion the police managed to capture the culprit and he was made to obliterate his work as part of a community service order.

I don't think Aubrey is able to differentiate between graffiti artists and bona fide street theatre artists, of whom the latter are fast acquiring cult status. For them, no subject matter is sacrosanct and I think that's a sign that freedom of speech is alive and kicking and the nation is all the better for it.

Benjamin is still unhappy about the situation. He even suggested that we should covertly fund a pro-government troupe to balance the left-wing rhetoric! Well really, what nonsense, and there's me thinking he was a smooth operator, a wise sort of spin-doctor. He would be much better occupied formulating a strategy to counter the scurrilous reports about Amelia that are now surfacing in the general press. I am not so naïve as to think that the hacks would not notice Amelia's absence from number ten without making comment before long, particularly as she has been her usual vocal self in the Sutchworth Arts Centre bar. Fortunately, the threatened strike has been averted and the grand opening night is next Saturday. Amelia was clearly delighted when she rang me about this.

"Off course you're invited you big floppy loon, we've got centre front seats in the dress circle."

"That's nice."

"Ambrose darling, how could I possibly forget that you hate sitting in the stalls."

"Straining the neck is an impediment to concentration."

"Absolutely and now you can wave grandly to your adoring public."

"You make me sound like royalty."

"Nonsense, they've got nothing to wave about whereas you have been virtually tectonic in your achievements."

"Have you been drinking?"

"Yes, and what's more we'll have champagne together after it's over."

"I miss you."

"Don't be daft, you sentimental old sausage."

"The press are speculating dangerously."

"Bugger the press, get Benjamin on the case, look I've got to fly now, catch you later."

She rang off before I could say that I had already taken that decision.

When there was a knock on the door I half expected it to be Benjamin, so I was a little surprised to see Mallard and Helga instead. Helga was her usual stunning self and gave me the most beautiful of smiles. Verily, she is a goddess. Mallard is far too pompous to smile but even if he had wanted to I doubt that he could do so now because the whole of one side of his face was puffed up like red party balloon. It was difficult not to snigger, so I feigned surprise instead.

"Good Lord Mallard, what have you been doing to yourself?"

He attempts to reply but clearly his condition is not conducive to the execution of normal speech. The swelling is so profound that it has squashed his mouth into a little cupid shaped spout that whoffles pathetically like a steam kettle about to expire.

"It's not whoff I've fleen doing but whoff offers have."

"I beg your pardon?"

"Off floff fof floff's fake."

Helga steps in to save us all further embarrassment.

"What Mallard is trying to say is that he's been physically assaulted by Hugo Snatch and Hugo has now been summarily dismissed pending a formal disciplinary."

"Good God!"

"I was witness to the event, Ambrose, and I can assure you that it was an unprovoked attack and naturally I will give evidence accordingly."

"Good Lord!"

"As you can see, Mallard is in no fit state to carry out his duties and in view of the pressing needs of government he has appointed me as acting cabinet secretary until further notice."

"I think he's in need of urgent medical attention."

"I have already arranged for a car to take him to hospital, but he is anxious that you endorse my appointment as a gesture of solidarity even though it is not required constitutionally."

Unless I'm not mistaken, Mallard's face looks as if it is about to explode any second. The poor man is on the brink of collapse and suffering incredible pain. The least I can do is give him the assurance he needs.

"Mallard, I am delighted that Helga should take over the reins of higher office, she has my utmost support and so do you too, now please, be a good chap and pop off to hospital as quick as you can."

"Ah floff floff floff floffff."

"What did he say?"

"He said, tell Hugo Snatch he can fuck off for good."

Before I can reply, poor Mallard collapses on the floor with an excoriating sigh of mammalian proportion. Helga gives me her winning smile.

"Looks like it's just you and me Ambrose."

I am too emotional to mention the rest of the cabinet.

24

At the next cabinet meeting, Rashidi can hardly contain his fury. We have already spent over an hour in heated one-to-one debate about the dangers of Helga becoming the acting cabinet secretary. To be accurate, the heat is all on his side. I merely continued with the same nonchalant attitude that I had adopted when he first contacted me on my mobile. If other cabinet members shared his concerns they certainly did not show it. It made me feel that I was right to be suspicious of him.

 News of Helga's appointment whizzed through the Whitehall grapevine as fast as heated mercury from a glass pipette, and within the hour, I received an extremely intriguing call from Rodney Snodder, the Head of MI6. He was his usual veiled self but ended up by saying 'she's a safer pair of hands than Snatch'. I did not take the bait but could barely suppress a chuckle, knowing, as I did, that Kevin, that malevolent Commissioner of Police, had been spotted by Gloria's boys with 'the safe pair of hands' entering an Iranian restaurant.

"It is not for me to comment on these things Rodney," I reply calmly, "as long as you're keeping tabs on our enemies, then it is in your hands that we shall all feel safe."

I can practically hear his brain ticking over as he analyses my reply for double meanings. He is such a cold, calculating man that I can't imagine he would be capable of physical love, let alone with someone as tempting as Helga. It made those rumours that he was sleeping with Gloria seem even more far-fetched as well, although, if they did have such a liaison which subsequently broke up, perhaps he bedded Helga out of spite?

There is always the possibility that Gloria falsified the photos she showed me in Finland to spite Rodney and bring about his downfall.

Perhaps it was Rodney and his MI6 agents that discovered the drugs money laundering operation of messrs Mboya, Fynch-Chilling and Napper, and Gloria simply claimed credit for it? And yet it was Kevin who claimed credit for that and Rodney has certainly never mentioned it (unless he has some ulterior motive?)

But why would Helga seduce Kevin unless it was to control all the angles as Gloria's reports suggested?

Perhaps Gloria also had an affair with Kevin, which hit the buffers when Helga seduced him? To a driven woman like Gloria it would doubtless drive her down a path of jealousy and revenge.

And then again, why would Gloria pursue an affair with Rashidi? On the face of it, they seem such an unlikely couple. However, as Deputy Prime Minister, with critical policy initiatives in his brief, he has the attraction of power, and maybe, for Gloria, this is the ultimate turn-on?

The more I distance myself from the hopeless machinations of human relationships, the more I am inclined to follow that which arises as a reality.

It is only on the so-called evidence of others that Helga's conduct could be called into question and therefore I shall trust my own counsel and no other. Besides, as is so often the case in politics, the pervading culture is one of being less than economical with the truth.

I think Rashidi is up to something and perhaps I should not groom him for higher office as originally intended? However, now that Helga is acting cabinet secretary, I am confident he will not out-manoeuvre me. Needless to say, since she is not kindly disposed towards black men, he won't be slipping her a length either, perish the thought!

As my mind wanders on the delights of being in bed with Helga and how long it has been since our last ravishing encounter, Rodney's cold voice interrupts my reverie.

"Of course, I shall remain as vigilant as ever, but do you have any particular concerns Ambrose?"

Translating the word 'concerns' from intelligence-speak into plain English means that Rodney is really asking me whether I know something that he does not. Since I rarely know what he knows because he is so guarded, I choose words that are more opaque than transparent.

"It's more a question of whether we share the same concerns, Rodney."

"Ambrose, as you know, all my concerns are included in the security briefings that cross your desk daily."

"Indeed, but events sometimes move quicker than paper, don't they?"

"Are you saying I don't know something that I should?"

"Well, let me put it this way, an Arab and a Jew are unlikely to share the same soup spoon."

". . . . Has somebody been stirring it in the Middle East?"

"That could be the case if one of them is a Mossad agent and the other a fundamentalist mullah."

"Is this unsubstantiated intelligence?"

"That is not for me to say, that is for you to find out."

"I share your concern."

"Thank you Rodney, I thought you might."

When the line went dead it was difficult not to chuckle.

Perhaps if I were not Prime Minister, I might make a rather good double agent? Tee hee hee. Anyway, it serves him right for being so lapse in matters of state security. Tee hee hee. And who says that what is arising should not be contributed to in the first place? I will seek guidance from the Buddha tonight. Meanwhile I have a cabinet meeting to run.

Lucy Bowens is tying everybody up in knots with endless questions about the cost of the civil service. Considering this is Aubrey's axe to grind, I'm now wondering if indeed those two haven't metaphorically climbed into bed. Lucy is like a minute Rottweiler when it comes to fighting her corner, especially when she needs large dollops of treasury cash to keep the welfare benefits system afloat.

"Lucy, are you saying that we should no longer fund the national identity card programme in favour of social security payments?" booms Hattie, who, since her appointment as Defence minister, has taken to stuffing herself with jam doughnuts to the extent that she is now as large as the battleships she fights to save, "and are you aware that the defence budget of the United States is fourteen times bigger than China and twenty-two times bigger than Russia and we, on the other hand, have virtually languished since 1913?"

"What I am saying," chirrups Lucy, "is that the cost of funding single parent families and job seeker allowances annually, is equal to a one hundred and sixty-three percent increase of the total annual salary bill on a monthly basis of those civil servants working directly on the national identity card project."

"A lot of single parent mothers have shown interest in joining the police now that we are offering free child care and the promise of a new stylish uniform," chirps George gaily, throwing me a little smile.

"And we shall have stylish uniforms for female train drivers too," says Christopher Meelybean, (who is currently giving daily press conferences since the re-nationalisation of the railways was announced) "and they won't be restricted to a national dress code either, it will be regional."

"What Lucy is trying to concentrate everyone's mind on" interjects Aubrey in his customary disdainful tone, "is that we have yet to agree on the funding of payments to GP's if the legalisation of drugs bill goes through."

The room falls silent. Everyone knows that the doctors have virtually been holding the government to ransom over this matter and the bill will be unenforceable without their cooperation. I am about to step in when Rashidi gets there first by slamming his papers on the table.

"And let's not forget that the world's drug supply lines are not exactly controlled by men of honour. It's up front payment or no deal."

His remark is tantamount to open opposition to the whole concept of the bill, which, as every minister knows, is a key element in my Great Thrust Forward programme. I decide to observe his arising temper for what it is.

"And don't kid yourself," he continues, his outstretched arms and huge hands anchoring the edge of the table in an image of power, "that a heroin addict that doesn't get his fix is going to settle for a drugs credit note. No way. He'll be rearranging the doctor's back teeth or ramming a stolen four-by-four into the nearest bonded warehouse. If you think that binge drinking is a problem, you ain't seen nothing yet."

I remain calm and silent but the tension is too much for George who pops like a bottle of fizzy.

"We have enough police to deal with any form of public disorder, enough prison space to hold those convicted of crimes and more to the point, a judiciary willing to pass custodial sentences."

"Very touching George," says Rashidi, "but I don't think we'll win any votes simply because the junkie population is either tearing the place apart or going cold turkey in a prison cell."

"You know as well as I do," retorts George, getting very het up, "that thanks to the professional services of the Kaya Centre for Mindfulness, we now lead the world in prisoner rehabilitation."

"Oh yes," sneers Aubrey, "and some of them even perform Beckett."

The cabinet breaks out into a titter. It's a cheap joke but nobody likes it when petty sniping replaces informed debate.

Faces then turn towards me as if to say, you are the Prime Minister, please lead us forward. But I remain composed and contained. I am observing non-judgmentally and unconditionally the arising of that which arises.

Susan Palmero, no doubt being an ex-actress, (or should I say actor?) senses that centre stage is there for the taking, and takes it. Usually her ripostes are forthright and fiery but on this occasion she adopts a quieter note. I wonder if she has picked up on my passive aura?

"Well Aubrey," she begins quietly, "whilst it is true that a growing band of prisoners are beginning to appreciate the therapeutic effect of self-expression through dramatic art, even greater are the numbers in the public domain. Surely you cannot have forgotten our manifesto statement that a nation that cannot express itself is a nation in decline?"

Aubrey does not answer, but the flicker of discomfort in his eyes reveals that he has already been reminded of that self same claim by me but cannot, as yet, accept it. Susan pushes home her advantage.

"Since we took office, the performing arts in general have experienced an unprecedented surge of creative expression. It's as if a massive yolk of repression has been lifted from young and old alike and we are witnessing not simply an artistic renaissance but a freeing of the nation's very soul. It is no less than a social phenomenon whose benefits go way beyond the humanistic aspiration of our manifesto. Far from becoming a society of barbarian binge drinkers versus a totalitarian police force, as our critics claim, Great Britain has become a model for freedom of expression."

There are mutters of approval around the table. Aubrey does not like this.

"Yes, I have seen some of those very expressions daubed across the M1, not something I would feel particularly proud of but I suppose some of us aspire to higher standards."

"The point is Aubrey," says Susan, fixing him with glowing eyes, "the fact that it can happen in the first place without fear of brutish reprisal is recognised throughout the civilised world as a benchmark for democracy."

"And great entertainment!" bursts forth George who is loving every minute of Aubrey's come uppance.

"And the tourist revenues are soaring and filling the treasury coffers as never before," says Susan.

"And Elton John is performing at the opening concert of the Sutchworth Arts Centre next Saturday and I've got a ticket!"

cries George, beads of happy perspiration trickling from beneath his tousled mop.

That raises a laugh. We all know that Elton will be in Las Vegas and George is going through one of his fantasy phases.

"I hope you've all got tickets," says Susan, "because it's a sell-out."

The atmosphere is nothing if not jolly as various voices are heard saying 'I've got one'. I feel this is the moment to make my contribution.

"Me too," I say, "and I shall be there with Amelia in the front row of the dress circle."

Spontaneous applause breaks out. Susan blushes and Helga smiles.

She has a ticket too.

25

The Sutchworth Arts Centre in Shropshire was not designed by Sir Norman Foster; his fee was too big. Nevertheless, the project was awarded to Norman Balls, a high flying graduate from the Telford College of Architectural Design. Not without reason was lottery money not going to be squandered and, as a consequence, Norman produced a building of such cutting edge technology that the main entrance consisted of a giant chamber in the shape of an egg. Arriving visitors would be given the sole option of seating themselves in soft spongy pods that would be whisked, as if by magic, through a huge celestial womb, replete with blue skies and cumulous clouds, directly to the foyer. The experience proved to be so uplifting that many folks became addicted to the ride and would spend hours sailing back and forth, even though the management subsequently imposed an automated one-pound entry charge. In spite of this, the centre soon became famously known as the Egg Whisk. Such was the extent of the architectural innovation that even managers from Disneyland took the first flight over from Orlando, Florida, to marvel at its wonders.

Norman Balls turned down an OBE and a commission for a new parliament building in Baghdad. The former rejection was rumoured to be the reason why the royal family was to be noticeable by their absence at the grand inaugural concert.

Meanwhile, every other celebrity from A to Z was scrambling desperately to get a ticket. To be present at the opening of the Egg Whisk was worth ten on the Richter scale of social achievement. As Prime Minister in the front row of the dress circle, it would be like sitting on top of the detonator. What fun!

When it first became apparent that Amelia's attraction to everything that the Sutchworth Arts Centre (or perhaps I should say the Egg Whisk) represented, was no mere passing fad, we had a long discussion on the practical ramifications of her passion. Even the greatest of enthusiasm could not counter the sheer grind of relentless motorway driving and so, as a commonsense measure, she purchased a flat. The press hounds were on the trail straight away, sniffing and fanning the rumours of marital breakdown.

Benjamin was in his element batting that one off. 'You should see the size of Amelia's telephone bills' he quipped, 'they talk for hours like a pair of young lovers.'

The Independent snidely suggested that perhaps I ought to spend more time talking to heads of state – *he is the most parochial of prime ministers in living memory* – and allocated many column inches in criticism of my foreign policy, or rather, the lack of it. Benjamin had to remind them that the hotlines to Bush, Putin, Chirac, Schroeder et al, were alive as never before. He was being less than economical with the truth when he said that, but it would be silly to suggest otherwise.

Investigative hacks sought out their international colleagues and I was rather dismayed when the press officers for messrs. Bush, Putin, Chirac and Schroeder issued rather ambiguous replies. The Guardian printed a cartoon of me on the hotline, with the caption - *put the president on hold, I'm discussing ballet positions with Amelia.*

The fact of the matter is that I have no need of international support as Great Britain is fast becoming the envy of the world. The forces of negativity and despair that were so prevalent when I took office have been resolutely kicked into touch. We have turned the corner and everyone knows it. Of course, the task is far from complete but the dye has been cast and The Great Thrust Forward will guarantee our continuing success. No longer can anyone doubt this. They have only to look at our tourist revenues which are rocketing ten-fold as millions of visitors flock to our shores to savour the delights of a positive, vibrant society, revelling in freedom of speech and expression.

As the opening of the Egg Whisk approaches, I can put my hand on my heart and say, with pride and humility, this administration has established a renaissance of the human spirit itself.

In the same breath I will readily admit that the trains do not, as yet, run on time, but we are working on that too.

I must say that since the announcement of our renationalisation plans, the Trades Unions have bent over backwards in support of this endeavour. In fact two of them have put forward suggestions for the siting of the proposed National Train Drivers' School. The RMT favours Cricklewood - *a much loved railway depot carved indelibly on the minds of train enthusiasts everywhere* - whereas ASLEF is pushing for York - *a national railway centre of consummate historical pedigree and affordable housing.*

I shall be happy to leave that decision to Christopher Meelybean whose last thought on the subject was to hold a public ballot amongst all rail union members. The unions are fêting him at every opportunity and the irony is that it's not left him much spare time to go chasing steam engines with Mangal Bali Chakkar, who has become rather jealous of his high profile. We still haven't found a suitable wall on which to secure Mangal's Shariputra elephant and I think that's also got something to do with his dyspeptic behaviour.

Not surprisingly, Mangal wrote a letter to Railway Magazine suggesting that Crewe would be the best location for the National Train Drivers' School; there was a lot of steamy

Victoriana in his argument. Whatever the merits of the case, the fact remains that my vision for the railways has every chance of remaining on track, if you'll pardon the pun.

It's a pity that I can't be so assured about air travel. With tourism producing such high revenues there is an urgent need to develop another international airport. Meelybean is on the case however, and has already produced a consultative paper to commercialise RAF Manston. I think it makes sense as it's already got the longest runway in the UK and the surrounding countryside is flat and uneventful as far as the eye can see. No doubt Bill Oddie and his fellow twitchers will claim that we are destroying the natural habitat of the greater crested oik but there are occasions when even our feathered friends have to take the rough with the smooth. It is not that I have no feeling for birds, in fact I love the cheeky, bright-eyed robin that perches on the fence as you dig the garden, waiting to snatch a fresh wriggly worm. And many is the summer evening when I have sat in the garden with a glass of wine and been enchanted by the beautiful song of the blackbird. The barn owl gives me much pleasure too. I love its gentle hooting, its flat, round face and bland expression; like Charles Kennedy at a late night sitting. But I must confess that after that, my appreciation leap-frogs the remainder of our native birds and I yearn only to see a hundred thousand pink flamingos rise above the great lakes of the Ngorongoro Basin. It is a fact of life that the Isle of Thanet holds no such spectacle.

Ironically, it is another species of bird that also stands in the way, and that bird (if you will pardon my sexist vernacular) is Hattie Chapplethwaite. As Minister of Defence she will fight her corner relentlessly and even though I may remind her that I have allowed the Nimrod project to continue at great cost, I have no doubt that she will respond by citing every defence cutback since 1913. But for the moment I set these concerns aside as I look forward to the gala opening of the Egg Whisk.

As you can imagine, the security arrangements are extraordinary, one might even say, over the top. Kevin Doppler certainly won't be making the same mistake as his predecessor Trevor Skidmarsh. Unlike the disastrous visit to the Hindu temple in Leicester, this time we shall fly direct by helicopter.

"Let's hope there's nobody with a grudge and a rocket thingummy," says Amelia, flippantly, as we gather ourselves together. I don't know if she's taking a swipe at me for insisting that she return to Downing Street in order that we may travel together safely. She has been absent for so long that I almost feel as if we are strangers in our own bedroom. It is a passing thought and I am soon caught up in the general excitement.

"I heard the SS rehearsing Wagner the other day," says Amelia, bubbling with enthusiasm, "they were fantastic."

I know she is referring to the Sutchworth Sinfonietta, the Egg Whisk's resident orchestra and I think it's a tribute to our artistic culture that a one hundred piece band of professional musicians can be created from scratch and on such a viable financial footing, but I am unhappy about their sobriquet.

"I do wish you wouldn't refer to them as the SS, it has the most awful connotations, especially in the Wagnerian context."

"Oh don't be so ridiculously PC, nobody pays any attention to that sort of thing nowadays."

"That's what concerns me."

"For God's sake, Ambrose, chill out. No one is going to be wearing swastika arm bands, including Holocaust Harry, not that he's coming anyway, or any of the royals for that matter, and neither will Princess Michael of Kent who tried to get a ticket under a false name."

"I didn't know that."

"She was very pushy and kept on insisting that she had been allocated one of the special reservations until the box office manager came on line and told her that they had all been allocated to patrons from our former colonies."

"If only Norman Balls had accepted his OBE such unpleasantries would never have arisen."

"Oh whatever, whatever . . . can you do me up?"

I can see there's no point in pursuing the matter so I attend to the zip and clasp on Amelia's evening dress. It has a plunging neckline and an even deeper cut at the back. She has a beautiful back, just like Helga's, and I cannot resist the temptation to gently run my hand down the curvature of her spine. She moves away without comment. There has been no intimacy between us for many months, possibly even a year. On reflection, that is probably all for the best. However, it occurs to me that we have not appeared in public together for an equal period and Benjamin's assertion that we spend hours talking romantically on the telephone has long since lost its credibility.

I attempt to raise the question of our public persona as a couple before leaving, in the hope that Amelia will not behave indiscreetly as she is wont to do, especially when fuelled by alcohol.

"Are you aware that Hello! Magazine is covering the event, my sweet?"

"Yes, so may I suggest you don't start pawing my back and drop all the coochy coo stuff."

"I am merely reminding you that people will be reading our body language, it will not be in our best interests to spend the entire evening three feet apart."

"You mean in *your* best interests."

"Please Amelia, let's not argue, I'm actually looking forward to tonight."

"Me too, so let's drop the lecture and go party."

I remain silent and adjust my bow tie.

Something tells me the way ahead is about to become hazardous.

26

The helicopter rota blades thrash the air and suddenly we are up and away with a jerk. Sergeant Pickering and his mute companion are with us again but this time the officer holds an evil looking machine gun at his side, not the sort of thing to warm the cockles of one's heart.

"Are we expecting trouble?" I enquire.

"Standard procedure," replies Sergeant Pickering, and jabbers nonsense into his mobile.

The Sutchworth Arts Centre looks truly magnificent from the air, its egg shaped dome bathed in coloured floodlights. As we begin our descent, it becomes bigger than I had anticipated, in fact, as we touch down on the nearby helipad, I realise it is enormous, its dimensions are truly awesome.

"Wait till you see inside," squeals Amelia with delight, "it gives a whole new meaning to cutting edge."

I could see what she meant the second we entered. I was so thrilled by the ride in those soft, spongy pod seats that I insisted on repeating it several times.

"Three is ENOUGH, Ambrose," she yells, as the press photographers have a field day.

"But I'm recapturing my youth, it's great – WHEEEE!"
When we finally emerge into the main foyer, there is Susan Palmero with a host of local dignitaries ready to greet us.
I give Susan a big hug as the flashing cameras flash away.
 "This is truly amazing," I exclaim, "what happens next?"
 "The concert starts in half an hour but I'd like you to meet some people first."
 "Okay, fine."
Susan and Amelia embrace amid more flashing cameras. If I'm not mistaken, I think I hear Amelia address Susan as darling. I suppose that's inevitable, given her prolonged exposure to the arty types. Everything and everyone seems very glittery and jittery and, how shall I put it, abnormally exercised, perhaps?
 Norman Balls is presented to me. He is very small, very shy, and very short sighted. He dresses like a 1950's librarian and looks no more than twelve years old.
 "This is a wonderful building," I say.
 "Thank you."
 "I can't wait to see all of it."
He smiles nervously and says nothing. A strange little chap.
 "And this is Quinlan Frick, the centre manager," says Susan, indicating a tall, gangling figure with huge fish-like eyes and albino colouring so acute he almost appears translucent. He sort of swims into view.
 "Hi there Prime Minister, how goes it?"
 "Very well thank you."
 "I see you got off on the pod rides."
 "Yes."
 "We all do, they're such a fix, aren't they?"
 "It would seem so."
 "Well you enjoy the rest of the building, it's sheer temptation."
 He floats away. It's almost as if he views the building as some kind of living entity rather than bricks and mortar.
An odd character, that's for sure.
 More dignitaries come and go and I nearly end up being introduced to my own cabinet. I'm so pleased to see so many of them out in force; Susan must have really whipped them into

action. She is looking stunning tonight and as we take our seats, I give her a little thumbs up sign. She returns a radiant smile, a wonderfully attractive woman.

And then the orchestra launches into Wagner's Die Meistersinger overture. Massively impressive. Likewise the applause. The front row of the stalls leap to their feet, cheering and shouting (the conductor having encouraged the brass). The next move is a bit of a surprise. Before the audience settles down, the orchestra strikes up with some Offenbach (Gaiety Parisienne, if I'm not mistaken) which is entirely inappropriate in my opinion. The audience starts to titter and then breaks out into peels of laughter as the entire orchestra and the platform on which they are seated begins to sink slowly out of sight! The last time I saw anything like that was forty years ago at the Grand Theatre in Leeds. Even then it was only the mighty Wurlitzer organ that disappeared into the orchestra pit in front of the proscenium arch.

As the entire Sutchworth Sinfonietta descends into some kind of Bayreuth inspired cavern, a huge stage floor rises from the back and unfolds across the top of them like a giant Swiss roll. The audience gasps and responds with tumultuous applause. The conductor is the last to disappear and just when it looks as if the stage floor will squash him like so much cream in a sponge, he turns and waves. It is all the more funny because he has a very odd shaped head, bald, pointed and shaven, like an artillery shell.

"That's Karl Dung," says Amelia, shouting in my ear.

"Never heard of him."

"He's on loan from the Schleswig-Holstein Radio Orchestra."

"I bet they miss him."

Amelia ignores my comment. Actually, I think she was too excited to heed it. She continues to chat animatedly.

"There's a great dance troupe next, they're fantastic, practically triple-jointed. Did you like the way the orchestra disappeared?"

"Amazing."

"It's all done by sand."

"Sand?"

"Yes, Norman Balls was telling me all about it. He got his inspiration from the ancient Egyptians. When they buried their pharaohs they sealed off the tomb by releasing tons of sand which allowed these huge blocks to drop down and stay put for ever."

"Does that mean we won't be seeing any more of Karl Dung?"

"No, don't be silly. Norman says the sand runs into a counter-balance chamber which sort of swings up and over somehow and dumps everything into this vast egg-timer affair at the top of the building, that's why it's egg-shaped of course, and then it's ready to run down again."

"Sounds rather archaic to me."

"Nonsense, sand is much safer than hydraulics because it doesn't burst or degenerate, anyway, the health and safety boys just love him."

"You certainly got more out of Norman than I did."

"He's a little genius – ooh look, its Sylvester Maloney, how about that for a torso?"

I settle in my seat to admire the spectacle of lithe, scantily clad dancers gyrating about the stage in movements of liquid fluidity. I share Amelia's love of ballet and am pleased that at least one contemporary choreographer has resisted the temptation to emulate the sand dancing of Wilson, Kepple and Betty, hugely entertaining though they may be. There is much to delight the senses in all that follows, solo and ensemble alike.

Gradually, the dancers depart and with extraordinary swiftness the backdrop and lighting changes as actors begin to strut their stuff. Satirical sketches and stand-up comedy begin to dominate, and very soon is becomes apparent that I, and my government, are the focal point of attention. Or should I say abuse? Political sideswipes soon degenerate into cheap mockery and eventually, full blown vilification. And this continues relentlessly, cruelly, until it reaches a peak of public humiliation the like of which no Prime Minister or political party has ever had to endure before. To make matters worse, the audience is hooting and braying with laughter. To my horror, even Amelia joins in, screaming and screeching like a buzzard claiming a freshly killed carcass.

Freedom of speech is one thing, a controversial handling of contemporary issues another, but what I have just experienced is a public execution. It's as if the entire artistic company are incapable of thinking beyond the narrow confines of political satire, no other source of inspiration has occurred to them.
I am even attacked personally.

As the performance progresses, what little wit existed at the beginning, now degenerates into facile buffoonery. Drama gives way to song and dance, but gone are the skills of ballet, replaced instead by the sort of banality that once passed for entertainment on Saturday Night at the London Palladium.

I see from the programme that there is no interval and as the final tableaux unfolds, I realise that I am to be treated to a spectacle of unsurpassed tastelessness.

A group of male dancers cavort about the stage, the traditional pantomime horse replaced by a monstrous mobile phallus. Slung around its testes is a big floppy bow tie, just like the one I am wearing tonight. Opposite them, a group of female dancers come together in coquettish symmetry to create a shimmering vulva with their fluttering, long-feathered fans. The male ensemble makes masturbatory movements, the phallus grows erect, the labia majora of the body politic quivers and the audience shrieks as the finale is consummated. The message is clear – I have raped the country for my own gratification.

As the house lights come up, I struggle to contain my anger and humiliation. I am on the point of storming out when some inner instinct prompts me to let go of my emotion. I do not know what feelings my expression may display but I am aware that flash photography is popping all over the place. Clearly, the press corps are inside the auditorium in force. Amelia appears immune to the grossness of the show, laughing and gesticulating and making ridiculous comments about what happened at the dress rehearsal. I snatch a glance at Susan and, to my horror, she too is convulsed with mirth. Can I really have no sense of humour?

"The helicopter's on standby Prime Minister," says Benjamin, in grim monotone.

"Thank you," I reply, "but I intend to maintain my dignity and will not be rushing immediately to the exit. Please pass the word around for cabinet ministers to do likewise."

"I will."

"And tell them to smile at the cameras as much as Susan Palmero is doing. We do not recognise gratuitous insult and will ignore it completely."

Eventually, I manage to rise above it as much as the bubbles in the champagne glasses at the reception afterwards. I drink more than I should but in the event, I find it helpful. Amelia stays by my side laughing and joking with all the bonhomie of someone who has just enjoyed a Gilbert and Sullivan operetta directed by Jonathan Miller. She too is drinking heavily (as is every guest) and when it looks as if the reception is about to give way to ballroom dancing, she whispers rather indiscreetly in my ear 'if I don't have pee in the next ten seconds I'll wet myself'. Naturally, I let her go. As couples begin to take to the dance floor, Benjamin approaches.

"The helicopter is ready when you are, Prime Minister."

"It's okay Benjamin, I'll wait for Amelia."

As he merges into the gathering throng, Helga appears.

As always, her beauty is ravishing but her usual composure is not entirely intact.

"Shall we dance?" I say.

She smiles gamely as I take her in my arms amid yet another outbreak of flash photography.

"There can be no forgiveness for what happened tonight," she hisses, as we circle in a gentle waltz, "you must sack Susan Palmero immediately and cut off all funding to this heinous place."

I feel the intensity of her anger physically transmitted at every turn, and there is no doubting the strength of her conviction Now more than ever, I am convinced that she remains true to me and those ghastly photos and insidious security reports are all part of a plot to overthrow me.

I glance amongst the whirling couples to see if my enemies are about. The floor is packed and it looks as if the party will continue well into the night. I recognise various celebrities, all of whom preen in front of the constantly flashing cameras. I catch a glimpse of the strange, fish-eyed figure of Quinlan Frick, who appears to be dancing with another man. Or is it a two-legged jellyfish? I think the heat and the champagne must be going to my head. Out of the swirling crowd comes Rashidi, who is partnered not by Gloria Fitzbagley but Angela Basoutar. I try to steer Helga away but Rashidi brushes past me.

"Wrong move," he snarls, then sails away, flashing his big smile for the cameras.

I can feel Helga tense in my arms. The music stops and I bow and kiss her hand in an old-style gesture of thanks.

"Amelia has gone to the loo, perhaps you could find her, I think it's time go."

"I'll check things out."

We move through the breaking crowds and Benjamin appears like a genie out of his lamp.

"Security is all in place Prime Minister."

"Excellent, Helga has gone to find Amelia, I think she's in the loo."

"I believe she was spotted heading for the upper gallery."

"Oh, well, I'd better wander up there."

As I make my way to a moving staircase, I'm aware of plainclothes policemen hovering in the background. Big guys with big feet that aren't made for dancing. Well, you can't be too careful these days.

The upper gallery is very much upper and I count at least four moving staircases before I alight on the appropriate floor. A sign indicates that this is indeed the upper gallery, underneath it, a notice saying: The Sutchworth Family Heritage. I can't imagine why Amelia persevered all the way up here with a full bladder, especially as there are a Ladies & Gentlemen on every level.

When I arrive at the end of the gallery, I pause to admire the main foyer which I can see way below through a huge smoked glass window. Such are the dimensions of the building that the people below look as small as, well, maybe not insects but certainly bumblebees, all massing and buzzing. The ladies jewellery sparkles in the spotlights and their translucent stoles twinkle like dragonfly wings. Notwithstanding this fascinating panorama, I decide it's a bit of a wild goose chase and turn to go; I think the bees have spotted me anyway.

As I proceed along the circular corridor, which is more like an open gantry, I realise I am right at the very top of the egg-shaped dome which has become such a landmark for the area, visible even from Wales on a fine day, or so I am told.

I hesitate in front of a door marked Sand Chute No.6. Can all that stuff about Norman and the pharaohs really be true? My inquisitiveness gets the better of me and I push open the door.

I know that light travels faster than sound but it is the sound that reaches me first. The unmistakable sound of a woman in ecstasy. And then the door swings open to reveal a sight that I shall never forget for the rest of my life. Amelia and Susan half-naked in each other's arms! Susan's mouth gorges on Amelia's breasts, her tongue circling and licking with unbridled passion. Amelia's head is thrown back in wild abandon, her hands grasping and plunging at Susan's hair. And then they see me. Amelia cries out and frantically tries to slam the door shut, but in her haste, loses her balance and topples to the ground, dragging Susan with her. The two women crash through the doorway and collapse in a heap, their coitus emphatically interrupted.

Now it is my turn to gasp. I hear footsteps running and voices shouting and, horror of all horrors, the lightning snap of flash photography. I try to move but remain transfixed like a traumatised rabbit.

God alone only knows what tomorrow's papers will say!

27

Benjamin looks like the Grim Reaper as he hands me the newspapers. He has been analysing them since they rolled off the presses in the early hours of this morning. He has tactfully placed the tabloids at the bottom of the pile but I turn to them immediately.

My worst fears are confirmed. The photographs leave nothing to the imagination, the headlines nothing to doubt.
I feel physically sick. I read the broadsheets in the hope of some encouragement. Alas, their sanctimonious tone makes me feel even worse. The Guardian can hardly contain its smugness:

To be cuckold as a public figure is a cruel blow, but to be cuckold when the relationship involves a lesbian lover must surely turn that humiliation into a personal tragedy? We can but sympathise with the Prime Minister who, prior to the extra-marital sideshow, had to endure ninety minutes of public ridicule, the only possible description for the much-trumpeted gala opening of the Sutchworth Arts Centre. Rumours of his close liaison with Helga Vine, the dauntingly beautiful acting cabinet secretary, may add a further dimension to this unfolding drama. Meanwhile, we can only speculate on how long it will be before letters of resignation and divorce papers start flying.

Needless to say, there is a half-plate photograph of Helga and myself dancing. As for other exposés, I suppose I should be grateful that the picture editor chose not to reveal Amelia's breasts although one has only to glance at Susan's to appreciate the level of passion still burning.

Breakfast TV merely adds to my agony. There are my political enemies scrambling to be the first to express their concerns with such cloying unctuousness that one can practically hear the programme editor gagging. I bury my head in my hands.

"I know this is a very difficult time for you, Ambrose," says Benjamin, quietly, "but whenever you feel like talking, you have only to buzz for me."

I find his calm detachment strangely consoling.

"Thank you Benjamin, that is very kind of you. I appreciate that political considerations will have to be addressed sooner rather than later."

He nods politely, makes to go then pauses at the doorway.

"Was there anything else you required?"

His diplomacy is admirable since he knows that I was consoled by Helga and a bottle of Korskenkorva vodka well into the early hours of the morning.

"Is Helga about?"

"Yes."

"Ask her to bring some Nurofen in with her."

Benjamin smiles and exits.

Press photographs of Helga and myself were limited to the dance floor as she was still checking the downstairs cloakrooms when the incident occurred. Fortunately, she had the good sense to remain in the background during all the kerfuffle but was already belted up in the seat behind me by the time the helicopter took off.

As soon as it became apparent what was happening, security officers had surrounded Amelia and Susan and bounced the paparazzi off the walls. In response to my cry 'get me out of here' I was whisked down a service elevator into the waiting helicopter. From that moment on I didn't really care what happened to Amelia or Susan.

According to reports, i.e. the newspapers, they both made an early exit under cover of tablecloths and a police van. The media lay siege to Amelia's flat following a tip-off and breakfast TV showed they were still camped out there this morning, their lenses trained on the front door and the heavily curtained windows. A pity the lovers' sense of privacy could not have prevailed earlier. Well, that's coke and champagne for you.

Given the furore that I knew would erupt the following day, I suppose it would have been more sensible to remain sober and clear headed, but I am only human like the rest of us. The vodka anaesthetised the pain whilst Helga provided much needed support.

As my emotion began to flow and Helga became not only a source of consolation but omniscience, I felt the hand of destiny on both our shoulders. For better or for worse, I raised the issue of her alleged infidelity. Her reaction was vigorous and unequivocal.

"Those bloody bastards," she snarled, "they are even more evil than I had imagined. You must not believe what you have seen with your own eyes, Ambrose, with digital photography you can transform or create anything."

In a way I was relieved to hear such a vociferous denial as it confirmed the validity of my gut instinct. Nevertheless, I pressed on.

"But what about Gloria's security reports, the ones she showed me in Finland, surely she couldn't assume that I would accept them at face value, that I wouldn't ask for more?"

"And did you?"

"Er . . . no, now you come to mention it, I don't think I did."

"And did she leave the reports with you?"

"No, she took them back, she put them safely in her bag, together with the photos. I suppose I was too shocked to understand why."

Helga clasped my hands in hers, a look of deep earnest in her eyes.

"Ambrose, you have been manipulated by a master of manipulation."

Blunted though my senses were by alcohol, sufficient nerve ends were still exposed for me to feel an awful jolt of reality. As I tried to unravel past events, I felt myself reeling under the mental onslaught of it all.

" – But - but, what about the murder of poor old Buttocks and other members of the judiciary? Those are facts that nobody can deny. Who is responsible for that?"

"Aubrey Fynch-Chilling."

"What!"

"He is behind everything."

"Everything?"

"Yes, he wanted to be Prime Minister and is consumed by hate and jealousy. He has never forgiven you for passing him over as Chancellor of the Exchequer. He is the one behind the temple bombing, the exposure of Jocelyn's sexual peccadilloes and the plundering of government money into off-shore accounts."

"But Kevin Doppler told me about those."

"He is Aubrey's stooge, he cannot be trusted. He is a heroin junkie. That's why he's so anxious to see the legalisation of drugs."

"But what about Rashidi?"

"He has no political skills whatsoever, he is a fixer, plain and simple. Aubrey needs him at the moment but will drop him when it comes to the crunch . . . when he stages his political coup."

My head really begins to spin now. I can feel the blood pulsing through my temples. Whatever is arising, I am no longer in control.

"And Amelia and Susan?" I cry, "who is to blame for that?"

"I am sorry Ambrose, I cannot answer that."

At which point, the floor rises to meet my face.

28

"One capsule or two?"

I give a victory sign and take the glass of water that Helga offers me. My hands are a bit unsteady but I raise the glass and take a resolute swig.

"Kippis," I say, with a stab at heartiness (kippis being the only word in the Finnish language that I have mastered with any confidence, although why I am resorting to this remote tongue when I can hardly articulate in my own, I have no idea), "how's your head?"

"It's fine, you did most of the drinking."

"What do I look like?"

"A wreck."

"Oh dear."

"Don't worry, it doesn't matter, I've cancelled all your appointments."

She smiles and pours the coffee. It smells delicious. And she looks beautiful.

Sunshine streams through the open window and the sound of chirruping birds is most reassuring. It is then that I realise I am still wearing last night's dress suit. My shirt collar is unbuttoned and I can feel the itch of unshaven skin. I don't appear to be wearing any shoes either. My jacket is slung over a chair and a duvet lies crumpled on the sofa.

The second coherent realisation of the day is that I am not in my office but in my private apartment. I try to focus on my wristwatch but the figures shimmer with all the colours of the spectrum. I sip on the strong, dark coffee. Somehow, my lips don't seem to be functioning properly and I dribble into the saucer. Taking stock of the overall situation, I conclude that at this moment in time I am unfit to run the country. I am not sure about much else either. Such memories that I can muster are more like a cavalcade of phantasmagorical images than a recollection of a gala night out. There is something surreal about the whole event but the weirdness disappears instantly as the press photos lay cruel testament to what actually happened.

I try to stand but my sense of balance is found wanting.
I flop back into my chair, spilling more coffee in the process. Helga dabs my chin with a tissue and places another one in the saucer. I feel like an invalid.

"Oh God, how long before the nurofen kick in?"

"Drink as much water as you can, all that alcohol has dehydrated you," I accept a large tumbler and try to swallow generously without gagging, "take your time, there is no need to hurry, your equilibrium will gradually return and then you can shave and shower, that will make you feel much better."
Words of wisdom indeed.

In politics, timing is everything. That may be so. In my experience, most political actions seldom occur as purely self-starting initiatives. The vast majority are knee-jerk reactions to unfolding events which are then portrayed as carefully considered decisions arising from sound advice and superior assessment.

I certainly feel refreshed after my shower but some inner voice tells me that there is no necessity to rush into the business of the day. The fact that Helga also subscribes to this view reinforces my feeling that right now, meditation is the next best thing.

After sixty minutes I come to the conclusion that my marriage is over but my premiership is not. We have both been unfaithful and the fact that Amelia has chosen to swap horses mid-stream does rather alter the terrain somewhat emphatically as we clamber up the banks to an uncertain future. Recrimination and blame is pointless. Forgiveness is the middle way. It is not for me to fathom the seeds of the gender bender although I wish it had not manifested itself quite like a prize exhibit at the Chelsea Flower Show. If they can be happy together so be it.

The political humiliation I have suffered is another matter entirely. This was premeditated and conceived on such a scale that I am in no doubt that it amounts to treachery. Susan Palmero will have to accept responsibility for her actions.

It is almost three p.m. by the time I sit down with Helga and Benjamin to discuss the way ahead. The frustration of the media at the delay in issuing any comment has apparently whipped them into a state of lather. Even Buckingham Palace has rung twice to find out what's going on.

"What did you say?" I ask Benjamin.

"I told them you were feeling pretty horribilis but remained mindful of your duty to the nation and Her Majesty. They were pleased to hear that."

"One is not surprised. Anybody else rung?"

"No." (They both know who I meant).

"Any leaks?"

"None."

"Any messages of support?"

"The Home Secretary was practically in tears. He said this sort of thing would never have happened if Elton John had been there."

"Poor George. I wonder which bit he was referring to?"

There is a pause whilst I stir my tea and take a first considered sip. I've always felt that high grown Assam has a quality about it that calms and stimulates the mind simultaneously, provided it is brewed correctly. I pause to savour its effects before continuing.

"I have decided that personal matters will remain personal and the only statement to be made in that respect is that I am disappointed at recent developments. Susan Palmero is to be summoned immediately and if she does not offer her resignation, I will sack her on the spot; a letter should be prepared to cover that eventuality. Make sure it's legally watertight," I add, "conduct unbecoming for a minister of state and failure to support government policy in a public and positive manner, or something like that."

"I'll get on to it right away," says Benjamin, "and I'll prepare a press statement too."

"Thank you, you can also add that I have called a full cabinet meeting for nine a.m. tomorrow morning. If George is the only minister with the decency to ring me, perhaps the others will be watching television."

Benjamin leaves us.

"What will you do about the Sutchworth Arts Centre?" says Helga, when he is gone, "are you really going to allow that despicable show to continue?"

"Yes, I shall rise above all that. Most of the theatre critics have condemned it as tacky stunt. I doubt if it will last long.

I intend to ask the cabinet for their opinion however, it's about time I started to flush out the traitors."

Helga moves closer and gently massages the back of my neck.

"I'm so pleased you've found your fighting spirit again Ambrose, you must be careful though, your enemies are resourceful and remember, even as we speak, Aubrey is plotting your downfall."

Benjamin gives a typically calm and assured performance on the early evening news and not long afterwards all ministers confirm their attendance at number ten tomorrow morning. All ministers with the exception of Susan Palmero. I demand to know why.

"The whole world knows she's in hiding at Amelia's place and she has full security coverage, surely it can't be that difficult to make contact?"

Some while later, a rather embarrassed security official informs me that Susan and Amelia have been airlifted by helicopter to East Midlands Airport and are on their way to Malaga.

"Malaga!"

"In Spain."

"Yes, I know where it is, you bloody idiot, but on whose authority?"

"Apparently yours, Prime Minister."

"Mine? MINE? Jesus bloody Christ!"

The official scuttles away as I send papers flying across the desk in a torrent of secular expletives. Helga rushes in alarmed.

"Ambrose, what is it, what's happened?"

I am so consumed with anger that I can barely spit the words out, but when I do, I find myself shrieking at the top of my voice.

"You were right about that pock-marked, needle punctured, bastard of a police commissioner, he is not one of us –
AND I WANT HIS BOLLOCKS ON A PLATE!"

29

There is nothing quite like a long session of meditation at midnight to calm the nerves. Even though my earlier outburst has subsided as a result of the natural arising and cessation of emotion, I know there is still some way to go before true equilibrium can be achieved.

I have rather neglected my Buddhist shrine of late, (always a sign of a distracted mind), and so I spend some while replacing the wilting evergreens and decaying fruit. With care and attention I dust the surfaces and reposition the bronze bell on its cushion. Similar consideration is given to the candles and incense and, before long, everything is as it should be. Clean, uncluttered and settled. Shortly before midnight, Helga joins me and we prepare ourselves for meditation.

I think it's a popular misconception that meditation is something that happens easily. Even after years of practise the mind can find itself wandering down blind alleyways, which is to say, they didn't appear blind at first. Some feeling, some idea, some notion, (I struggle to find the right word), some something seems to beckon, to persuade, to lead one gently on, as if to say – yes, this is the way to go, I am free of all attachments, this is the path to follow. And then, suddenly, with no subtlety at all, there you are, slap bang in the middle of a dead end. Irritation and sometimes anger immediately arise with the realisation that your mind has been hijacked. And who is to blame? You? Somebody else? Be honest with yourself. The answer is no. Nobody. And so you try again to concentrate hard to banish all external trivia. Perhaps it's better this time and you begin to feel good and you say to yourself – oh yes, now I am meditating. But of course, that only leads to another dead end. To feel that you are meditating merely reveals that you have not cleared the mind at all, you are still hanging on to some intellectual concept of what you think meditation is. Alas, you remain deluded until you realise that to meditate is simply to be. To be aware. To see the truth.

The problem tonight is that the truth is so bloody awful that I'd rather open another bottle of vodka. In such circumstances it is better not to meditate alone, and that's why I am pleased that Helga is with me now. Enough said.

The pressures of the day have been considerable and I suspect that they will increase tomorrow. News of Amelia and Susan's flight to Spain has now become the big story everywhere. Scotland Yard has been pressed to make a statement about the security arrangements and Kevin Doppler has had the effrontery to say on camera that his officers were acting in accordance with instructions from Downing Street. Jon Snow, that bicycling hack from Channel 4 News has already posed the question *"why would the Prime Minister send his wife and her lover abroad, yet in the same breath summon the latter to number ten?"* How does he know that?

I fear there are fifth columnists everywhere and it's still only Sunday.

But these issues no longer clamour for attention as I settle myself in the lotus position and begin my journey to the far side. There is no striving, no urge to achieve a goal. There is just the nature of the moment to observe. The essence of the moment itself. That is enough. There is no desire to experience more than that. Now is the moment. Now is the knowing.

Helga is with me on the far side. It has been a long while since we were together here. Her presence is reassuring. Once again she is bathed in brilliant white light. I feel her aura arising. I connect with her chi. It's like plugging into the national grid. The power is awesome. A vista of endless possibility opens up before me. There is nothing to fear now. There is no need to seek solutions to problems that do not exist. The truth of the moment has no such complication. Only as a politician am I deluded. As a human being I see the truth. I am simply passing through the universe. Alive today, dead tomorrow. Why should I care about the next general election? I still have the biggest parliamentary majority in political history, so what's to stop me changing the constitution? No more elections this century! That would stuff Aubrey Fynch-Chilling well and truly, wouldn't it? Tee hee hee.

The following morning in the cabinet room you can cut the atmosphere with a knife. I am completely unaffected by this but totally aware of it. Totally. In fact, the totality of my awareness is beyond their comprehension. They do not know what I know. Nor do they know that I know what they do not. They are in the dark whereas I am in the light. That is because I have been to the far side with Helga and together we have come back.

This morning I am sitting at the head of the long table instead of my usual position in the middle of it. My ministers must either sit to my left or to my right. They can choose to sit alongside a particular colleague or face them. The dynamic created by this simple move is most revealing.

Aubrey sits on my left, half way down. He is flanked by Rashidi on one side and Claude Napper, the Foreign Secretary on the other (to give him credit, Claude has established considerable entente cordial with his opposite number in Paris and reports that President Chirac is desirous of placing a French company on the tender list for the next round of mega-prison building).

Lucy Bowens the Health and Social Services Minister is sitting on the left too, next to Leonard Welling the Treasury

Secretary (rumour has it that she is driving the poor man mad with her relentless cross-examination of budget figures).

And there is Harold Plumrose the Industry Secretary, who doesn't know what time of day it is but tries to give the impression that he is the only one who does.

Facing Aubrey is Hattie Chapelthwaite who has now swelled to the size of an aircraft carrier. She is flanked by Scott Rignold who must be wondering what is going on with overseas development these days.

And there is Christopher Meelybean, preening himself like there is no tomorrow, I am sure he must be spending more time in front of a sun lamp than is good for him.

And there is his estranged bosom buddy, Dr. Mangal Bali Chakkar, down the other end with an extra large blotting pad.

Mervyn Mallatratt, the Employment Secretary is shuffling papers about with a permanent furrow on his brow (he's not managed to say anything for a long while now).

And next to me on my right is George, dear George, my ever-loyal Home Secretary who popped in earlier this morning with a large display of lavender 'to assist the senses'. He confided that ever since the closing scene of the Egg Whisk gala night he has been suffering high blood pressure and asked me not to mistake his florid complexion for pent up anger in spite of the fact that he remained outraged at the spectacle. 'I can never forgive Susan Palmero for what she has done to you, Ambrose, I blame her Italian blood, but even so.' He mops his brow with his handkerchief. Poor, dear George, I assure him I will be mindful of his condition (even though he looks like a roman candle in mid flight).

As I adjust my spectacles, I notice that Clive Smeelie, my morose Lord Chancellor has chosen to sit opposite at the far end. A consummate fence sitter if ever there was. He does not know that I know that traces of his DNA were found on the abandoned motorbike that was used in the assassination of poor old Buttocks, Lord Justice deceased. Well, I told you that the vista on the far side contained endless possibilities. Tee hee hee.

"Good morning everyone, let's get down to business."

All eyes are on me as I test my fountain pen. It is a little ritual I have developed to concentrate their minds. A purple snake emerges on the blotter. Purple, the colour of Roman Emperors. I am ready to begin.

"You are all aware of the events of the past forty-eight hours, it would be ridiculous of me to assume otherwise.
I have already summoned Susan Palmero to give an account of the proceedings that culminated in the opening of the Sutchworth Arts Centre but she has not complied with this instruction, choosing instead to take an unauthorised holiday in Spain."

"And we all know why," interjects Aubrey, with a mocking sneer.

"I beg your pardon, Aubrey, is there something you wish to say?"

The knife that has already cut the atmosphere slices through the ether again. No pins can be heard to drop. Aubrey rises to his feet, presumably to affect more gravitas and authority. I notice his flies are almost undone. What a shabby individual.

"Prime Minister, I will not mince my words. The last forty-eight hours are merely the inevitable result of your disastrous management of this administration. There are those among us who do not share your view on the state of the nation, nor can we find it in ourselves to subscribe to your Great Thrust Forward initiative. In short, you have engendered a crisis of confidence and I hereby serve notice that I am formally challenging you for leadership of the Conservative Party."

The purple snake grows bigger. I watch it calmly before looking up with a smile as warm as the English Channel.

"So, Aubrey, you have finally revealed your hand. Well, I suggest you get on with it."

Not a word is uttered by mouse or minister as I replace the cap on my fountain pen and affix it to my inside jacket pocket. As I rise to go, George stands smartly to attention, followed by everyone on his side of the table. I can tell that was a gesture Aubrey had not bargained for.

I ignore him completely and make my exit.

30

As you can probably imagine, by now the press and media were into a full throttle feeding frenzy. Gloves and morals were off in equal measure. Politicians of every party and position were swapping blows and ditching the dirt in dumper truck sizes.

When I saw Angela Basoutar dancing with Rashidi on that infamous night, I wondered whether he had persuaded her to join his camp? During the ensuing days that proved not to be the case. A tabloid newspaper that I will not stoop to name, offered her twenty-five thousand pounds to spill the beans about my relationship with Helga, and then upped it to one hundred thousand to include Amelia.

"I do not comment on such matters," she said firmly, as she made her way into number ten, chased by the usual posse.

But they kept on digging and prodding and stirring and fabricating. They even ran a readers' opinion poll with the scurrilous question *"Who do YOU think was unfaithful first? Ambrose or Amelia?"* It was little comfort to me that the vote went 70/30 in my favour.

Nor was I encouraged by the news that tickets for the Egg Whisk cabaret (as it was now known) were completely sold out and the season had been extended indefinitely. The Egg Whisk itself was saturated with reporters (much to the delight of the performers) all looking for the inside story. A chorus girl said copulation of infinite variety was always taking place wherever a couple could find a vacant spot of sand on which to hastily throw a beach towel.

Norman Balls declined to appear on News at Ten to discuss the erotic qualities of sand, so they wheeled in a Professor of Egyptology who opined that the ancient Egyptians probably did it on some kind of mattress made from camel hide and stuffed with papyrus reeds.

Magazines the length and breadth of the country ran endless stories about sex and sand. Even The Psychiatrist Monthly magazine jumped on the bandwagon with an article about the problems encountered in adult life by those who had been denied access to a sandpit during nursery school years. Anything vaguely Egyptian was given air space.

The Tatty Gallery in Hoxton displayed a painting by Najmah al-Haqq of two bare-breasted women embracing between the humps of a camel; the consenting beast wore a burka. Unfortunately, local Muslims did not appreciate the humour but the gallery remained open in spite of several riots. Meanwhile, the leadership race continued.

I was not fazed by the fact that I did not win an overall majority at the first ballot. I was half expecting it. Aubrey had been scheming and plotting and undermining everything I had done from the moment I took office, so it did not surprise me that the first flush had merely revealed the success of his covert operation. However, it cannot have pleased him that two of his cabal mates saw fit to break ranks and thus dilute his vote at the first fence. Ego has a lot to answer for. That is something that I understand but he does not. I came second by a margin of only eight votes. Claude Napper was a credible third, whereas Rashidi Eaglescliffe Mboya was an ignominious fourth. Before the next round commences, I think we shall see a shifting of the sands, if not the parting of the waves.

Sure enough, there is a tap on my office door late one night. It is Claude Napper and slightly sozzled if I'm not mistaken.

"Come in Claude," I welcome him cheerily, "I was just about to take a bottle of Chablis from the ice bucket, would you care to join me?"

"That would be most welcome, Prime Minister."

"Oh Claude, it's Ambrose please, after all, you are still my Foreign Secretary."

He looks suitably sheepish and I notice a slight tremble of the hand as I pass him a full glass.

"Thank you Ambrose, that's most generous."

"Well, I see no reason not to be, do you Claude?" He shuffles about a bit. "Oh please do sit down, try that leather armchair over there, it's most comfortable."

I remember Lord Carrington, a previous Tory foreign secretary of some pre-eminence, saying that diplomacy was the art of pouring emollient into an open wound as if it were a privilege, even if the person sitting opposite had caused it; the rationale being that magnanimity before actual victory was often the catalyst to achieving it.

The trouble with Claude, as I perceive it, is that he's easily led astray. He's an inveterate gambler and I have no doubt that plundering the defence procurement budget to see off his many creditors had a twisted logic that he could not resist. Perhaps it was made all the more resilient by the fact that the number crunching was being master-minded by the Chancellor of the Exchequer. Was it these factors that convinced him to back Aubrey in the first round instead of me? I felt I was owed some explanation. Knowing that he was something of an empire patriot I chose an appropriate toast.

"Mud in your eye."

"Not too much I hope."

We raise our glasses together and take our first swig. A piquant nose.

"So, what's on your mind, Claude?"

"I wish to state my position clearly vis-à-vis the leadership contest."

"I am grateful for that much."

He pauses before beginning. I am on tenterhooks

"I no longer believe that Aubrey will lead a future government in the best interests of the nation and the Conservative party."

"Oh really, now what makes you think that?"

Claude takes a big swig, not even pausing to savour the bouquet.

"He believes in a strong federal Europe, he owns two chateaux and six commercially operating vineyards in France which he has not declared in the register of members interests."

"That's a bit naughty."

Claude takes another big swig.

"And he has a twenty percent share in a French engineering company that supplies nuclear reactor components to Iran."

"Good Lord!" Now it's my turn to take a liberal swig of the Chablis, not even pausing to establish its country of origin, "how on earth did this come to light?"

"He was convinced that he would win the first ballot outright and accused me of ruining his chances. When our conversation looked like it was getting out of hand, I decided the most prudent course of action was to share a spliff. Fortunately, he went along with this and . . . well, I had some pretty mind-blowing Lebanese and I guess it made him rather light-headed and indiscreet. He loves to brag, as you know."

I do indeed know all about the ins and outs of Aubrey's not entirely endearing personality, but what Claude has just said casts a more Machiavellian shadow on the proceedings.

"You appreciate I shall have to check this out, Claude."

"Of course."

"Is there a possibility that he will recall your conversation?"

"Absolutely none whatsoever."

Claude swills the contents of his glass about in a series of counter-intelligence circles before meeting my eyes with a sure and steady gaze.

"Well, in that case, mud in your eye."

We drain our glasses. Claude makes to go.

"I'd better make a move Ambrose, I know you've got a lot on your plate at the moment."

"Yes. Jolly nice of you to drop in though."

"I felt it was my duty."

I open the door for him. We shake hands.

"Are you happy in the Foreign Office?"

"Yes, very much so."

"I understand that my dear compatriot Jacques Chirac holds our penal system in high regard?"

"Yes, I believe that to be the case."

"Well, I think it's time we forgot about those nasty Exocets in the South Atlantic, don't you?"

"I couldn't agree more."

"Jolly good. Well, I'm sure I can rely on you to keep up the good work Claude."

"Absolutely."

As he wanders off into the night, I have to say that basically I think he's a pretty good egg.

He's just fallen off the wall rather too many times.

31

Previous governments have been criticised for formulating policy behind closed doors instead of discussing them in open cabinet. Well, cabinet per se, is suspended due to the leadership contest and nobody can take issue with that. That does not mean that the traditional lines of communication with the civil service should be similarly held in abeyance, so naturally I appraised Helga of the latest developments at the earliest opportunity. This occurs about five minutes after Claude has left.

"I already asked Rodney to brief me on the Iranian question some days ago, I'm surprised he hasn't told me about Aubrey's little arrangement by now. Is Rodney one of us?"

Before Helga replies I think I glimpse the tiniest flicker of hurt in her eyes. Perhaps that photograph of her and Rodney indulging in sexual gymnastics remains as disturbing to her as it does to me.

"You can trust him to deliver the goods," she says, "he is doubly suspicious now that Kevin has encroached on his territory."

I make no comment. Reference to Kevin reminds me that I am still surrounded by my enemies, however, there is no need to panic since I have taken the noble sword of justice from its scabbard and before long they will fear the righteous cut of its blade. *Life's a pudding full of plums, care's a canker that benumbs.* Think positive is the mantra. Yes, I am looking forward to tomorrow.

Tomorrow comes and with it the morning post. I am handed an A5 size envelope addressed in a familiar hand. Inside is a holiday post card from Amelia featuring a municipal fountain in the whimsical art nouveau style, to wit, a little boy with tousled oxidised curls urinating with considerable vigour into a pool, his aim apparently to the delight of waiting dolphins, frozen in mid curtsey. If there is a subliminal message in the imagery there is no mistaking the tenor of the text:

Having a raunchy time – glad you're not here. Up yours! Amelia.

I confess I am rather hurt by that. Just because our marriage didn't entail swinging naked from the chandeliers every Saturday night doesn't mean that it was devoid of any shared happiness. No point in walking down memory lane now, I suppose, but why does she have to be so spiteful?

I think Susan Palmero has a lot to answer for. News of the leadership contest is worldwide and if she cannot even be bothered to vote then presumably she is no longer interested in politics? I have decided to sack her. It is the only possible course of action left open to me. It is so sad really, after all the support I have given to the arts, she might at least have the decency to return to Westminster to acknowledge that. I have said as much in my letter which I anticipate will reach her through the good offices of Francis Lilac, our ambassador to Spain.

He telephoned Claude this morning to say that she had been spotted shopping with Amelia in Madrid and wondered what security arrangements were in place as it would appear they were both unescorted, apart from about fifty photographers.

I cannot believe such reckless behaviour, they must have taken leave of their senses. I really do have to struggle to contain my anger. After a slow count of ten I request to be put through to George.

"George, I am not in any mood to talk directly to the Police Commissioner but I need to know as a matter of some urgency what exactly he is doing to protect my wife from kidnapping or assassination."

"I'll get on to it right away, Ambrose. Please try not to worry too much."

There are times when I can really do without George's touchy feely approach and this is one of them. Whatever disaster has become of my marriage I have no wish for anything harmful to happen to Amelia. I know she can be spontaneous and impulsive but disregarding all security just beggars believe. She cannot be of sound mind. Does this mean she is in love?

I am trying hard not to hate Susan Palmero. I am trying very hard indeed. Her actions have caused a crisis in government and what looks like an irretrievable breakdown in my marriage. On reflection, perhaps her actions are not the only ones to blame? I admit I have neglected Amelia badly but then, on those occasions when I have tried to do something about it, she has rejected me. Can I really be such a boring old fart? Helga doesn't think so, and that must count for something. I wonder how different everything would be if Helga did not exist? Or Susan Palmero, for that matter? No point looking backwards. Now is the moment to focus on.

I know I love Helga. I know I still love Amelia. I also know I hate that bitch Susan Palmero. Oh my God, I'd better have a strong cup of tea. I'm so unbalanced right now.

I'm about to buzz for one when Angela buzzes me first.

"The Secretary of State for Health and Social Services is here to see you, Prime Minister."

"Who the hell's that?"

". . . er Lucy Bowens, Prime Minister."

"Righto, send her in, and with a strong cup of tea, please."

Lucy can be very demanding at the best of times and right now is not one of them. However, I have to remind myself that she chose to sit on Aubrey's side in cabinet and therefore her presence could signal an interesting turn of events. Is she about to follow in Claude Napper's footsteps?

I do not rise to greet her as is my custom. I've heard say that she interprets such action as a male ploy to dominate her. I remain seated behind my desk.

"I've ordered some tea, hopefully we'll get two cups."

"Hope is something I beginning to weary of, Ambrose."

"Oh dear, you never struck me as being cynical Lucy, things must be bad."

"Things are a total mess, to put it bluntly."

Her little voice is as clear as a piccolo but I know it will not detract from what she has to say. As I've said before, she is as lethal as a rattlesnake and right now her tail is trilling like a Mexican maraca. I wish the tea would arrive. If I had any aces up my sleeve I doubt if I could produce them now, so I decide to lay my cards on the table.

"Lucy, am I to understand from that remark that I cannot rely on your vote?"

"The only thing that needs understanding right now are the figures that I get from the treasury and why I should be met with constant obfuscation and procrastination whenever I challenge them."

I say nothing as Lucy unfolds her papers and begins to quote figures and percentages and dates and calculations and comparisons and cabinet minutes and inter-departmental memoranda and emails and on and on relentlessly until I feel like screaming stop, I can't take it anymore. Fortunately the tea arrives before then. It is already poured and as my need is somewhat acute, I do not stand on ceremony. I grab my cup and gulp away. Meanwhile, Lucy stirs hers in quick, precise circles and then sips with little pernickety movements, fixing me with her bright, beady eyes. When I have drained my cup I feel it is safe to comment.

"I know just how you feel."

"You do?"

"Yes, I'm afraid so and I share your frustration. I rely on accurate financial information, whether it be forecasts, trends, results or whatever. Without it, I find it very difficult to govern the country."

"Of course."

"The point is Lucy, I have no wish to indulge in character assassination, nor do I think it would be appropriate for me to comment on any individual minister's performance, however, suffice to say, if Jocelyn Hubbard were still chancellor, you and I would not awaken every morning feeling that yet again we were up that well known creek without a paddle."

I pause to gauge the effect of my remark. Lucy replaces her cup in the saucer. Her eyes are less beady now, her voice less shrill.

"I just wanted to make my position clear," she says.

"Likewise," I reply, "and when I am returned as Prime Minister, as I have every confidence that I shall be, I will be in need of a new Chancellor."

I give her a smile as warm and glowing as the tea inside me. The honesty of my remark percolates the atmosphere until total ambience is the brew.

"You can count on me, Ambrose," she replies, in flute-like tones as soft and subtle as Debussy.

"I'm so glad we understand each other, Lucy . . . I suggest we keep this conversation under wraps, don't you?"

"You won't hear a squeak from me," she says, grinning from ear to ear as she passes through the doorway.

A dynamo in waiting, if I'm not mistaken.

The feel-good factor is immediately shattered by the telephone.

"Yes?"

"The Home Secretary for you, Prime Minister."

"Put him through."

George bursts on line in a paroxysm of emotion. I can tell today is not going to be constant.

"Ambrose, oh my God, Ambrose, I have terrible news, I don't know where to begin."

"Just calm down George, take it easy, just start from the beginning, is it something to do with Amelia?"

"Yes - I mean no - I mean, oh God we need this like a hole in the head."

"What George, what? For God's sake get a grip of yourself and tell me what's happened."

"It's Kevin Doppler, the police commissioner."

"Yes, I know who he bloody well is, what about him?"

"He's dead!"

"What? How?"

"An overdose of heroin."

"Are you sure?"

"His driver found him this morning, needles and stuff all over the bed. Looks like he choked on his own vomit."

"Who else knows about this?"

"Probably everyone by now."

"Why? How?"

"The police arrested a rent boy shortly afterwards, stoned out of his mind, he had Kevin's wallet in his pocket."

"Who's in charge now?"

"I've no idea, I mean, isn't it a bit early to talk about replacements?"

"I don't mean that, you twerp, I mean who's in charge of the investigation?"

"Damien Chick, head of the drugs squad."

"Tell him to speak to Benjamin immediately, we've got to keep a lid on this."

"Oh my God, I can't believe this is happening, we need this like a hole in the head."

"You've already said that George – "

"I know, I know but it's true, isn't it?"

"George, for God's sake pull yourself together, get a grip on things, stick your head in a bucket of lavender or something but whatever you do, DON'T PANIC."

32

Unfortunately, George panics big time. I don't know why I thought it would be any different. The feeding frenzy that the press and media have been indulging in ever since the notorious opening of the Sutchworth Arts Centre has now become a feeding orgy. There are so many splattered entrails that nobody can decide which is the best one to gorge on first. Not without reason is the choice of lead stories different.

The tabloids are going berserk about Amelia and Susan whilst continuing to dig frantically about Helga and myself. The Evening Standard, meanwhile, is crowing so loudly about its 'exclusive scoop' on the death of Kevin Doppler that it prints three different spellings of his surname in one column; you can practically hear The Guardian journalists wetting themselves.

So far, I have managed to avoid giving any press conferences, largely on the advice of Benjamin who I am more than happy to follow.

Others are not similarly restrained, Aubrey being one of them. He's going for my jugular. Well, he would, wouldn't he? It's the leadership race and he's been bloodied at the first fence. I am not surprised that he has decided to criticise George, everyone knows that I tolerate him more than it is politically wise to do so. Poor George cannot defend himself very well, he is just too honest and decent. The Kevin Doppler situation is spiralling out of control and the government is fast losing credibility. I feel I should step in but Benjamin says no, not yet, and so does Helga.

George has already been mauled by Jon Snow on Channel 4 News but continues to express admiration for Mr Snow's ties whilst ignoring his choice of socks. By some mishap, the poor man then appears on Newsnight like a sacrificial lamb to the slaughter. It's just his luck that Jeremy Paxman is anchoring the show tonight; when it comes to blood lust, our Paxo is leader of the vampires.

"So what you're really saying Home Secretary, is that you've completely lost control of the situation and the country faces anarchy."

"Ah, well, not exactly."

Too late, the severed head drops into the basket. By the time George returns home from the studio I am on the phone to Damien Chick offering him the job of Police Commissioner. Somebody has to head this crisis off sharpish or before long I'll be facing a vote of no confidence in the House.

"The job's yours if you want it Damien, your track record is good and your expertise in the field of drugs will be a great asset when the Legalisation of Drugs Bill becomes law."

"I wanna bullet proof Humvee okay?"

"I'm sure that can be arranged."

"With SAT-nav and snakeskin upholstery?"

"Everything's possible."

"What abart a Mini Cooper S for me girlfriend?"

"That does seem a little excessive."

"Oi, is this an offer I can't refuse or what?"

"I'll see what I can do."

"Right, what about me pay?"

I begin to sweat a bit. This man is not so much in your face as tearing one's features apart. I reply cautiously.

"That is not under my direct control, it's set by an independent panel of experts appointed by the - "

"Bollocks, I know what Kev's screw was, I want double."
"Damien, it's not quite as straightforward as that."
"Course it bloody is, you're the Prime Minister intcha?"
"I don't think you quite understand the situation."
"Don't patronise me, you old wanker."
"I beg your pardon?"
"You need me more than I need you."
"Damien, I now realise that this telephone call was ill-advised and I bid you goodnight."
"Yeah, fuck off then."
I bury my head in my hands. Whoever handed me his CV must have picked up the wrong file. It is one thing to work your way up through the ranks but another thing entirely to do so without picking up at least some modicum of good manners. I cannot believe that he went to Harrow. There must be a mistake. One can legislate for education, but not for breeding. Oh dear, now what?

I miss Helga. She is not about tonight. I take myself upstairs. Number Ten seems very quiet. I wonder what Amelia and Susan are doing? The mind shudders. I think a spot of meditation would not go amiss. It is way beyond the stroke of midnight when I realise why today has been so fractious. It is because I continue to take hold of things, to direct and control them instead of letting them be as they are. Events have their own dynamic. They should be left alone. Why is it so difficult for me to understand that? As I extinguish the candles, I determine that from now on I shall go with the flow. Once more, without feeling.

I wake up to the sound of clinking china. It is Florrie Finch the housekeeper with a cup of tea. She favours PG Tips in pyramid shaped bags but I'm not going to say anything. I'm going to let things be as they are. The sun seems higher in the sky, it must be later than usual. The bedside clock says ten a.m. Oh well, never mind, there must be a good reason for that.

"Good morning, sir, I thought you might like a cup of tea."
"Thank you Florrie, that's very kind of you."
"I've already stirred it."

"Thank you, much appreciated."

"Well, every little helps, as they say."

"That's very true."

"And you need all the help you can get these days, don't you?"

I assume this is a rhetorical question since the entire world knows that my private and public life have become one and the same thing. I don't think she means this unkindly so I just sip my tea.

"Any chance of some more sugar, Florrie?"

"I think one's enough, sir, too much sugar gives you diabetes."

"I just thought I'd ask."

She draws the curtains and sunshine floods the room. It really is remarkable weather for this time of year. On her way to the door she picks up my socks and stuffs them in my dressing gown pocket. This strikes me as rather odd but I make no comment.

"Right, there's a bit of a hullabaloo going on downstairs so I'll leave you to sort yourself out."

I remain mute as she exits. I wonder what type of hullabaloo she is referring to? Is it confined to the kitchen or does it exist on a grander scale? Florrie is a woman of fixed routine so almost anything beyond the absolutely predictable has the potential to become a crisis.

I finish my tea (it's actually quite nice) and take a long hot shower. The bathroom mirror is all steamed up so I clear a circle with my flannel to inspect the visage of the day. Not too impressive. I wrap a towel around my head like a turban. Amelia always did that after washing her hair. Since I am almost bald, apart for a whispery valance around my lower cranium, this does seem a somewhat whimsical gesture.

I enjoy it nonetheless. I fumble for my dressing gown and turn again to face the mirror. It is semi-opaque.

Give me my robe, put on my crown: I have immortal longings in me.

I fear I am barking up the wrong tree already. I clear the circle in the mirror a second time and peer closer.

To be, or not to be: that is the question:
Whether 'tis nobler in the mind to suffer
The slings and arrows of outrageous fortune,
Or take arms against a sea of troubles,
And by opposing end them?

Haven't I already tried both those tactics and failed? Do I really care how my mind perceives my actions? Should I mind about the minds of others? Does being a politician give me an automatic mandate to persuade other minds to think as I do? Isn't democracy about letting people make up their own minds? Surely I have given everyone the freedom to do that much? And still I am attacked – even from within. Is it really worth it?

I dress slowly, choosing a particularly flamboyant bow tie to add sparkle to the sartorial picture. A secretary whose name I cannot remember waits for me at the bottom of the stairs.

"Good morning, Prime Minister, the Foreign Secretary is anxious to speak to you, he is waiting in the main reception room."

"Then I will go straight there."

Claude is looking rather harassed when I enter the room.

"Hello Claude, how goes the day?"

"Bloody awful so far Ambrose, there's been an unexpected turn of events."

"Oh really?"

"Susan Palmero has returned to Westminster and entered the leadership contest."

"Impossible, I have sacked her."

"She says your letter is invalidated by a clause in the leadership rules relating to the suspension of executive powers."

"Nonsense. It's a smokescreen, we'll soon sort her out."

"I've heard she's gathering support already."

"Don't panic Claude, she just being theatrical, it's the Italian in her."

"That's what I fear."

Another secretary whose name I can't remember either, enters through a far door to enquire whether we would like some tea.

"No thank you. Please get hold of the Lord Chancellor immediately."

"Yes sir."

"And please tell the acting Cabinet Secretary I would like to see her."

"I believe she's gone to the Harvey Nicks sale – oops - sir."

By the time Claude and I reach my office the first secretary approaches looking rather flushed.

"I've just spoken to the Lord Chancellor and he says he's rather tied up at the moment but if you would like to drop by his office at your convenience he will do his best to see you, sir."

Claude swears long and malevolently under his breath. In contrast, I merely take long and deep breaths and begin a process of mental disengagement from the unfolding events. They have a life of their own and I have mine. I intend to stay sane.

When my car swings into the Palace of Westminster, the police have difficulty in containing the hordes of press photographers outside. We disembark from both sides of the car amid a huge barrage of flash photography. If there was a red carpet it would be like BAFTA night at the Odeon Leicester Square, as it is, there are rather more empty McDonald's cartons than usual. Am I the only person to be offended by litter? In the circumstances it is difficult to make a dignified entry but we do our best. Reporters shout provocative questions at me but I pretend not to hear them, especially the one – *what's it like being married to a lesbian?*

Inside the building we make no delay in making our way to Clive Smeelie's office. Claude bangs vigorously on the door; clearly he is still riled by Clive's overt snub. A haughty voice from within says 'you may enter'.

"Too fucking right we will", hisses Claude as he holds the door open for me.

At the far end of the office sits Clive, on a huge throne-like chair on top of a raised dais and he is dressed in the Chancellor's full official regalia. Claude virtually bursts a blood vessel at the sight but I remain calm and disconnected. Here is a man, I say to myself, whose ego is so great that he has to fast forward his life to some point of pomp and circumstance that he cannot wait naturally for.

"Is he sad or mad, or both?" whispers Claude.

"He is deluded," I reply.

Clive gestures us to sit down in front of him. I get straight to the point and tell him that in my opinion I have the authority to sack any member of the cabinet whether there be a leadership contest in progress or not.

"Depends which set of rules you're referring to," says Clive imperiously.

"He's referring to these," snarls Claude, seizing a bundle of papers from his briefcase and almost throwing them at Clive.

Clive picks them up matter-of-factly and turns to the back page. He squints through his gold-rimmed half-moon spectacles.

"Wrong set. Out of date. Tough titty."

This is an insult too far for Claude who leaps onto the dais, white with anger.

"Don't talk to the Prime Minister like that, you fucking pantomime dame, that is a genuine original document with all appropriate signatories and witnesses."

"So's this," says Clive, producing another set from a voluminous pocket inside his garment, "and it's stamped with the Conservative Party seal and, most significantly, a later date. Temper, temper, don't snatch."

Claude leaps off the dais with ungainly haste. We inspect the document closely. It looks genuine in every respect. I take a dignified stand.

"I don't remember discussing this version, let alone signing it."

"It's a bloody forgery!" yells Claude.

"Prove it," says Clive.

"Too bloody right we will," shouts Claude, "and meanwhile you can put a stop to this farce of a leadership contest."

"No can do old boy, see page three, clause six, paragraph eight. You're both stuffed."

This is another emotional break point for Claude. He grabs a ceremonial gavel from the table and launches himself towards Clive. I do not know how I manage to restrain Claude from bludgeoning Clive to death but I do so with words alone.

"Don't do it Claude – we're on CCTV!"

33

Faced with such treachery, most Prime Ministers would sack their Chancellor immediately. Unfortunately, Clive has manipulated me into a position where I cannot do so, at least not without invoking a constitutional crisis. Knowing what I do about him I have little doubt that his version of the leadership rules are a fake. I would never agree to the suspension of executive powers, even for twenty-four hours, it is too preposterous for words. The parliamentary party wouldn't stand for it either and I daresay the Queen wouldn't be overly ecstatic. As for the reaction of constitutional lawyers, well, the mind boggles. All I have to do is call his bluff. Parliament would have to endure organised chaos for a few weeks but our majority is such that we could easily ride the storm. However, it would mean that I would have to re-engage my mind to a purely political construct and this is not the path I wish to follow. I have a higher calling. I felt it tangibly in the steam of my bathroom and again, more strongly, in all my meditations since then. Helga is appalled at my attitude. There is a noticeable friction in our relationship of late. As far as I am concerned, that is something else that will have to work itself out in the natural order of things.

"I cannot believe that you're not going to do anything about him," she says angrily, "the man is a lunatic, he's not fit to hold office, you should expose him immediately."

"In due course he will do that himself."

"Quite possibly, but are you really telling me that in the meantime you are prepared to let Susan Palmero steal not only your wife but also your premiership?"

"I am not aware that she has that much support."

"For God's sake Ambrose, these days you're not aware of anything."

"Please calm down Helga, your emotion is clouding your judgment. The truth of the matter is that I am aware of more than you or anyone else gives me credit for."

"Oh get real, Ambrose, for God's sake, GET BLOODY REAL!"

And following that rather untypical outburst, Helga storms out of the room. So be it. She does not understand that Clive Smeelie is a negative force and, as such, should not be resisted. On the contrary, I shall simply redirect his energy by allowing him to continue in his present trajectory and, ipso facto, impale himself on his own ego. A sort of yang on yang approach with a positive outcome.

After Helga has disappeared (metaphorically of course), I'm quite relieved to see Angela Basoutar's cheerful face poking round the doorway.

"Time for a cup of tea, perhaps?" she says, a little mischievously.

"Absolutely, come and join me."

In no time at all we are dunking our chocolate chip cookies and chatting about this and that and some of the other.

"Have you spoken to Amelia since the Egg Whisk debacle?" she enquires solicitously.

I am not offended by her directness, in fact I am rather relieved that someone has finally broken what was fast becoming a taboo subject.

"No, she sent me a rather hurtful postcard from Spain and I can only assume she is co-habiting with Susan, somewhere or other."

". . . She is staying at Susan's flat in Maida Vale."

". . . Thank you for letting me know."

We dunk the remainder of our biscuits and our hands collide as we both go for another. It's a funny but rather cosy sort of moment. She has a warmth and humanity about her that I really like.

"If it's any consolation," she says, as half-a-dozen silver bracelets dive centipede-like into her mug, "I lived with a guy for three years until one Christmas, right out of the blue, he tells me that he's fallen in love with another man, a DJ as it happens, and they're going to run a nightclub in Ibiza, so thanks for the memory but tootle-loo and all that."

"How awful."

"Shit happens."

"What did you do?"

"Nothing. I told him if that was the way he wanted to swing then go swing and enjoy it."

"That was very forgiving."

"No point being otherwise. I didn't take it as a slur on my womanhood and I couldn't see the point of saying, hey, would it help matters if I strapped on a dick?"

At which point I fall about. This little interlude is a much needed tonic. The affairs of state and the machinations of politics can become overbearingly tedious at times. A good dose of laughter can put so many things into perspective. So we up the dosage with another cuppa and carry on laughing. Eventually, by the time we have tired ourselves out, I find it easier than ever to confide in Angela.

"Do you think it's wrong of me not to get worked up about this leadership contest?"

"Not if you're not bothered about the outcome."

"If my colleagues don't know what I stand for now, I don't think I should attempt to persuade them otherwise."

"But Ambrose you haven't even served one full term yet."

"I know, but that Egg Whisk gala was such a humiliating experience that I can't see the point of carrying on if people believe I've damaged the country so catastrophically."

"Ambrose, you've been in politics almost as long as my adult life, surely you must know it's a dirty game?"

"Yes, of course I do, but it's not because I can't stand the heat in the kitchen, it's more to do with what the others are cooking. It stinks."

A certain pall descends on our conversation. My guess is that Angela has read between the lines and understands the real cause of my despondency. She knows from her own experience that, in spite of making light of it, the breakdown of a relationship due to one partner's discovery of their true sexuality is pretty earth shattering. One needs time to adjust.

"Well," says Angela, shaking the crumbs off her skirt, "it's a three horse race but the word on the street is that Susan is gaining ground steadily."

I shrug my shoulders.

"Considering that the vast majority of back-benchers are male and from a background and age group that is not naturally inclined to favour gay relationships, I find that rather puzzling."

"The times they are a-changing Ambrose and not everyone trusts Aubrey Fynch-Chilling, including me."

Enough said is unsaid. It has been a chummy intercourse and I am grateful for that.

Over the next few days the race hots up with a fervour and intensity that would do credit to a general election. I continue to feel insulted that Susan has still not had the decency to speak to me face to face, if only to formally declare her candidacy. Perhaps the personal issues are her reason for avoiding me? All the same, I find it incredibly disdainful and not a little cowardly. When she starts giving press interviews and openly discusses her affair with Amelia, my blood nearly boils over. Somehow I manage to pull back from the brink. If only Amelia would answer my telephone calls and letters, I would feel so much better one way or the other. Although Amelia is an independent spirit in the very best sense of the word, throughout our entire marriage, ups and downs included, she has never ignored me like this before. I can only conclude that I have totally underestimated Susan's influence over her.

Meanwhile, Helga continues to castigate me.

"It's too late now, you should've cut Clive Smeelie's balls off when I told you too, and hers with it."

"Aren't you becoming a little gender confused?"

"She's making a laughing stock out of you."

I sense the beginning of the end has already started yet I do not fear it.

34

I always thought leadership contests were supposed to be relatively dignified affairs, public scalping not being in the party's overall best interests. Alas, it is a case of *cry havoc and let loose the dog's of war.*

Tensions have been rising all week and the real blood letting begins when The Sunday Times publishes an article accusing Aubrey Fynch-Chilling of illicit share dealing in the international arms trade. In the course of its exposé, it claims that Aubrey owns a twenty percent stake in a French engineering company called Axiales Speciale, who are manufacturing parts for a nuclear reactor in Iran. How dreadful. No prizes given for knowing the source of that little bombshell.

Within hours, the proverbial brown smelly stuff is not only hitting the fan but covering the whole of Westminster in a sanctimonious cloud of outrage. There is uproar in the House as that redoubtable Labour backbencher, Dennis Skinner, leaps to his feet to condemn the government in vintage sneer:

It's a pity that the high cost of living caused by this corrupt Tory government means that most of us have difficulty in paying our food bills, never mind having a few thousand left over for the purchase of nuclear reactor parts to flog to our enemies.

The Speaker calls for order amid cries of 'untrue, untrue, apologise, apologise,' but to no avail.

I have a nudging respect for dear old Dennis, at least he tells it how it is. At times like this, the greedy ones with their noses in the trough do more than pause to look over their shoulders as he swings into action. Such a pity he's on the other side. A few years ago I remember expressing that view to him in person, when we were queuing together in the bar. 'I'm on the side of fairness and justice, Ambrose,' he growled, 'd'you have a problem with that?' I didn't pursue the argument.

Not surprisingly, Aubrey begins a series of forthright denials which are soon compromised when The Guardian somehow acquires a copy of his share certificate with Axiales Speciale. The French become indignant and the Iranian Foreign Minister rings Claude to say that he thought they were supposed to be friends. Claude gives appropriate assurances in the House whilst I enjoy a moment of quiet irony. A hare has been sent running and, whatever the final outcome, most backbenchers have already decided who is not going to make it to the finishing post.

These are emotionally charged times and the prevailing mutterings are very much of the 'no smoke without fire' variety. In desperation, Aubrey agrees to an internal inquiry but everyone knows he's toast. In reality, it's Susan or me.

A beast is always at its most dangerous when wounded and Aubrey is no exception. I say as much because it could not be anyone other than him to instigate such a devastating blow at my most vulnerable flank. In spite of continuing rumour and speculation about Helga and myself the press has not been able to unearth anything factual or conclusively damning about either of us. Until now.

The Guardian (who else could it be, one has to laugh) publishes photographs of the two of us together in Finland. There we are smoking our fish by the lakeside, and there we are sharing a spliff almost as big as the fish itself. And there we are again canoodling and stoned out of our minds. And there is Helga, emerging naked from the water whilst I watch adoringly from the bank, more Dr Yes than Dr No. Holiday snapshots courtesy of Gloria Fitzbagley and Rashidi Eaglescliffe Mboya and their associates, i.e. bent security guards; reliable and authoritative sources, as the Guardian coyly puts it. As if this wasn't enough, a further montage shows Helga, in disguise, entering Helsinki airport and disembarking at Luton. Flight and baggage details all included.

On seeing them, Helga goes berserk, storming around Number Ten swearing vengeance of the most unwholesome kind. I really am worried about her these days. She seems to have lost all her usual composure and is behaving like a demon possessed. Angela told me that the other day, when she was in the loo, Helga came straight out of a cubicle and kicked the sanitary towel disposal unit right across the floor for no apparent reason. On another occasion, she threw a letter knife at one of the secretaries for nothing more than some minor administrative error. It's almost as if she is undergoing some kind of major personality change. She refuses to join me in meditation and has become openly scornful of my practice. I fear that unless she modifies her behaviour, something highly regrettable might happen.

As head of the civil service, Sir Mallard Kane has a duty of care and responsibility towards her. He is fully recovered from his fountain pen attack and now that Hugo Snatch has been despatched to the department of weights and measures following a successful appeal against his dismissal, Mallard has regained some of his former aplomb.

When I approach Mallard, he seems strangely reluctant to address the issue. Perhaps he feels that Helga, being of unstable condition, might take exception to his words of consultation and launch a sharp-pronged attack of some kind against his person. Even the most level headed of us are conditioned by past experiences to some extent and I would not blame him for being apprehensive about the situation. Nevertheless, she is a member of the civil service and not the Conservative party so there can be no question of whose responsibility it is. Besides, I have decided to make a clean sweep of things at a special press conference before the final leadership ballot is taken. If nothing else, I think the party and the country needs to know where it stands. I also feel that Helga should be aware of my intentions. It is only fair. When all's said and done, what have we to be ashamed of? We fell in love. I am married, she is not. It happens to so many couples these days. I am not condoning extra-marital behaviour, but I am prepared to say, in public, that I have participated in it.

Unfortunately, Helga has a different perspective on the matter. When we meet, she is not backward in coming forward.

"You don't love me any more."
"I do, but I have to come clean, I am the Prime Minister."
"Not for much longer."
"Thanks for your vote of confidence."
"If you'd listened to me we wouldn't be in this mess."
"So it's all my fault is it?"
"There you go, twisting my words, typical politician."
"Look, I know we're both under a lot of pressure but you've been behaving so strangely of late, I just need to know why."
"You're having an affair with Angela Basoutar, aren't you?"
"Oh my God, so that's what this is all about? That's it. Enough. Conversation ended. I have a press conference to give."
"See – I knew I was right."

The press conference goes badly. I would rather not say too much about it. I try to conduct myself with dignity but I am boxed in and pummelled from all directions.
I signal the end but still they keep coming.
"Do you think you'll win the leadership contest?"
"Let's wait until tomorrow's vote."
"Will you serve under Susan Palmero if she wins?"
"I am not prepared to answer hypothetical questions."
"Will Amelia live with her at number ten?"
"Good evening."

The following day the final ballot is taken and the result is declared at three p.m. Susan wins by a margin of sixty-two votes.

Pretty conclusive, wouldn't you say?

35

My car pulls up outside Buckingham Palace in the early morning sunshine. A liveried footman moves forward to open the door. He is surprised to see that I am not there. That is because I am sitting in the front. Perhaps I should explain that Susan Palmero has already commandeered my ministerial car and the chauffeur that goes with it. As a mere backbencher I am no longer entitled to any kind of official transport. Not wishing to create a scene, I accept George's kind offer of a lift and insist on sitting in the front whilst he drives. I think he appreciates that. These days he is isolated enough.

"Five minutes to eight, couldn't be better, thanks a load George."

"I'll park somewhere behind those wheelybins if there's room, if not, I'll sort of hover until you reappear."

"I shouldn't be that long, apparently Her Majesty is exercising her horses in Windsor Park at eight forty-five."

"Okay, catch you later then."

"Take care – by the way, I hope you've paid the congestion charge?"

"Oh my goodness, I never realised, I mean surely we're exempt?"

"Just winding you up George."

He laughs as the liveried footman holds the front door open rather sniffily and then shouts through the window, "you look great."

I am pleased to receive his compliment as I spent some while in selecting an appropriate bow tie. I have chosen one of my favourites. Pink raspberries on a lemon background. Very upbeat.

The Queen has invited me personally to join her for breakfast. It is not every ex-Prime Minister who is accorded this honour, in fact I may be the only one.

A butler in full morning dress ushers me into a large room overlooking the gardens. A table is set for two by the window. I notice there are various items of Tupperware on display and the electric toaster resembles a corgi dog.

"Her Majesty will be with you shortly, sir, would you like a fruit juice? I recommend the pineapple."

"Thank you, that will do nicely."

He pours one out and hands it to me just as Her Majesty arrives.

"Good morning Ambrose."

"Good morning ma'am."

"Please sit down."

"Thank you."

The butler takes two medium-cut slices of Kingsmill white, places them in the toaster and then stands to attention.

"How would you like your toast?" she enquires.

"Well done, if I may."

"Try number six," she says to the butler, who obliges accordingly, "do you prefer Cornflakes or Frosties?"

"Cornflakes, thank you, ma'am"

The butler is about to uncap the Tupperware when Her Majesty intervenes.

"Thank you, Snelgrove, you may leave us now."

He bows politely and exits inconspicuously as only a royal butler can.

Her Majesty tips a generous portion of each cereal straight into the bowls. There are two milk jugs on the table.

"Semi-skinned or full cream?"

"I have a weakness for full."

"Me too."

She pours with equal generosity. I notice she prefers Frosties.

"Do you take sugar?"

"I'm trying to give it up, ma'am."

"Me too, but I think we can spoil ourselves for today, don't you?"

I smile gratefully as she applies sugar from a shaker as big as one's forearm, the crystals appearing from out of a clenched fist. It is rather cannibalistic. Quite a bit misses the bowl and cascades over the tablecloth.

"This was a present from an African chief, I use it daily, I think it's great fun. Snelgrove hates it."

I make no comment and we settle down to breakfast. Suddenly I am aware of acrid blue smoke pouring from the toaster. I am about to cry out but cannot do so because I have a mouthful of cornflakes. I gesticulate wildly with my spoon. In the event this proves unnecessary as Her Majesty is already stabbing the eject button. There is a loud metallic ping as two blackened slices go sailing through the open window with uncommon grace. Her Majesty grins and waves her napkin about in the manner of a cheerleader. It disperses the smoke most effectively.

"Strictly speaking, that smoke detector alarm over there should go off but I disconnected the batteries because I can't stand that awful whistling first thing in the morning. Don't tell Snelgrove."

"My lips are sealed ma'am"

"I'd offer to have another go but these days I'm limited to two slices only, my auditors insist I cut back on domestic expenditure and you have to start somewhere don't you?"

"The cornflakes will be more than sufficient, thank you, ma'am."

We carry on munching.

Through the open window I can hear the distant rumbling of the rush hour traffic. The sound of people with jobs to go to, tasks to perform, decisions to take. Having given my constituency party notice of my intention to quit politics altogether at the end of next month, I am looking forward to a change of tempo and scene.

Her Majesty interrupts my musing to offer a choice of coffee or tea. I have already noticed two large chrome thermo-flasks with automatic plunger type dispensers positioned on a nearby trolley. By now the tea must be stewed beyond even the most rustic of palates so I decide it's safer to plumb for the coffee.

I pass on the milk but accept two large cubes of brown sugar served from a pink Tupperware with matching plastic tongs. The teaspoons are plastic too. It feels like a picnic. It is unexpected but not altogether unpleasant. I am grateful.

"Well, Ambrose," says Her Majesty, dabbing her mouth with her napkin, "what are going to do with yourself?"

I pause before replying. It is important that I do not convey a sense of pointlessness in having pursued a career in the service of Her Majesty and her subjects, only to have it nose-dive in such lurid and sensational circumstances.

"In the not too distant future I shall return to the Kaya Centre for Mindfulness to take up a position of pastoral care."

"Oh really, how nice."

"Yes, I'm looking forward to it."

"Weren't you the founder of the centre?"

"Yes ma'am, I was its chairman for twenty-five years."

"Of course you were and I didn't I knight you for services to the community?"

"Yes ma'am."

"Well, well, well, fancy that, and now you've come full circle."

Now it is my turn to dab my mouth with the napkin.

"That is indeed so, ma'am, but I have arrived at a different point in its circumference and can therefore enjoy a fresh perspective."

"How interesting. You must have a talk with Charles sometime. He seems to be going round in never ending circles, it can't be any good for him."

"I shall be happy to help in any way I can, ma'am"

"That's very kind of you. I'll drop him a line."

Her Majesty rises and our breakfast is concluded. We exchange farewells and I thank her for inviting me. She wishes me good luck.

On my way out I notice two corgis scampering around the corner of the building, each with a blackened slice of toast in its jaws. There is connectivity in everything. I will speak to Charles about that.

I am sure if he visited his mother more often he would soon become king.

36

Winter always turns to spring.

What a beautiful sentiment, and even more so in the actualité. The winter has not been too harsh although February gave us all a shock with its arctic winds and swirling snowstorms. Now it is April and there is so much promise in the air as blossoms bloom and people smile and even sing.

I am very happy at the Kaya Centre for Mindfulness.
I have been reunited with many old friends and made numerous fresh acquaintances. I can't tell you how delightful it is to be with my dear friend Jocelyn again. I have missed his great lumbering frame and chortling subterranean voice.

As he was such a brilliant Chancellor of the Exchequer, it is hardly surprising that he has excelled as Financial Director of the Kaya Centre. One can only describe our profits as stratospheric. This is entirely due to the revenue received from our counselling and rehabilitation contract with H.M. Prison Services. Jocelyn has invested some of it in capital projects for the centre and we now have an indoor swimming pool in addition to the saunas and massage parlours and sundry other rooms set aside for prayer and meditation.

We also have an extensive library and several clinics dedicated to homeopathic and oriental healing.

I live at the centre. Nothing extravagant, just an apartment with en suite facilities and a generous lounge. My Blochstein mini-grand piano fits nicely in one corner. I have a Bang and Olufsen eight-speaker stereo system and a wide screen plasma television to fill those moments when one seeks relief from the rigours of spiritual assignments.

It is a light, airy room with floor to ceiling double glazed windows and electrically operated curtains; I quite like playing with those during idle moments. Two sliding patio doors lead to a wooden veranda that offers a panoramic view of the incessantly manicured Hertfordshire countryside.

On a fine day, such as now, I like to sit outside with a cup of tea and admire my turbo-charged Bentley Continental parked in the courtyard below. Such a handsome car with its British Racing Green coachwork and cream leather upholstery. It is really gleaming today, having just been cleaned by two young Thai girls who are attending a beginner's course in Qi Gong.

The Centre has a high intake of foreign students, particularly from South East Asia, due entirely to the efforts of Jocelyn who has an abiding interest in their culture and has travelled extensively throughout the region, mainly on package holidays, or so I understand.

Amelia is coming to see me this afternoon. I am pleased to say that following our divorce, which was as amicable as it was possible to be, given the continuing media interest, we have managed to establish a cordial relationship. I'm not saying it was wine and roses all the way, but it could have been a lot easier were it not for Susan's jealousy. Underneath her feisty personality is a woman with severe insecurities. Jealousy is such an insidiously destructive behaviour that I can only hope and pray it will not drive a wedge between them.

Amelia never stays for long, for reasons that you will now understand, and this afternoon she is just popping in to say hello and goodbye before she travels to Shropshire.

Although I do not have the fondest of memories of the Sutchworth Arts Centre, I am truly delighted that Amelia has recently been appointed as its new artistic director. She has assured me she had nothing whatsoever to do with that dreadful opening gala night and I have no reason to doubt her. She has good taste and an eye for talent and I know she will make a success of it. At long last she will be fulfilled in every direction.

I am at the Blochstein playing Lizst when she enters. Earlier on I had been dabbling in Chopin but felt he would be rather too sentimental for the occasion. Before that, I had discarded Schumann on the basis of melancholy. After today I do not know when I will next be seeing Amelia so I feel that something bravura like a Hungarian Rhapsody will be just the ticket. Up and down the keys I go, what a swine of a piece this is. Amelia sits beside me on the piano stool, (the familiarity of her perfume is most intriguing) and she begins to laugh at my mistakes, which of course, are plentiful. I start to laugh too and eventually she seizes my hands and drags them away from the keyboard.

"Oh Ambrose, you're priceless, you really are. Stop now, please, for good."

"For good, was it that bad?"

"Utterly excruciating."

"How about a spot of Scarlatti? that's very sparkly."

This suggestion gives us the giggles again. I don't know exactly why, it just does.

After we have calmed down a bit, I pose Amelia a question in all innocence.

"Have you missed my playing?"

She looks at me with genuine tenderness. I can even detect a certain moistness in her eyes.

"Ambrose," she says quietly, "when will you realise that you can't play the piano at all, you just bash the keys like a three year old child."

"I think it's my sight reading that lets me down."

"No, it goes way beyond that."

She points to the musical score.

"What note is that?"

"F sharp."

"How do you know?"

"Well, I just do."

"Ambrose, the music is upside down," she takes it off the stand and turns it over, "how about that, can you spot the difference?"

I can't say as I do, but then again Liszt is notoriously chromatic and these are very dense runs. My dilemma is obvious.

She takes my hands in hers and shakes her head. It is a very touching moment and brings a lump to my throat.

"Sit there Ambrose, while I make you a nice cup of tea."

I do as I am told. It is a strange interlude. All time seems suspended.

When the tea finally arrives it is remarkable, the most wonderful brew I have ever tasted. We drink in silence until our cups are empty. Then Amelia takes my right hand and places my thumb on a white key that sits so conveniently in front of me.

"Play that note."

I press the key.

"Do you know what that is?"

"Not really."

"It's middle C. Now Ambrose, for your own sake and everyone else's, whenever you feel the urge to play, will you promise me, from the bottom of your heart, which I know is very big, that you will only ever play this one note here, middle C, and then remain silent. Will you promise me that?"

For those of us who have opened our minds to the universal force of love, there comes a moment of enlightenment that is so profound it cannot be articulated. Middle C is middle C. Being in the middle it contains all that I need to know. I can embrace the whole universe from that position without moving a finger.

I look at Amelia. She is smiling but awaiting my reply. After all that we have been through together I cannot refuse her this one last request. And yet there is a question that must be answered first, if my heart and my head are to be in this together. She will understand because she knows I am ambidextrous, even though, pianistically speaking, it is a thwarted skill.

"Amelia, my sweet, does it matter which hand I use?"

"No Ambrose. As a beginner, you'd play middle C with the thumb of either hand, depending on what the other one was doing, if you see what I mean. Before long there is no rule at all, it all depends on what position your hand needs to be in at any given moment, so middle C is actually the key most likely to be played by any finger on any hand."

"Such freedom – how wonderful!"

I play it now with the middle finger of my right hand and I press the loud pedal with my foot to show her that I have taught myself how to prolong a note. It is the most beautiful sound I have ever heard.

"Well done Ambrose, that's very good"

We are both smiling now.

"Thank you Amelia, you are such a treasure. From now on, I promise, from the bottom of my heart, that I will only ever play middle C.

oooOOooo

All power corrupts and absolute power is an absolute nightmare

> *Ambrose Covey-Crump*
> *Spiritual Healer Emeritus*
> *Kaya Centre for Mindfulness*

Beyond the S-Bend
Copyright © 2006 Martin Pilcher
AADVARK-ZAP PUBLISHING (UK)

If you have enjoyed this novel, why not visit the author's storefront:
www.lulu.com/aadvarkzap

Other novels by Martin Pilcher

Read a preview then purchase on line from the author's storefront
www.lulu.com/aadvarkzap

The Banana Skin Tango

Melvin is a stressed out executive with a broken marriage, a fading career and a nicely developing drink habit. When he beds the local bar maid, he ignores the fact that her boyfriend is a psychotic bi-sexual gangster with half London's bent coppers in his pocket. When finally ensnared, both sexually and criminally, he is at last forced to confront his own dubious morality. Redemption occurs when he realises that if you want to stay alive, you must treat women with respect.

Up a Yum Bum Tree

Freddie is a missile scientist with a mad idea. When the British Government rejects his plan, he signs up with Boris Blodvrinsky, a mega-rich Russian Mafia boss. But nobody could envisage the effects of the mysterious Yum Bum tree which grows to become an icon of peace for the 21st Century, visited by world leaders desperate for good publicity. When its sap is discovered to contain a volatile compound for rocket fuel, as well as being a fantastic body cream - greed, ambition, lust and loathing all combine to produce a human drama that climaxes in front of the world's media.

AADVARK-ZAP PUBLISHING (UK)